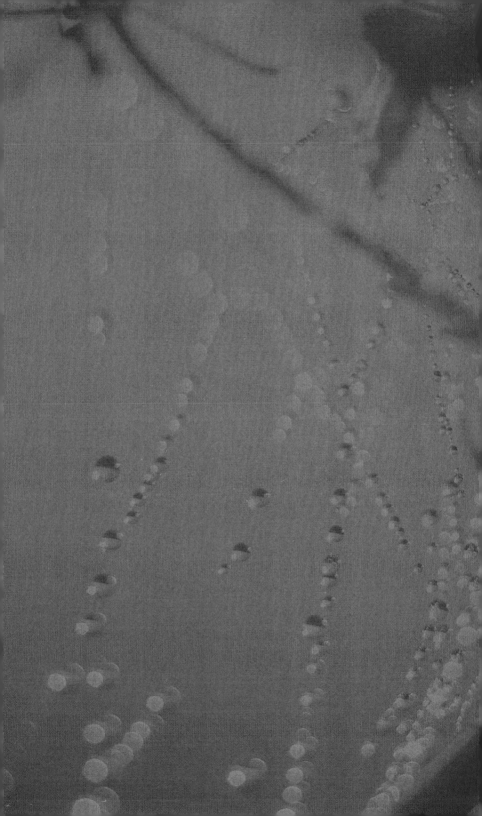

PROLOGUE

COHEN

"Just for a minute," I plea, rocking my newborn son in my arms. "Hold him for one damn minute."

It'll change your mind.

It has to change your mind.

Heather sneers, refusing to look at us, and crosses her arms, as if she's scared I'll push him into them.

I count to ten, my jaw clenching harder with each number. Ten hits and I blow out a series of calming breaths.

Not that it works.

I'm fighting to keep my cool.

For him.

Not her.

Fuck her.

"Enough is enough, Heather," I say.

Her green eyes, void of emotion, narrow when they meet mine. "I told you, Cohen, I wanted out. I can't do this—"

"You decided out of the fucking blue that you wanted out *two months ago*. A little too late to change your mind about having our baby."

"I don't want him. You agreed to accept all responsibility, and

I expect you to keep your word." She uncrosses her arms and rubs her hands together. "My job is done. I'm leaving."

I trace the tiny features of Noah's face with the pad of my thumb. "Give it a week. *Please.*"

"My flight leaves in three days."

"Heather—"

"If you hoped me seeing him would change my mind, you were wrong." She tips her head toward the little man in my arms. "Neither will holding him."

Revulsion seeps through me when she turns around and walks away without giving us another glance.

How did I ever love this woman?

That love splinters into disgust.

Trailing a finger over Noah's peach fuzz, I whisper, "Looks like it's just you and me against the world, buddy."

STIRRED

USA TODAY & WALL STREET JOURNAL BESTSELLING AUTHOR
CHARITY FERRELL

Editor: Jovana Shirley, Unforeseen Editing, www.unforeseenediting.com

Proofreading: Jenny Sims, Editing4Indies

Cover Designer: Mayhem Cover Creations

CHAPTER
ONE

JAMIE

Five Years Later

Nine hours down.

Three to go.

Three hours until I can go home, finish that box of Thin Mints I shouldn't have bought, and binge-watch a show on Netflix.

Netflix and cookies.

Netflix and single.

Netflix and story of my life.

"Tell me he finally agreed?" Lauren, our charge nurse, asks—referring to the appendicitis patient who's been refusing an appendectomy all night.

I nod. "After his wife promised to buy him a new TV."

She scoffs. "I'd love to say someone being bribed to have life-saving surgery is a shocker, but after working in the ER for so long, I'm not easily shooketh."

"Tell me about it." I glance around the emergency room. "What's next for me?"

It's been a slow night at Anchor Ridge Memorial Hospital, and as much as that's a good thing, it can get boring.

She points down the hall. "Exam room three. Five-year-old

with a fever." Her tone turns bubbly as she wiggles her shoulders. "Dad is *super hot*, by the way."

I shake my head and tap my knuckles against the triage desk. "I'll let you know if I need anything."

"Ask him for his number," she half-whispers with a thumbs-up.

I roll my eyes and dismissively wave my hand. "Absolutely not."

"All work and no play makes Jamie a grumpy doctor."

"Yeah, yeah, yeah." I spin on my heel and walk to the room.

The door is cracked, and I knock, snatching a pair of latex gloves on my way in.

"Hello, I'm Dr.—" I stop, stumble back two steps, and cover my mouth with my hand.

Holy crap.

My body tenses, and as soon as my gaze meets his, his jaw flexes.

I struggle for words as anger and disgust line his face.

Words I'd planned if this moment ever happened.

Unfortunately, those words become a scared bitch and run away.

"Cohen," is all I manage in a whisper.

He stands tall from his chair, his narrowed eyes pinned to me, and moves to the side of the bed, blocking my view of the patient.

Lauren's words hit me.

"Five-year-old …"

My attention slides from Sir Pissed Off, and I shift to the left.

"Oh my God," I whisper, gaping at the little boy in the bed.

A little boy whose eyes are sleepy and nose is red and irritated.

Those sleepy eyes, a walnut-brown with a slight slant, match his father's.

The same with his thick ash-brown hair.

But the dimple in his chin and heart-shaped face match *hers*.

"Is this …?" My hand shakes when I point at him.

It's a dumb question.

Even if he says no, he'll be a liar.

"What are you doing here?" he repeats, his tone harsh.

If I wasn't at a loss for words, my smart-ass self would throw out something along the lines of, *What do you think, dumbass? I'm sporting a doctor's jacket with my name embroidered on it.*

But I don't.

Because I can't.

It's a challenge, wrapping my head around them being here, let alone dragging out my sarcasm.

"I'm your doctor," I finally say before signaling to the boy. "I'm *his* doctor."

Sound cool. Confident.

You're the fucking professional here, Jamie.

"We want a different doctor," he hisses, his voice low enough so only I can hear.

"I'm the *only* doctor on shift tonight." I'm speaking to Cohen, but the boy holds my interest.

He's watching this exchange, his eyes pinging back and forth between his father and me with curiosity on his tired face.

"We'll go to another hospital then."

"Why, Dad?" the boy whines, sniffling. "I don't feel good, and what if I puke in the car?"

"I want another doctor." His broad shoulders draw back.

He raises a brow when I hold up a finger, turn, and scurry out of the room.

I rush over to Lauren. "Can you watch the boy in three for a minute? I need to talk to his father privately."

She peeks up at me from her computer and tilts her head to the side. "Yeah … sure."

Cohen is pacing the room when we walk in.

"A word," I say, jerking my head toward the doorway.

Cohen's attention darts to the boy, and he delivers a gentle smile. "I'll be right back, buddy." He gives him a quick peck on the head and swings his arm toward the door, his eyes cold. "After you, Your Highness."

Lauren throws me a curious glance when he walks past her, and I shrug as if this isn't about to be awkward city up in here.

As we leave, I hear Lauren asking the boy what his favorite cartoon is.

Cohen keeps his distance while I lead us into a private room, the one reserved for breaking bad news to families.

I speak as soon as I shut the door, "Cohen—"

Too bad he doesn't let me get more than his name out.

Rude.

His deep-set eyes level on me. "This is a conflict of interest, Jamie. The nurse can help us. We don't need you."

"We don't need you."

The memories of the last time he said those words to me smack into me like a headache.

It was the last time I saw him.

The last time he looked at me with the same resentment.

Either he doesn't realize how hard his insult hit me or he doesn't care.

I snort, anger biting at me. "What do you think I'm going to do, huh? Kidnap him?"

"Considering who you're related to, who knows?"

"Wow." I clench my fists to hold myself back from smacking him in the face since his words are like a slap in mine. "You have some nerve."

It'd make for some bad headlines if a doctor slapped a patient's father.

There's no apology on his face when he holds up his hands. "Just saying it how I see it."

"Then allow me to *say it how I see it.*" I thrust my finger toward the door. "You have a sick son in there, and it's *my job* to treat him. Don't like it? I don't give a shit." I shove past him, stalk out of the room, and don't check to see if he's following me.

"Everything okay?" Lauren asks, her eyes glancing over my

shoulder, and I realize Cohen is behind me, still keeping his distance.

"Peachy," I chirp before approaching the bed and smiling down at the boy. "What's your name, honey?"

"Noah," he croaks.

Even though I was sure it was him, my head spins at his confirmation.

I tenderly squeeze his arm, and my tone turns cheerful. "Hi, Noah. I'm Dr. Gentry. Can I ask some questions about how you're feeling?"

He nods.

Cohen stalks to the other side of the bed, his eyes on me, and Lauren migrates to the corner, her nosy ass interested in this shitshow.

"He has a fever," Cohen tells me, his tone softer.

"For how long?"

He scratches his scruffy cheek. "Over twenty-four hours."

"Appetite?"

He shakes his head. "Not even sugar. I can hardly get him to drink, and he has no energy, which is *very* rare for him."

"Cough?"

"Yes."

His jerk attitude settles while we turn our attention to Noah. I ask question after question as I take his temperature and go through all the motions.

"Symptoms tell me it's the flu," I say, removing my gloves and tossing them into the trash. "We'll do a test, and I also want to run some blood work to make sure we're not missing anything."

Cohen nods. "Thank you."

I smile at Noah. "We'll get you back to feeling good in no time." I give Lauren, who's gathering supplies for the test, a head nod and leave the room.

I'll definitely be pairing wine with those Thin Mints tonight.

Lauren comes scurrying into the doctors' lounge ten minutes

later. "Whoa, what was that about? Dude was super nice to me but acted as if you'd pissed in his Cheerios."

Here goes.

A chill sweeps up my neck. "That's my sister's ex … and her son … the ones she left."

"Oh, Jerry Springer."

CHAPTER
TWO

COHEN

O ut of all the doctors, it had to be her.
   Jamie fucking Gentry.

Heather's younger sister.

A woman I demanded stay the fuck away from Noah and me.

I moved two towns over from Mayview to Anchor Ridge, Iowa, to prevent this shit from happening.

The last time I saw her was a few days after Noah was born. That was five years ago, and even though she's changed, there was no disputing it was her when she walked in. The moment our eyes met, I jumped to my feet, dread spilling over every rational thought in my head.

She can't see him.

She can't know him.

Anger shook through me as we stared at each other. Her eyes —so similar to the woman's I despised—only pissed me off more.

Noah is sleeping, and my back straightens in my chair at the sound of a tap on the door. I slump in relief when it's my younger sister, Georgia, coming into view and not Jamie.

Hopefully, Jamie listened and won't come back.

"I came as soon as I left work," Georgia says, collapsing in the chair next to me.

I shoot her a stressed smile. "Thanks."

She bites into her lower lip, her gaze sweeping from one side of the room to the other, and taps her foot. "This might sound super random, but did you know that Heather's sister is here?"

"Yep." I stretch out my legs. "She's Noah's doctor."

"Wow." She whistles. "Awkward."

"Tell me about it."

"I wish I had been here at that first exchange."

I drop my head back, hoping to release the tension in my neck. "I nearly had a heart attack when she walked in."

I'm positive she felt the same.

Jamie's face revealed every thought running through her head.

Shock, hurt, anger.

The same shit her sister made me feel.

"Did you ask for another doctor?"

"She's the only doctor here tonight."

She lowers her voice. "Does Noah know who she is?"

"No, and it'd better stay that way." I move my neck from side to side before standing. "Can you keep an eye on him while I grab a quick coffee from the waiting room?"

"No, there's no way I can handle him," she says with a roll of her eyes. "He's acting like an animal. Too much energy."

I ruffle my hand through her hair, and she smacks it away.

"Fucking smart-ass."

"Grab me a coffee too. Please and thank you."

I pour our coffees and almost make it back to Noah's room Jamie-free, but she steps in front of me before I do.

Determination is set on her too-pretty face, and she crosses her arms. As much as I'd love to tell her to fuck off, I can't. The nurse's eyes are glued to us like we're her favorite soap opera.

There sure is enough drama for us to be one.

"Cohen, we need to talk," Jamie says.

I match her stance, folding my arms across my chest, and grip the coffees tight in each hand while adding a scowl to one-up her. "If it's not about Noah, I have nothing to say to you."

She stretches out her hand and separates her fingers. "Five minutes. That's all I'm asking for, and it *is* about Noah."

"Three minutes." I'm not doing shit on her terms.

She throws her arms up before collapsing them to her sides. "Fine, three minutes."

I trail her when she starts walking, and the nurse smirks when we pass her. We're back in the room she dragged me into earlier, and she shuts the door behind us. I can't stop myself from chuckling when she stands in the doorway, crossing her arms again as if she's geared to stop me from leaving.

As if she makes the fucking rules.

Her thick honey-brown hair is longer than it was so many years ago and swept back into a ponytail, a few curly strands loose around her face. She's wearing blue scrubs—even though they shouldn't look hot, they do on her—and a white jacket, the words *Dr. Jamie Gentry, MD, Emergency Medicine* embroidered on it in red stitching.

She's gorgeous—even with the similarities between her and Heather. Prettier—because she doesn't have a black fucking heart. Long gone is her geeky phase. Now replaced with a beautiful, confident woman, and by the look on her face, she is about to be a pain in my fucking ass.

"I tried calling you for months, Cohen," she snaps before raising a finger. "No, wait. I tried calling you for *years.*"

"What did I tell you?" I reply, setting the cups down on a table. "If it doesn't involve Noah, I have nothing to say to you."

"Seriously?" She grimaces. "Act like a grown man here."

"Trust me, I *am* plenty of a grown man."

"Really? Because your behavior screams more of a child's than a man's."

"This conversation is what's childish. What do you want me

to tell you, Jamie?" I scrape a hand through my hair and blow out a stressed breath. "I changed my number."

"Thank you, Captain Fucking Obvious. *Why* did you change your number?"

"Put two and two together. You're smart."

She shoots me a cold look. "Asshole."

I shrug.

"He's so big, Cohen." Her features, along with her tone, relax. "And he has your eyes. Fatherhood suits you."

If this is her trying some reverse psychology shit, it won't work.

"Fuck your compliments, Jamie," I snarl. "Saying nice shit to me and being Noah's doctor won't change anything between your family and me... between *you and me.*"

"Why?" she questions with disdain, taking a step closer. "What did I do to you to take away the chance of knowing my nephew? To take away my parents' first and *only* grandchild? We never turned our backs on Noah when Heather said she was leaving. We opened our arms—"

"And asked to fucking adopt him!" Anger fires through me. Anger that's been embedded in me since Noah's birth and can finally be released. "You wanted to take him from my arms!"

"That isn't fair to say it like that," she states, repeatedly shaking her head while delivering a pained stare. "They were worried."

"They had nothing to worry about."

"With your job—"

"My job makes me incompetent of being a father?" I snort and scowl at the same time. "If anything, it's given me patience. I can easily clean up spills and vomit, and I have no issue dealing with a lack of sleep. My job has made me the *perfect fucking parent.*"

She stays quiet as worry covers her face. She's searching for her next words, wanting them to be perfect.

"I can expect you won't tell Noah who you are?" I ask.

She doesn't answer.

"Jamie"—I seethe—"you're his fucking doctor. That's it."

Her face turns stern. "I won't say anything."

I tip my head down and grab the coffees. "Thank you. Now, I need to get back to my son."

She jumps in front of me when I attempt to beeline around her. "If you change your mind—"

I hold up my hand and talk over her because I'm a jackass like that., "Not fucking happening, so don't bother finishing that sentence."

"Jesus, Cohen, will you stop interrupting me?"

"You can't see him, Jamie. It'll only confuse him."

"Why?"

"You're seriously asking me that fucking question?"

"Say I'm your friend." She edges closer, and I retreat. "Say I'm his aunt Jamie. Say whatever you want."

I lower my gaze on her. "I appreciate your help today, but that's all we need from you."

She glares at me, unblinking. "Oh, I get it. You're selfish ... just like her."

My face burns, and I reply through gritted teeth, "Excuse me?"

"Withholding Noah from having grandparents," she says, my temper not scaring her off. "Withholding an aunt—"

"Georgia is a perfectly good aunt."

She digs in her pocket and pulls a card out between two fingers. "Noah has the flu. The nurse will go through the details for treatment with you. Here's my card if you need anything. Call me, day or night. If Noah is sick. If he isn't. If you change your mind."

I scoff., "Not happening."

She shoves the card in my shirt pocket, pats my chest, and turns to leave. I still, staring at her as she walks away.

Cursing under my breath, I stroll back to Noah's room. Jamie is gone, and the nurse delivers a hesitant smile before giving us the discharge information.

"What's that?" Georgia asks when the nurse leaves, referring to the card sticking out of my pocket.

"Jamie's card." I snatch the card and glare at it like it's ruined my night.

Georgia stops me when I start crumpling it in my hand. "Don't do that. She's a doctor. If you ever need help, you can call her."

"Noah has a doctor. There's no shortage of them around."

"Keep it." She pats my chest the same way Jamie did. "Don't be dumb."

CHAPTER
THREE

JAMIE

"Y ou're a doctor, huh? Does that mean you like blood and can stomach gory shit?"

I'm a firm believer in not wasting wine, but the longer my date speaks, the higher the chance he'll be wearing mine by the end of the night.

It wouldn't be completely wasted if it taught him a lesson, right?

Reason four hundred and fifty-three of why I hate blind dates: I'm set up with idiots who ask if I get pleasure from blood and gory shit as if I were Rob Zombie.

Hell, I'd rather be on a date with Mr. Zombie than this expensive-suit-wearing prick.

A suit that'd pair nicely with a soft red, if I do say so myself.

Normally, I'd roll my eyes and ignore his remark, but today is not my day. Thanks to a bolt of lightning striking my townhome's power line, I got ready for this joke of a date with no electricity—my iPhone flashlight and a sugar cookie-scented candle my only light sources.

All that trouble for this smug dick to smirk and ask me ridiculous questions.

On paper, he's perfect—wealthy, successful, handsome.

Realistically, he's a major tool bag.

"You're a criminal defense attorney, huh?" I relax in my chair and deliver a smirk more asshole-like than his. "Does that mean you like convicts and can stomach illegal shit?"

He lifts his chin with pride and waggles his manicured finger my way. "I see what you did there, beautiful."

Gag me.

He grabs his scotch from the table and casually leans back in his chair, and the glass dangles from his fingers. "Baby, there's no denying I love when the law is broken. The criminals, they flock to me. I'm damn good at my job, which means I make damn good money." His eyes brighten as if he's gearing to reveal a secret. "You know Freddy Louda?"

Who doesn't?

"The millionaire who trafficked drugs and murdered two women?"

"*Allegedly* trafficked drugs and murdered those women. I got him off with not one charge." He swipes invisible dirt from his shoulder. "I love it when the bigwigs with fat bank accounts need legal counsel. Hell, I bought a new Mercedes S550 from his case alone."

I grimace.

Lord, if I have to continue listening to his bullshit, I'll be joining the criminals he neglected to keep out of jail.

We can form a We Hate This Asshole gang, play poker, and share ramen noodles. Fun stuff.

I jerk my napkin off my lap, slap it onto the table, and snatch my purse. "Excuse me for a sec."

Forever actually.

"Sure." He licks his lips. "I'll cover the check. We can have dessert at my place."

Gag me again.

And not in the exciting, sexual sense.

Not that that's my thing, but still.

Gag me in a way that this is the worst date I've had—and there have been some terrible ones.

I roll my eyes, stand, and walk away without another word. A crowd surrounds the hostess stand, and I duck my head while passing them before rushing out of the restaurant.

I'm not dining and dashing.

I'll pay Asshole-at-Law back for my meal, but if I'd spent another second with him, my knee would have had a date with his balls.

I curse Ashley with every step while dragging my phone from my clutch.

"Listen, Ash," I screech when my best friend answers, "you're officially cut off from setting me up on dates. I should've ended it after the last disaster."

"Hey, he wasn't *that* awful," she argues around a laugh.

"He drew out a deck of cards at dinner and spent our meal showing the entire restaurant offensive magic tricks." I snort. "Oh, and after that lovely dinner, he was generous enough to suggest we go to his place to show me his best trick of them all. It wasn't pulling a rabbit out of a hat—"

"Which is unfortunate," she cuts in. "I've always wanted to learn how to do that."

"It was pulling his *magic snake* from his pants." I shudder, the memory of forcing back vomit hitting me, and my hatred toward the Houdini wannabe resurfaces. Asshole ruined chicken Bellagio for me, and damn it, pasta is my favorite carb.

"You are a Harry Potter fan."

"And you're clearly a fan of me being single for the rest of my life."

She sighs. "Look, Gregory works with Jared, and everybody says he's a nice guy. He's the best attorney at their firm. I even made Jared search his office for magic wands."

"A nice guy?" I scoff. "Have *you* had the pleasure of meeting my lovely dinner date, Gregory?"

"Well"—she pauses—"no."

"He's scum, and Jared should fire him."

"He's a partner. Jared can't fire him."

"Then tell Jared his partner sucks when he asks why I dipped out on our date."

"What?" she shrieks. "You can't *dip out* without saying goodbye."

"The dipping is done. My current situation is me standing outside, missing the glass of wine I deserted."

I should've chugged that shit before leaving.

Thou shall not waste wine unless it's throwing it at a bad date.

"He'll be insulted."

"Good. He deserves it for how many times he insulted me tonight. Consider us even. I'm ordering an Uber. Fingers crossed my driver has a better personality than my drug lord-loving date."

"Maybe you can ask him to show you his magic snake."

I groan and shiver, running a hand over my arm. "Tell Jared I'll Venmo the money back to Douchebag-at-Law for dinner. Love ya."

I hang up, and before I tap the Uber app, my phone rings with an unknown number calling.

"Hello?" I answer.

"Jamie, it's Cohen." His voice is low-toned, as smooth as my abandoned wine, and hasn't changed since high school. "Are you busy?"

I sway slightly, not from being drunk, but from the shock of this call. "No ... not at all."

"Noah was starting to feel better, and his fever went down. He returned to school, but earlier, they called, saying he had a fever again. I picked him up, but I'm unsure if we should make another hospital visit or ride it out as the flu again."

"Any vomiting?"

"A few times on my couch, yes."

"I can ..." My heart pounds, and I can hear my pulse in my ears. "I can come over and check on him if you want?"

A chilly silence consumes our call.

His answer could change everything.

Noah's life.

His life.

My life.

If Cohen opens this door, there's no going back.

"I'll text you my address."

Cohen lives fifteen minutes away from the restaurant.

Twenty away from my house.

I thank my Uber driver when we pull into the driveway of the brick home with a bright yellow door, black shutters, and a beautifully manicured landscape. A light shines over the front door, making it easy for me to follow the path up to the porch, and I climb the concrete steps.

I know where he lives.

His number.

I'm about to become a major pain in the ass for Cohen Fox.

A knot ties in my belly when I knock, and my stomach clenches hard when he answers the door. Our eyes meet, a brief pause passing before either of us says anything.

Exhaustion lines his perfect face. His eyes are heavy, his cheeks and strong jaw unshaven, and his hair is messy. Even run-down, the man is handsome—exactly my type. Although I'm not sure if Cohen is *exactly my type* because I've crushed on him since I was sporting braces and wearing training bras.

"Hey, Jamie," he greets around a stressed breath. "Thank you for coming."

"Of course," I blurt out, the words coming out as one.

He retreats a step, straightening his back against the door as he opens it wider, allowing me room to walk in. I follow him through entry, a living room, and down a short hallway, the walls lined with framed photos of Noah. Cohen's house is nothing like I expected—nothing you'd see from a man who's spent years working in bars.

He stops in a bedroom where Noah is snuggled in his bed, sleeping and facing us. A lamp—surrounded by a thermometer, bottle of water, and a box of tissues—on the nightstand gives me decent light as I glance around the room. It's clean. The walls and ceiling are covered with glow-in-the-dark stars, and a chest overfilled with toys is in the corner. A long shelf hanging on the wall is lined with action figures.

A light laugh leaves me when I hear Noah snoring, and he slightly stirs when I settle on the edge of his bed, pressing the back of my hand to his forehead. When I brush away strands of his hair, his eyes slowly open.

"Hey there," I whisper with a smile, placing my clutch on the nightstand.

"Hi," he rasps out around a yawn. "You're the doctor from the hospital."

I nod. "I sure am."

I peek over to see Cohen standing in the doorway.

Please tell him.

Tell him who I am.

That I'm not just the doctor from the hospital.

He stays quiet.

Just as fast as Noah's eyes opened, he's back to sleep. I check his temperature, return the thermometer to the nightstand, and grab my clutch, and as I'm about to stand, I spot Cohen at the foot of the bed. His hands are in the pockets of his sweats, and his gaze is leveled on me, his face indescribable. When our eyes meet, all the tension that filled his face when he opened the door softens.

Melts away.

I do a once-over of the room, stupidly making sure it's me he's looking at like this and not some random-ass ghost in the corner.

My cheeks turn as warm as Noah's forehead while the room falls quiet—an agonizing silence I'm unsure of how to break. Blame it on the lack of light, the slight darkness encompassing us, but in the still of this bedroom, in the faint light of glow-in-the-dark stars, we share a moment.

A moment that stalls my breathing.

One I'll never forget as I search his eyes for *something.*

Questions?

Answers?

What-ifs?

What if Heather had never left him?

How could someone leave this man ... this family?

The cord of this—*whatever it is*—snaps when Noah coughs. I tense, common sense smacking into me with a reminder to pull my shit together. Cohen steps forward, and our attention diverts to Noah. We wait as if his next move will be life-changing.

He doesn't wake up.

I cast a nervous glance at Cohen, and just as I do, he shakes his head and curses as he stalks out of the room. I place a gentle kiss on Noah's forehead before tiptoeing out.

Cohen is slumped on the couch when I walk into the living room, his hands clasped between his open thighs, his head bowed.

"No more fever," I say, proud of my voice for not wavering. "I think he'll be okay. Just keep him home for a few more days."

He lifts his head, the tension from earlier reappearing, now stronger than when he answered the door.

He rubs his eyes with the base of his palms as if trying to scrub away the connection we shared. "I'm sorry, Jamie."

"For ... for what?" My pride of not stumbling over my words has left the building, ladies and gentlemen.

"For taking you away from whatever you were doing." His gaze flicks down my body, and he signals to my short black dress and heels. "You obviously weren't home."

"What?" My next words come out in nearly a yelp as I force a casual smile and pull at the bottom of my dress. "This old thing? I hang out at home in it all the time. It's pretty much my pajamas."

He snorts while standing. "I took you away from a date, didn't I?"

I hold up a finger. "*Technically*, you took me away while I was *bailing* on a date."

"That bad, huh?" His lips flicker into a slight grin.

"Dating blows," I mutter, moving from one foot to the other. "They need an app that screens for douchebags."

He pulls out his wallet, plucks a fifty from it, and holds it out to me. "For your troubles."

I swat the money away. "I'm not taking that."

"It's cheaper than a hospital visit."

"Whether or not you want to acknowledge it, I'm Noah's aunt. Even if I just met him, if he needs anything, I come here as that. Not as a doctor you need to pay."

He hesitates before shoving the fifty back into his wallet. "Thank you."

Silence fills the room until I clear my throat.

"Let me, uh … schedule my Uber, and then I'll be on my way." I open my clutch for my phone and unlock the screen.

"Whoa, you had to take an Uber here?" he asks as I focus on requesting a ride.

"It was no biggie," I answer with a dismissive wave.

I take Ubers all the time—to my waxing appointments, yoga, or when I've had too many glasses of wine after one of Ashley's terrible matchmaking dates.

I'm an *Uber out of desperation* kinda gal.

Thank goodness I snuck out of my date before I showed up as Jamie, Medicine of White Girl Wasted.

"Shit," Cohen hisses, scrubbing a hand over his strong jaw. "I'd give you a ride, but—"

"No way in hell am I letting you wake him up," I interrupt.

When I'm finished booking my ride, I smile. "Good night." I zip my finger toward the door. "I'll just wait outside."

He nods, and I feel him behind me as I walk to the door. I

glance back, a quick glimpse, and nearly trip over my feet when he doesn't shut the door behind me.

No, he walks outside, a jacket in his hand, and plops down on the porch step. When I join him, he drags the jacket over my shoulders, and neither of us mutters a word as we wait for my ride.

It's strange.

It's uncomfortable but comfortable at the same time.

There's newness to this, but the familiarity still lingers at the edges.

We know each other but not the new parts, the hidden parts, the hurt parts.

I peek over at him, biting into my lower lip. "Will you tell me how Noah is doing in the morning?"

He nods. "I can do that."

There's no holding back my grin.

Our attention moves to the driveway when the Uber car pulls up, and Cohen gives my thigh a light squeeze before he lowers his voice, and says, "Good night, Jamie."

CHAPTER FOUR

COHEN

Sleep is like a scorned ex.

It hates me.

Last night consisted of checking on Noah every few hours and thoughts of Jamie.

One of those I should've been doing.

The other I sure as fuck shouldn't have been doing.

For hours, I battled with myself on calling her, but finally, I broke down. For Noah. It was always a struggle to decide when to make hospital visits, and if I could get Noah checked out without dragging him to a hospital, I would.

Even when I'd crumpled up her card, I hadn't been sure if I'd actually toss it. It was more of a show for Georgia. An *I couldn't care less about Jamie* attempt. I'd shoved it into my back pocket and then slid it into my wallet when I got home—*just in case*.

Just in case I changed my mind, which was doubtful.

Or I needed her.

Or because I saw the love on her face as she looked at Noah that night.

That's Jamie's character—affectionate, caring, showing every ounce of her emotions on her face.

So I called.

I called, and she came.

Seeing her with Noah last night fucked with my head.

My chest ached, hurt squeezing my throat as I watched them. It was what I'd wanted from Heather—what I've desired for Noah to have. Someone who cares about him as much as I do, a nurturer who comes running in the middle of the night when he's sick.

Even after I was a dick to Jamie, she was here.

Dressed in a sexy-as-fuck black dress and fuck-me heels.

When she walked in, I knew she'd been out, and jealousy consumed me. Whoever she'd been with, I hated the asshole. I gulped, holding back a shit-eating grin when she revealed she'd ditched the guy.

These feelings are wrong.

So damn wrong.

She's the sister of my son's mother, for fuck's sake.

If anyone's off-limits, it's her.

The attraction is mutual, no question about it. Years ago, Jamie drunkenly confessed her feelings for me, and considering I was dating her sister, I shot her down. Sometimes, when I'm tipsy ... or lonely ... feeling sorry for myself, I wonder what would've happened if I'd chosen her—the other sister.

What if I had taken a chance with her?

Then I tell myself it doesn't matter.

That it never could've happened.

It'd have been wrong on so many levels.

So why did I feel so drawn to her last night?

It has to be my dick.

That's a lie.

It was more than me thinking with my cock.

My heart tightened as I thought about someone like Jamie in Noah's life ... in *my* life.

I shake my head, calling myself stupid for even considering it.

My love life is nothing to brag about. After Heather left, I trusted no one, except Georgia. She, Noah, and my job are my life. As Noah grew older, I dated around, but nothing worked out. My job isn't the best place to meet women, but since I'm there so frequently, it's typically where I do meet them. Georgia has attempted to set me up with her friends, but not fucking happening.

Her friends are as big of a pain in the ass as she is.

After checking Noah's temperature again without waking him, I jump in the shower. My mind races as the water pours down my body.

Jamie asked me to tell her how Noah was doing today.

I can do one of two things: ignore her and act like last night never happened or be a man of my word and text her.

In the end, while drying off, I decide to be a man of my word.

One quick text.

A thank-you.

That's it.

It's the least I can do.

Grabbing my phone, I turn it in my hand as if it had the answer for everything.

I owe her this.

> Me: Noah is doing better. Low-grade fever. Headache. No vomiting ... thank God.

There.

I kept my word.

Not even a minute later, my phone beeps with her reply.

> Jamie: Perfect! Just keep an eye on the fever, and I'm here if you need me.

"Here if you need me."

Why does she have to say shit like that?

I hesitate for a moment.

> Me: I was thinking …

Don't do it. Don't do it, dumbass.

My heart convinces me to do something my head would never do.

> Jamie: That's nice. You going to finish that sentence?

Fuck it.
Here goes.

> Me: If you want to see Noah, you can come over when Georgia is babysitting. Spend some time together when he's feeling better.

Holding my breath until she answers, I wonder when I lost my damn mind.

> Jamie: I'd love that! When is Georgia watching him next?

> Me: Wednesday.

> Jamie: I'll be there. Thank you.

I shove my phone into my pocket as Noah comes plodding into the kitchen.

Please don't break my son's heart.

Now, I need to figure out how I'll explain who Jamie is to him.

Twisted Fox Bar is my dream come true.

I always wanted to be a business owner—be my own boss.

In high school, I'd been clueless on what I'd do, but I started bartending when I turned twenty-one. It was fast money and fast-paced. That job turned into several throughout the years, and eventually, I fell in love with it. I managed to snag promotions where I learned the business side of things and met friends along the way—some I kept, some I didn't, and I'm thankful for the ones who've stayed by my side.

My friend Archer and I combined our funds two years ago and opened the bar. Archer, being Archer, demanded he be a silent partner. No one but our friends knows how much he's involved. The only role he wanted outside of investing money was bartending and living a stress-free life away from the public eye. Our friends Finn and Silas came along for the ride.

We're the sole sports pub in the county, and our only competition is a run-down business that doesn't hold one TV. We purchased the large building for pennies on the dollar, gutted it, renovated it, and filled it with state-of-the-art shit. We created an environment for people to have good times with their friends. Dozens of TVs hang along the walls. Wood stools line the bar, and pub tables are scattered throughout the room—two-, four-, and six-tops. Sports memorabilia from the town and pieces I snagged at flea markets fill the empty spaces on the walls. There's a separate room with two pool tables and an area to play darts.

With the bar and Noah, I don't have time for much else—not that I'm complaining.

Being busy prevents me from overthinking shit.

It helps me forget my problems.

"How's the little guy feeling?" Archer asks when I stroll into the bar.

"You mean, after he went all *Exorcist* on the couch?" I joke, shaking my head at the gross-ass memory. "He's feeling better, but I'm still keeping him out of school."

He nods. "I'm sure he loves that."

Out of everyone, Archer is my right-hand man. This bar is our life, and without him, Twisted Fox would've never opened.

Even though he put up most of the cash, he insisted we own the bar fifty-fifty. I argued that it wasn't fair, but he wouldn't budge.

Noah's babysitter, Sylvia, is hanging out with him today while I work. Paperwork isn't going to do itself. Archer manages the books, but I'm heavily involved in every aspect of the bar. It's my main source of income, my bread and butter, and I track every penny that comes in and goes out. Noah deserves the life I wanted growing up, and if I have to work my ass off to give it to him, then so be it. Maybe it's just me making up for his lack of a mother, but my world revolves around him and his happiness.

Plopping down on the chair behind my desk, I release a stressed breath. As funny as it sounds, work relaxes me. It derails my mind from the bullshit and makes me money. Win-win.

Single parenthood is a struggle. It was even harder when I didn't own the bar I worked in. Controlling my schedule wasn't an option then, and for the first three years of Noah's life, I was a bitter asshole. My tips lacked because I hated almost everyone.

And that was all thanks to Heather.

Never in my mind had I imagined her turning her back on us like she did.

Heather and I'd started dating in high school. Throughout the years, we'd broken up and gotten back together a few times, but we grew up. Three months after we moved in together, she became pregnant with Noah.

Everything was good.

Sure, the pregnancy was a shock, but we were excited about being parents.

Then, out of nowhere, she changed.

I should've known something was wrong when all baby-related interests stopped.

Hearing his heartbeat? No, thank you.

Making sure the car seat was properly installed in case she went into early labor? Not happening.

Like everyone else, I blamed it on the hormones. The baby

books warned us about mood changes, bouts of depression, and lashing out. In my dumbass mind, those books knew everything. Too bad there were no chapters on the mother bailing.

Two months before Noah was due, while watching one of her stupid-ass reality shows, she turned to me and asked if we could put Noah up for adoption. I nearly fell off the couch when she said she'd discussed the idea with her parents. She explained, frustration slashing through her, that they'd offered to adopt him. She didn't want that because she'd have to see him, and she was scared they'd push her to have a relationship with him later. To stop that from happening, she asked me to sign over my rights. That way, another family, no one related to us, could adopt him.

As I absorbed what she'd said, my pulse sped while I waited for her to tell me she was kidding. Instead, she jumped up from the couch. With a smile on her face, she returned with papers —*the papers*—her name already signed on the line.

She already had the shit drawn up.

I told her she'd lost her fucking mind. We argued, and with anger firing through me, I stormed out and walked to the bar down the street—my attempt to drink away the bullshit.

Maybe walking out on her wasn't the smartest reaction, but she had been fucking smiling. *Skipping* out of the kitchen as if she wasn't asking me to sign my life over—a person I'd fallen in love with before he was even here.

I'd give up Heather before I'd ever give him up.

Every day for the next week, she begged me to sign. We'd argue, and I'd head to the bar. I became the bastard in the corner, drinking away his problems. Eventually, I ripped up the papers while Heather sobbed, begging for an out.

And I'd given it to her when I promised we'd stay out of her selfish life.

Noah didn't need to be around anyone who didn't want him.

Heather signed over her rights, and three days after his birth, she moved to Vegas. That was when I learned the reason she'd wanted out. She had fallen in love with a man she'd met online. A man who didn't like children—*what a fucking winner*—so fuck our child.

I cut off all communication, and we moved on with our lives as if she never existed. As much as I didn't want my son growing up without a mother, I knew we'd survive. I'd give Noah a happy life without her, and my family and friends have made up for that void pretty damn well.

Better to be without someone than to be with someone who doesn't love you.

I don't hate Heather for finding someone else.

I hate her for not standing up to that someone else for our son.

I haven't spoken to the mother of my child since the day we left the hospital, and I plan to keep it that way.

CHAPTER
FIVE

JAMIE

My shirt is cute.

The sweat rings underneath my armpits? Not so much.

Those sweat rings didn't exist twenty minutes ago when I left my house.

Hanging out with Noah and Georgia today has me more nervous than any blind date I've gone on.

I park next to a red VW Beetle in Cohen's driveway. The car has black polka dots on it, like a ladybug, and is hideous.

I'm also pretty sure it belongs to Georgia.

I make a mental note not to tell her it's hideous.

I can't mess this up.

No one in my family knows about my visit with them. I kept my mouth shut, scared that Cohen would back out. Hell, who even knows if today is a one-time thing he's giving me because I came over when Noah was sick?

I fan out my armpits before performing a quick smell check.

Don't judge me.

A girl doesn't want to be known as the smelly … doctor … friend … aunt?

Note to self: figure out who the hell Noah thinks I am.

I shake out my hands, as if I were preparing to run a 5K—tried it once and gave it a zero out of ten for fun—and hope Georgia has a better response to me than Cohen did.

My pace is slow as I walk up the steps, and when the front door swings open, Georgia appears in the doorway.

My shoulders relax at the sight of her bright pink lips tilting into a smile.

A smile is good.

"Hey, Jamie," she says.

"Hi." I give her a shy wave like the awkward person I am before gesturing to her. "Wow, you look so different … grown up."

Georgia is a few years younger than I am, and while she's always been pretty, she's drop-dead gorgeous now. Her eccentric style hasn't changed much. Even when she was younger, she was always doing something different—pink stripes in her hair, intense makeup, pigtails with tinsel in them. Today, her hair—what had once been a similar color to Cohen's—is dyed blond and pulled into two buns at the top of her head, and she's wearing a crop top with a kimono wrap over it and jeans with holes down the legs.

"Same to you." She whistles. "You're hot as fuck."

My eyes downcast as I blush.

"Come on." She waves me inside, and I find Noah in the living room, surrounded by a pile of Legos.

He eagerly jumps to his feet, a handful of Legos dropping from his hand. "Hi!" His attention snaps to Georgia, and he points at me. "This is your friend? She was my doctor when I was sick! She even came to our house too!"

His excitement settles my nerves and melts my heart. His T-shirt is black and says, *Snack so hard,* his pants are ripped in the knees—somewhat like Georgia's—and he's wearing checkered Vans. Noah is for sure a mini Cohen, definitely a future heart-breaker.

Georgia snags her black fringed purse from a leather recliner and swoops it over her body. "We're going on a sugar run. You game?"

I nod. "I'm game."

Who turns down a sugar run?

Especially in a stressful situation.

Georgia's car is as uncomfortable as it looks.

I considered suggesting we ride in my car since it's not the size of a stroller, and the idea of being cramped in it with sweaty pits was nerve-racking. I kept my mouth shut so I wouldn't look like a pain in the ass already and loaded into her car, sweat pits and all.

Noah is in the back seat, rambling off his favorite snacks while counting them off on his fingers, "Cookies, cupcakes, cake, brownies, sprinkles."

I take in his every word. If Cohen allows me to see Noah again, I want to be the aunt who takes him out for sugar runs like Georgia.

When Georgia pulls into the parking lot of Sally's Sprinkles, my stomach twists, the urge to jump out of the car and run hitting me.

Out of all the places for a sugar run.

Georgia parks, kills the engine, and peeks back at Noah. "Remember our rule?"

Noah eagerly nods. "I get two cupcakes, but tell Dad I only had one."

He laughs, and Georgia high-fives him.

A wave of jealousy swims inside me.

If only Heather hadn't been so damn selfish, I could've had that with him.

Noah unbuckles his seat belt, and he holds Georgia's hand as we walk into the small cupcake shop. The bell above the door rings at our arrival, and small crowds are circled around tables, shoving their sugary goodness into their mouths.

The owner's eyes light up when she notices me.

I want to shrink and hide.

I was hoping it was Sally's day off.

"Jamie!" She beams, sporting the same blue eye shadow and pink lips she's had for years.

Noah darts to the counter, his feet stomping, and eyes the cupcakes lined up inside the glass counter. My stomach growls, and my mouth waters at the memory of how delicious Sally's cupcakes are when I stand next to him. The shop was once a weekly stop for me, but two years have passed since I've been here.

"Hi, Sally," I say.

Sally tells them hello, and her attention turns back to me. "I'm glad you came in. Just because you and my Seth broke up doesn't mean you can't stop in and enjoy your favorite dark chocolate, peanut butter cupcakes."

The mention of his name has my gaze darting from one side of the shop to the other.

So far, Seth-free.

The shop hasn't changed with its bubblegum-pink walls and bright red tables and chairs, and Sally is wearing her *Sprinkle Me Up, Baby* apron Seth bought her for Christmas a few years back.

Sally rubs her hands together. "What can I get for you guys?"

I peek over at Noah and tilt my head toward the counter. "Do you know what you want?"

"Hmm …" He taps his finger against his chin. "So many yummy choices." His attention flicks to Georgia. "How many am I allowed to have again?"

"Two," she answers.

He holds up four fingers. "*Please.* I won't eat them all today."

Georgia shakes her head while fighting back a smile. "Three, and that's final. We'll have to stash the third one somewhere in the house."

He jumps up and down and starts pointing at his cupcakes of choice for Sally—Funfetti, Oreo, and chocolate.

Just as I'm about to order the cupcakes I've missed so much —my ass, not so much—my name is called. I jump at the familiar voice, and my hand flies to my chest at the same time as Seth walks toward us from the back room. He stops next to Sally, wearing a stunned expression on his face.

It's not that we ended on bad terms. The shock is from not seeing him in so long, and I wasn't expecting it. I'm not rehearsed in the whole *running into your ex* thing since I haven't had many exes.

Sweat rings while running into your ex.

Good times.

I'll be taking six of those cupcakes to eat away my embarrassment later.

Noah peeks over at me with a raised brow. "How do you know him?"

As my mind is scrambling for the best lie, Seth laughs.

"I used to be Jamie's boyfriend," he answers for me.

"Well, shit," Georgia whispers, bumping her shoulder against mine. She lowers her voice. "You could've told me we were walking into your ex's lair."

"Boyfriend?" Noah says, sticking out his tongue. "Yucky yuck."

I give Seth a look, and he holds up his hands in innocence.

"What, babe? Just answering the kid's question."

Seth's face is unshaven, and his hair is shaggier. He looks good, mature, and the goofy smile on his face reminds me of why I was so attracted to him. We dated for almost two years, and this was where we met. I used to study here while eating my frustrations out on my homework. Sally had insisted on fixing me up with her son, but I'd declined. The next day, Seth had sat down at my table with my favorite cupcake in his hand and asked me out.

He was a good boyfriend, yet the day he asked me to move in

with him, I broke things off. I was too busy with med school, and he wanted more than I could give.

He deserved more.

Medical school and a love life don't go hand in hand.

"Cupcakes are on the house!" Sally squeals, packing up a box of cupcakes, adding plenty of dark chocolate, peanut butter ones.

"In that case," Georgia says, "can you add two more red velvets?"

I elbow her side as Sally snatches another red velvet. "No, you don't have to do that." I grab my wallet from the bag and pull out my credit card.

Georgia stops me. "I was totally kidding. I invited you on this sugar-binge trip. It's only fair I pay for it. Plus, you ran into your ex. You can't make a girl pay for sugar after that happens."

"It was good to see you, Jamie," Seth says, winking at me before returning to the back room.

Sally refuses to take either of our cards, and five minutes later, I reluctantly accept the free cupcakes.

"You know, he's still single and ready to mingle," Sally adds, wiggling her brows.

Georgia cracks up while I cover my face in embarrassment.

Our next stop is the park.

We sit at a picnic table, and Noah devours his cupcake in seconds. The frosting is smudged around his mouth when he asks Georgia for another. She shakes her head, and he frowns when she insists he let his stomach rest.

"I'm going to go play then," he says, grabbing his cupcake liner and crumpling it in his hand. "Johnny from school is over there." He tosses the liner in the trash and takes off toward the playground.

I swipe my finger through the frosting on my cupcake and

glance at Georgia from across the table. "What did Cohen tell Noah? Who does he think I am?"

She shoves a bite into her mouth and slowly chews it before answering, "A friend of mine." There's a hint of apology on her face before her expression turns serious as if something hit her. "And to be clear, you *can* be *my friend*—as long as you make sure your skank-ass sister stays away from Noah."

The protective aunt bear is coming at me, claws slightly drawn in warning.

"Heather lives in Vegas," I rush out, the need to assure her that'll never happen powering through me. "She, uh … married the man she left Cohen for and has only been home a few times."

"Good. I hope she stays there forever."

I only nod.

I have never been close with Heather, and our relationship turned sour after she left Noah. It put a strain on our family, nearly broke us, and she didn't talk to my parents for a year. It was two for me until my parents begged me to reconcile with her.

I did it for them, not her.

Making up is my tolerating her the few times she comes around—those visits typically when she needs money because her piece-of-shit husband can't hold a job.

"It was a big deal to him, you know," Georgia adds, "Cohen letting you see Noah. For years, he's called you the sworn enemy."

I lick frosting off my finger. "I never did anything to him."

"Directly, no, but your family did."

"We were in a tough spot. Heather swore they were putting Noah up for adoption. It terrified my parents."

"Cohen assured them *plenty of times* that wouldn't happen."

"We had Heather in our other ear, swearing he'd change his mind after Noah was born because he wouldn't want to do it alone."

She scowls. "You should know my brother's character better than that."

"I know." I release a heavy sigh. "It was chaotic for us, and all we had was Heather's side. Cohen would be a single father, and he was always in bars—"

"Whoa. I'm going to stop you right there. Cohen isn't *always in bars* like he's out partying. He works in one."

"I know that—"

"And now, he owns one," she adds, talking over me.

I pause, biting into my cheek. "Really?"

She nods.

I wait for her to tell me which one, but she doesn't. Not surprising. They're only giving me a glimpse into their lives, but I'll take it.

Is that desperate?

Maybe.

But this is what my family has wanted forever.

Noah has been the topic of countless conversations.

Now, I know what a great kid he is ... and I want to know him more.

"How late does Cohen work?" I ask Georgia.

We're back at his house, high on sugar, and Noah and I just finished a Lego house.

A badass Lego house if I do say so myself.

"It depends." She checks her watch while sitting cross-legged on the couch. "My guess is, he'll be home around nine. Archer, his partner, is working the late shift tonight. I work there too, and if I'm not working, I'm hanging out with Noah or in class." She smiles in pride. "We have a group-effort thing."

I return the smile. "I'm glad Noah has a good support system."

Noah loudly yawns. "I'm sleepy."

"Sugar crash," Georgia says around a laugh. Her phone beeps, and she glances at the screen before looking at me. "Cohen is on his way home."

I push myself to my feet. "That's my cue to leave."

She scrunches up her nose. "Why?"

"I want to dodge any awkward convos the best I can."

"You're leaving?" Noah asks, peering up at me with a furrowed brow. "Will you come over again?"

My heart hurts at the sad look on his face, and I run my hand through his hair. "Of course I will."

"Can we get cupcakes again too?" He jumps to his feet, nearly knocking over the Lego house. "Your old boyfriend can give us some!"

"We can definitely get cupcakes," I answer with a chuckle.

"I think you've won his heart," Georgia comments.

"When will you come back?" Noah questions, the words quickly falling from his lips. "Tomorrow?"

"I don't know about tomorrow because I have to work," I answer. "Let me check with your dad. Does that sound good?"

His eyes are alert, the sleepiness vanishing. "My dad will say yes! He said you're a nice doctor! I asked if you were his girl-friend, but he said no. I'll tell him he can't be your boyfriend now because you like boys who give you cupcakes. Dad doesn't make cupcakes." He stops and takes a quick breath before going on, "Maybe he can learn because I think you'd be a good girl-friend. I'll ask him!"

My eyes grow wider, the more he rambles.

"If you haven't noticed," Georgia says when he finishes, "Noah is bold and idealistic."

I'd say so.

I give him a hug, promise to see him again, and say good-bye to Georgia. When I get in my car, I pull out my phone and grin at the selfie we took at the park.

Later that night, my grin returns when Cohen sends me a text, saying Noah wants to hang out again.

CHAPTER
SIX

COHEN

"Drunk dude, Mohawk, at the pool table," Georgia calls into my office, barging in. "He's asked at least three women to suck his dick, he spit in a guy's face, and … I'm not even going to describe what he's doing now."

I stand from the chair behind my desk and stalk over to the camera monitors across the room. Spotting the culprit doesn't take long. A lanky guy sporting a Mohawk with a face tattoo is dry-humping a pool stick between his legs and twirling his arm in the air as if he were riding a horse.

Jesus, fuck.

Owning a bar is all fun and games until shit like this happens.

Goofy drunks? I can handle.

Sad drunks? I pat them on the back and pour them another beer on me.

Drunks who repeat stories? I nod and pretend I've never heard it before.

What I fail to have patience for are idiots humping pool sticks.

"Shit," I hiss, storming out of my office with Georgia behind me.

I cut through customers and head straight to Mohawk, who's still sliding the stick against his junk while grinding against it.

Yeah, that thing is going right in the dumpster.

"You," I yell when I reach him, gesturing toward the door with my thumb, "Stick Humper. Time for you to go."

He snorts and ignores me, but thankfully, he removes the stick from his legs.

At least we're getting somewhere.

"Out," I demand.

Like the douchebag he's proven to be, he doesn't listen. Instead, he snatches a beer from a pub table and chugs it, a smirk playing at his lips when he finishes.

"Come on, man," I say. "Don't make this complicated. You're drunk. Have one of your buddies drive you home, so you can sleep off the booze. You can't stay here and harass my customers."

Years of working in the bar industry have taught me the best approach to these situations is keeping my cool and suggesting a plan for them to get the fuck out.

Finn, my friend/bouncer/part-time bartender, appears at my side. "I got this, Co."

I swing out my arm, stopping him, and shake my head. "Nah, I think he'll listen."

"I don't," Finn states, straightening his broad shoulders and clenching his fists.

Mohawk slams the empty beer bottle onto the table, shattering it, and the people around him jump back. Finn shoots forward before I can stop him and captures the back of Mohawk's shirt, causing the stick to drop from his hand. Mohawk grunts when Finn jerks him away from the table.

"Time to go, asshole," Finn snaps.

The crowd breaks, and all attention is on Finn as he drags Mohawk toward the exit.

A few chicks in the corner clap their hands, and another guy yells, "About damn time!"

Their cheering is interrupted by Polly, my newly hired bartender, scrambling in my direction and yelling my name.

"Cohen!" she shrieks, her attention bouncing between Finn and me. "That's my boyfriend! Tell Finn to let him go!"

"Your boyfriend is out of here," Finn yells over his shoulder, her demand not stopping his mission.

Polly throws her purple hair over her shoulder and kicks out her hip. "If he's out of here, *I'm* out of here."

I scrub my hand over my face while groaning.

I don't need this high school bullshit today.

"What'll it be?" Polly asks. "Kick him out or lose a bartender?"

"I'll mail your last paycheck," I reply with no hesitation.

No way am I allowing a twit dating a Post Malone wannabe to give me ultimatums. I should've known it wasn't a good idea to hire Polly when she said she drank Fireball for breakfast.

"Are ... are you serious?" Polly's eyes widen at the response she didn't expect.

She picked the wrong bar to work in if she thinks her boyfriend can pull that shit.

I cross my arms. "Dead serious."

"Fine." She stomps her foot. "Good luck handling this crowd with one bartender."

My head throbs at the reminder.

It's a game day, and we're busy as fuck. Polly and Archer were my only available bartenders tonight. Finn is working the door, and I was finishing paperwork before leaving for the night. Noah's babysitter, Sylvia, is scheduled to leave in an hour, and I hate running late.

"Good luck with your scumbag boyfriend," Georgia retorts.

"Fuck you," Polly screams before shooting her glare to me. "And fuck you too, Cohen." She whips around and chases after her loser boyfriend.

I run my hands through my hair and suck in an irritated breath.

Georgia sighs, patting my arm. "Don't stress, big bro. I'll cover the bar."

I shake my head. "You're waiting tables, and you have class in the morning."

"And?" She flashes me an amused grin. "It won't be the first time I've pulled an all-nighter and then gone to class. I like to think that I'm a professional at it actually."

"I'll act like I didn't hear that," I say with a pointed look, and she follows me to the bar. "Not to mention, you and Archer will kill each other if I let you work with him. I can't be down two more bartenders."

"I got this, Co!" Archer shouts from behind the bar while two men argue over a game call in front of him. The way his eyes cut to Georgia in irritation confirms he overheard our conversation. "She's not working with me."

Georgia flips him off. "You're a dick."

Archer shrugs, pours a beer, and then slides it down the bar to a regular.

"Let me call Sylvia," I say, fishing my phone from my pocket and heading toward my office.

Five minutes later, I'm walking out of the office, my shoulders slumped.

"Is Sylvia staying?" Georgia asks.

I shake my head and scrub a hand over my face.

She pauses for a moment before saying, "What about Jamie?"

I move my hand to stare at her. "What?"

"Ask if she can watch him."

"Not a good idea."

"Oh, come on," she groans, tilting her head back. "She's been hanging out with him for weeks now."

"Not alone."

"It won't be that long, she's a doctor, and everything will be okay. Heather is still in Vegas."

I flinch. Not once since Jamie came into our lives have I asked about Heather. Just her name puts a bad taste in my mouth.

It's not that I doubt Archer can handle the crowd alone, but customers will bitch if it takes too long for their drinks. Bars aren't known for patient customers, and we can't afford to lose the business, especially on game nights. They bring in a shit-ton of money.

Archer shakes his head when I join him behind the bar. "Go home. I'll call Silas."

"Silas is at some convention," I reply, referring to our friend. Silas bartends, does all of Twisted Fox's marketing, and fills us in on the latest alcohol trends.

"*Or* I can do it since I'm *already here*," Georgia comments before cracking an arrogant smile Archer's way. "I promise to stay on my side of the bar, and I won't trip you this time—even though you deserved it last week … and will probably deserve another tripping … or a swift kick in the nuts."

There's no way the two of them can work together.

"Give me a minute."

I scroll through the Contacts in my phone and hit Jamie's name.

Here goes.

CHAPTER
SEVEN

JAMIE

I t's six in the evening.
   I'm living a very exciting social life by chilling in bed and watching Netflix.

Alone.

No Thin Mints this time.

They're all gone, and I'm all out of Girl Scout sources to get more.

Might have to search the black market later.

I'm licking Cheetos cheese off my fingers when my phone rings, and I nearly drop it when Cohen's name flashes across the screen.

He never calls.

We've texted a few times, but since I've started hanging out with Georgia and Noah, I communicate through her.

I'm unsure why I drag in a calming breath before answering, "Hello?"

"Jamie." My name sounds stressed, leaving his mouth. "Are you busy?"

"Nope." *Cleaning cheddar fingers doesn't count as busy, right?* "What's up?"

"An employee just walked out, leaving me stuck at the bar,

and Noah's babysitter can't stay any later. Is there any way you can hang out at my house until I can get there? If not, I completely understand. Georgia suggested you might be—"

"That's no problem," I interrupt before he talks himself out of the idea.

"I wouldn't ask, but I'm in a bind."

"I can be there in about ten minutes." I jump out of bed and scramble for clothes that don't make me look homeless.

"Thank you. I'll let the babysitter know you're coming. If you need anything, call me. If I don't answer, call Georgia."

"Gotcha. I'll be there."

A gorgeous, college-aged blonde answers Cohen's door.

No wonder Noah says he wants his babysitter to be his girlfriend.

She stands up straight, and her words are chirpy. "Hi! I'm Sylvia. You must be Jamie."

I nod, and when I say hello, it's not nearly as chirpy as hers.

She retreats a step, allowing me space to come in. "It's nice to finally meet you. You're all Noah talks about." She peeks back at me with a frown. "I feel bad I can't stay later, but I'm going out of town."

"Totally understandable. I'm happy to help."

"Jamie!" Noah shouts when I come into view. He punches his hand through the air before dashing across the living room to give me a hug.

Bending down, I hug him back, squeezing him tight and savoring the moment. The more we hang out, the closer we get. This little boy has sent a wave of happiness through my life, and moments like this, even though they're joyous, still send a flash of fear through me.

That motherly instinct has hit me.

The love for him in my heart is there.

Whether that's good or bad, I'm not sure.

I'm playing by Cohen's rules, going at it minute by minute.

Cohen could have a bad day and decide no more Noah visits for me.

I could say the wrong thing, and he could pull away the happiness we've created.

The thought is terrifying.

Never did I think I'd get so attached in such a short amount of time, but Noah has won me over with his radiant and childish heart. He's funny, a ball of energy, and the sweetest little guy. Cohen raised him right, and a sense of guilt twists my heart that we'd ever doubted him.

Noah gives Sylvia a hug good-bye along with a kiss on the cheek, and we make ourselves comfortable in the living room when she leaves. Cartoons are playing on the crazy-large TV, and Noah has his action figures displayed on the floor, perched up as if they were watching the show with him.

Cohen's house is warm and comfortable, very homey. The walls are painted a light gray throughout the entire house with the exception of Noah's blue bedroom. The couch is cushy, which I love. Nothing's worse than a stiff couch. Two brown suede recliners sit on each side of the couch. Blankets are everywhere—thrown over those recliners, a Spider-Man one spilling over the arm of the couch—and brown suede pillows that match the recliners are scattered around. Just like in the hallway, pictures of Noah are everywhere. School pictures, pictures of him and his family, and ones of him with others.

Twenty minutes later, Noah looks back at me. "I'm hungry."

"You haven't eaten dinner?"

"Sylvia made me chicken nuggets and gross broccoli, but I'm hungry again." He pats his stomach.

"What would you like to eat?"

He provides a sly grin. "Pizza."

I snatch my phone from my bag. "Let me check with your dad."

"Dad won't care. I'll save him a slice and a half."

Yeah, not pushing my buttons with this one.

I could see Cohen banning me for giving Noah a pepperoni instead of a broccoli sprout.

> Me: Is it cool if we order pizza?

He texts me back a few minutes later.

> Cohen: Since I'm sure he won't let you say no, that's fine.

> Me: He agreed to save you a slice and a half.

> Cohen: Tell him I appreciate his generosity.

"Good news," I tell him, pulling up the pizza shop app to order. "Pizza it is!"

This is my mom's third call.

Her seventh text comes through.

> Mom: Are you alive? I thought you had the night off at the hospital?

Knowing my mom, she won't stop calling until I answer.

"I'll be right back," I tell Noah before walking to the kitchen and returning her call.

"Honey, why have you been ignoring my calls?" she answers. "I've been calling you all day."

"Sorry," I grumble. "I've been busy."

"Doing what?" Her voice is stern and worried. "Are you working too many hours at the hospital again?"

That is a regular question from her.

"No, Mom. I'm working regular ER doctor hours," I answer.

"Which is too many hours! I don't understand why you won't work in a practice. Your father does."

"I don't want to work in a practice."

"Hey, Jamie!"

My hand tightens around my phone at the sound of Noah yelling my name, and I turn around at the same time he comes barreling into the kitchen.

He jumps up and down, his voice rising. "Can I have a cookie?"

"Who's that?" my mom asks.

I gulp, unable to speak. Instead, I nod as I give Noah a thumbs-up, and he dashes to the pantry. A package of cookies is in his hand when he turns and scurries to the table.

"Jamie!" my mom yelps.

I hear the wrapper opening when I speed-walk to the bathroom and shut the door behind me. "I'm babysitting."

"Babysitting? Babysitting who?"

"A kid." My stomach sinks.

My mother won't stop at that answer.

"I'd assume so. Whose kid?"

She's also always been a nosy one.

To lie or not to lie.

My pizza threatens to come up while I fight with myself on how to answer.

"It's Noah, Mom," I reply, resting my back against the door. "I'm babysitting Noah."

The line goes silent, and I double-check that she didn't hang up on me.

"I'm sorry." She clears her throat. "Did you say you're babysitting Noah?"

I nod even though she can't see me. "Yes."

Another silence.

"Heather's Noah?"

"Yes."

"What?" Her voice lowers. "How?"

I hold the phone closer to my face and lower my voice. "I can't exactly go into the details at the moment."

Her shocked tone morphs into an angry one. "How long has this been happening behind our backs?"

I shut my eyes, hating the betrayal in her voice. "It's not behind your backs." When she doesn't reply, I release a heavy breath. "It hasn't been long. I wanted to make sure it stuck before I got anyone involved. I plan to ask Cohen if you can see Noah, but you can't tell Heather about this, okay?"

"Jamie, you know I don't like secrets."

"If you want Cohen to even consider letting you meet Noah, you should start liking them with this one."

Noah yells my name again.

"Look, I have to go," I rush out.

"Call me when you leave. I want to know what he's like." She sighs. "Snap a picture if you can."

CHAPTER
EIGHT

COHEN

I t's after three in the morning when I pull into my garage.
After Noah was born, I saved every penny I could and
bought the three-bedroom brick ranch. For years, Noah, Georgia,
and I lived here together. She only moved out a few years ago.

Now, it's just me and my mini-me.

I texted Jamie a few times throughout the night to check on
Noah and make sure she was okay with staying so late. Around
nine thirty, she told me Noah passed out on the couch, and she
was putting him to bed.

Never in a million years would I have thought Jamie would
be in my house, watching Noah while I worked.

I hear the TV when I walk into the house, but there's no sign
of life in the living room. I circle the couch to find Jamie sleeping
with a Spider-Man blanket wrapped around her.

Staring down at her in curiosity, not creepiness, I absorb her
beauty. We haven't seen each other since the night she came over
when Noah was sick.

It's better that way.

I kept my distance to avoid what I'm doing now—drinking
her in as if she were the best drink I'd ever poured. Her golden-
brown hair spills over the edge of the pillow and covers half of

her tan face. Even in Jamie's dorky days, she was cute. Her lips are pouty, and I know she has two dimples that pop through her cheeks when she bursts into laughter. Her green eyes light up any room.

There's more to Jamie than her looks.

She has the warmest heart of anyone I've ever known.

I dip down and whisper her name, and her eyes slowly open, one at a time.

"Sorry." A deep yawn leaves her. "I dozed off."

I shove my hands into my pants pockets and chuckle. "He can be a handful."

She snorts, rubbing her sleepy eyes. "Oh, he's nothing."

I retreat a step when she rises and stretches out her arms. My eyes are on her when she stands, grabs the blanket, folds it into a neat square, and settles it on the end of the couch. Without a word and with another yawn, she snags a mug with the bar's logo from the table, and her fuzzy-socked feet pad through the living room to the kitchen.

My gaze is on her, my eyes taking in every inch of her ass, which makes me a rude bastard. Her black yoga pants hug her body, accentuating her plump ass, and I love how casual she looks tonight and how comfortable she seems in my home. Sure, seeing her in that black dress was nice, but this is so much more.

The kitchen is quiet as she rinses out her mug and places it in the dishwasher as if she owned the place.

My mouth turns dry as I rest my back against the cabinets and search for the right words. "How's life going?"

How's life?

Lamest fucking question.

When did I lose my game?

"Life is living at the hospital while playing Let's See How Many Coffees Jamie Can Drink Before She Has an Anxiety Attack."

My eyes return to her ass when she crouches down to shut the dishwasher.

"I get you on the coffee." I chuckle as I take the few steps to the kitchen table and collapse into a chair. I grab the pizza box, sliding it to me, and cringe when I open it. "What's this trash?"

She arches a brow. "Pizza."

"Did you torture my son with this *pizza*?"

"Uh ... yeah."

"Listen, there's a lot of shit I'll take, but feeding my son this pineapple demon of a pizza is where I draw the line."

"He loved it, thank you very much." She smirks and surprisingly sits across from me. "Have you ever tried Hawaiian pizza?"

"Nope, nor do I care to."

"What is it Noah said you tell him?" She taps the side of her cheek, thinking. "You have to try foods before you decide you don't like them. Practice what you preach, Fox."

Nausea turns in my stomach when she slides the pizza box closer to me.

I push it back. "Nasty-ass pizza. Hard pass."

"Cohen, try the damn pizza."

"Look, I don't want to be a dick and make you clean up my vomit after I eat this garbage. Plus, I don't want my house to smell."

"For a guy, you're dramatic as fuck."

I chuckle. "Oh, really?"

"Really."

"It's weird, hearing you cuss."

The Jamie I knew was shy, timid, definitely not this outspoken.

This Jamie is confident, funny, and a fucking smart-ass.

She scrunches up that cute nose of hers. "Why?"

"You hardly muttered a curse word in high school."

"Well, I didn't think you were dramatic as fuck then." A smirk plays at her lips, her dimples slightly making an appearance. "Had I, I would've told you the same."

I can't help but chuckle. "There's always been a little rebel inside you."

She rolls a hairband off her wrist, smooths her hair into a ponytail, and ties it back, stray strands framing her face. "*Puhlease.* The most rebellious thing I did in high school was go to that stupid party." Her cheeks redden before she buries her face in her hands, speaking through them, "Oh my God. I can't believe I brought that up."

Our conversation is about to grow more interesting than a damn pineapple pizza debate.

I straighten my shoulders, a cocky smile crossing my face. "I was your first kiss, wasn't I?"

When she uncovers her face, she's glaring at me. "You don't know that."

"I was," I state, matter-of-factly.

"Oh, piss off." Her hand waves through the air. "It sucked, by the way."

Leaning back in the chair, I'm already enjoying every word of this, knowing it'll just get better. "I don't doubt that. You cornered me in a bathroom and drunkenly stuck your tongue down my throat."

My breathing slows at the memory. Heather lost her shit when she spotted Jamie at that party, but I made her chill out. Jamie didn't have much of a social life, and I was happy that she was finally enjoying her teenage years. I plowed through the crowd and made it clear that she could only take drinks from me. Later, when I went to take a piss, Jamie shoved herself into the bathroom behind me and locked the door. Before I could stop her and ask when she'd lost her mind, she pushed me against the door and attempted to suck my face off.

It was bad.

She was so inexperienced.

I turned her down, she cried, and then I drove her home.

We never brought up that night ... until now.

"That's why I don't drink cheap vodka anymore," she says.

"Oh, really?" I lean back in my chair. "What's your drink of choice now? Pineapple juice to match your pineapple pizza?"

"Wine, thank you very much. It's never convinced me to stick my tongue down someone's throat where it doesn't belong." The blush on her cheeks hasn't disappeared.

"Does it make you stick your tongue down throats you should?"

She bites into the edge of her lip. "Can we stop talking about me, and you eat the damn pizza?"

I'd much rather talk about her sticking her tongue down throats.

And other places.

Well, not anyone's throat.

Maybe talk about her sticking her tongue down my throat.

Or vice versa.

I shake my head, mentally slapping my forehead. "If it's gross, you owe me fifteen mushroom pizzas."

"Ew." A fake gagging sound falls from her mouth. "I don't trust people who eat fungus on their pizza."

"Fruit on it is better?"

"Quit delaying and eat the damn pizza."

My stomach growls, but not because I'm hungry. It's tightening, gearing itself up to ingest something disgusting. Jamie's eyes are pinned to me, and she's nearly bouncing in her chair. My upper lip snarls when I pick up a slice, bite off the corner, and chew it as slow as Noah does his broccoli.

I'm making the same disgusted face.

"So?" she asks eagerly when I swallow it.

"Just as I suspected." I clasp my fingers together in a fist, hold it over my mouth, and make a choking noise. "Nasty as hell."

She rips off an edge of crust from a slice and tosses it at me. "You suck."

We're in need of a subject change. I can't have her asking me to try any more nasty shit.

"You know," I say, "I never told Heather about that night."

CHAPTER
NINE

JAMIE

I pull in a breath.

Whoa.

He said her name.

Not once in the six years they've been broken up has Heather said his name.

If it wasn't for Noah, you'd think their relationship never existed.

A few years ago, when Heather was in town, I asked if she regretted leaving them.

She answered with a friendly, "Fuck off," and stormed out of the room.

Her pig of a husband, the man she'd stupidly ditched Cohen for, grunted and muttered something along the lines of, "Fuck kids."

A real winner there, sis.

I told him to, "Fuck off," next, and the day was filled with everyone wanting the other to fuck themselves.

My eyes meet Cohen's, and a tingle sweeps up my spine. Even though this is an embarrassing moment, I have no compulsion to flee.

We're having a good time.

"I figured you hadn't tattled, given I wasn't strangled in my sleep," I say, cracking a smile. "Thank you for that. It's nice to be alive and breathing."

He shrugs. "We all do stupid shit the first time we're drunk."

"Fun fact: not everyone attempts to make out with their sister's boyfriend. Total slut move on my part, which I take full accountability for." I pause, holding up a finger. "To you, I take responsibility. With Heather, I'm taking that shit to the grave."

He's right about it being the first time I got drunk. For someone with a 4.0 GPA, I was clueless about how potent vodka was and how stupid it could make you. I chugged that shit down like it was Kool-Aid, trying to fit in, and then threw myself at a man who wasn't mine.

After our *incident*, I didn't drink for three years.

In college was when I realized that not all alcohol was cheap vodka that would have you puking up your guts and kissing guys.

"You were what"—Cohen scrunches his brows together—"sixteen?"

"Sixteen, stupid, and slutty."

I couldn't look at him for weeks. Anytime he came over, I left the room. I was ashamed and terrified he'd tell Heather. She would've tattled to my parents, and all hell would've broken loose. But Cohen pretended it never happened, and at times, I wondered if he even remembered.

Maybe I wasn't that memorable.

"What if I told you it was the best kiss of my life?" Cohen asks, grinning playfully before licking his lips.

I flip him off. "Shut your mouth before I shove that pizza in it."

"I know it was the best kiss of yours." His smile turns cocky.

"Please. It lasted five seconds before you shot me down."

"Yes, because you tasted like pineapple pizza."

"And you tasted like cheap beer and tacos. Not hot."

"I won't argue with that. I had some shitty taste in liquor back then."

And shitty taste in girlfriends.

He clasps his hands together, resting them on the table, and it reminds me of a dad about to give their child *the birds and the bees* talk. "Seriously, though, pineapple breath and all, thank you for coming tonight."

"Thank you for letting me in his life," I whisper. "I know it was hard for you."

His gaze darts to the other side of the kitchen.

Whenever I bring up Noah, Cohen changes.

Vulnerability flashes in his eyes.

He's unsure if me seeing Noah is the right thing to do.

Please don't doubt me.

I'll never hurt either of you.

I swear it.

I'm playing, and I will always play by your rules.

He knocks his knuckles against the table before sliding out of his chair. "Sorry for taking you away from whatever you were doing by asking you at the last minute. I'm sure you were busy."

"Nope, just in bed." I chew on the inside of my mouth.

He tilts his head back. "Now, I feel like shit for dragging you out of bed." His head lowers as if something quickly hit him. "Wait, why were you in bed that early?"

A strangled laugh leaves me. "I was awake ... just chilling."

A low chuckle from him eases me a bit. "Just chilling, huh?"

"Yep."

His lips twitch into a relaxed smile. "What does one do while *just chilling* in bed?"

"Eat ice cream." I wrinkle my nose while rambling off my list, "Complain about insomnia." I snap my fingers, and my voice hitches. "Oh! And eat Cheetos—the puffy kind, of course. Sometimes, if I'm feeling crazy, I throw Netflix into the mix. My shifts have been chaotic lately, and it's been difficult to maintain a normal sleep schedule."

Last week, we were short a doctor and two nurses in the ER, so I picked up the slack.

He scratches his chin. "What does Jamie watch in bed while chilling?"

"*The Office* reruns usually or a serial killer documentary."

"You have no idea how much I'd pay to binge-watch a show that isn't cartoons or even eat in bed. If Noah catches me snacking in bed, he'll try to do the same. Kid's a messy eater. In all seriousness, though, I'm proud of you for going for your dream."

Rising from the chair, I clap him on the shoulder. "You sound like a proud dad at graduation."

He clasps his hand over mine, squeezing it. "Hey now, I heard you babble on about wanting to be a doctor for years. I'm glad it worked out."

As happy as his words hit me, my attention is pinned to his hand over mine.

To his touch.

The way his large hand perfectly blankets mine.

The warmth of his skin over mine.

I shut my eyes, telling myself to pull away but not having the strength to.

He blows out a long breath at the same time he releases my hand. "It's late."

I retreat a few steps, maintaining distance, and groan when he pulls out his wallet.

Not again.

"Nope," I say, pushing the wallet away. "If you even think of taking anything out of that, I'm kicking your ass."

He snags a bill and slides it between two fingers, holding it out to me. "For taking you away from your Cheetos and Netflix."

I narrow my eyes on him. "Put it away."

"Jamie—"

"You can pay me back by allowing me to see Noah more. How's that?"

He stiffens at my response, and his face changes into a look I've only seen once—when we were in Noah's bedroom. We lock eyes, and I feel my pulse in my throat.

"I'll give you that." His voice is gentle when he reaches forward, wraps a strand of my hair around his thick finger, and clips it behind my ear. "Good night, Jamie. Get back to your Cheetos and Netflix."

I suck in a breath.

Cheetos?

From the way he's looking at me, I'll be getting back to my vibrator.

His eyes are half-lidded and tired when I tell him good night, and he walks me to the door, standing on the porch until I drive away.

When I get home, I pour a glass of wine to pair nicely with my Cheetos and go to bed.

CHAPTER
TEN

COHEN

"I understand you want to wear your Spider-Man light-up sandals, buddy, but it's cold outside. Your toes will freeze off."

I'm crouched on one knee and having a standoff with my five-year-old son about fucking light-up sandals at the ass crack of dawn.

Noah scowls at me. "I don't care. I don't need all my toes." He holds up his tiny hand and separates his fingers, wiggling them. "I got ten of 'em."

I scrub a hand over my cheek. I'm functioning on three hours of sleep, and I still need to make breakfast and drop Noah off at school on time. "How about this? I'll buy you Spider-Man boots if you put *those* boots on. Neither one of us is getting our way here, bud."

He tilts his head to the side, thinking. "If I listen, *you* are getting your way."

Schooled by a kindergartener.

I stare at him, searching for my next move, but he sighs as if annoyed with me.

"*Fine,*" he groans. "I'll wear the boots *if* you put an extra pudding cup in my lunchbox."

"Sold!" I high-five him and stand. "Put on your boots, and let's get moving."

Noah pulls the bright red boots up each foot and stomps into the bathroom. I spike his hair with gel and spritz cologne on his wrist, and we head into the kitchen, the smell of his cologne filling the hallway when he sprints down it. I bought him the cheap shit last month in hopes that he'd stop stealing mine.

He dances in his seat at the kitchen table while I heat his oatmeal—the kind where the dinosaurs hatch from their eggs after it's warm—and I make his lunch while he eats. Normally, I have everything ready the night before, but the fiasco with Polly and Mohawk fucked up my schedule. I was exhausted and crashed into bed as soon as Jamie left.

After Noah scarfs down his oatmeal, he jumps from his chair, and we load into my Jeep. The drive to school isn't a quiet one while he talks about how pretty his babysitter is and then complains that I'm not bumping Kidz Bop.

After I drop him off, I head to the bar for another day of work.

"Hey, big brother."

I glance up, drying off a glass, and set it to the side as Georgia skips over to me.

She plops down on a stool, sets her salad container on the bar, and opens it. "How'd last night go?"

I grab another glass. "You were with me last night. Remember?"

"How'd your night go with *Jamie*?" She stabs a piece of lettuce and shoves it in her mouth.

That's where she was going with that.

Not surprising.

"I went home. She went home. That's it," I lie with a shrug.

That's it.

That's definitely not it.

We talked. We laughed. We joked.

We brought up secrets.

Even though I had been tired as fuck, ready to collapse into my bed when I walked into the house, I could've sat at that table and talked to her all night.

Then we started talking about our kiss.

The kiss we'd shared years ago that was anything but hot.

My chest expanded, and my dick stirred at the thought of kissing her again—better this time.

Hotter this time.

Me not pulling away this time.

I prayed she didn't notice me staring at her plump lips as I wondered how it'd feel to brush mine against them.

"Lame," Georgia groans, breaking me out of my thoughts before dropping her fork and staring at me, a shit-eating grin on her face. "I have a great idea."

"Keep that idea to yourself," I grumble.

"Ask her out."

Georgia liking Jamie surprises me. When Noah was a baby, Georgia sided with me about Heather's family—including Jamie —not seeing Noah. Like me, she saw them as a threat.

"Mind your business."

"She doesn't know how to do that," Archer says, strolling behind me to grab a cocktail shaker.

"And just like that, my appetite is ruined," Georgia snaps, her cold glare pinned on Archer as she slams the lid back onto her salad.

I gear up, ready to block it because her face suggests she's about to throw it at him. As annoying as it is to hear them argue like fucking children, it at least takes the attention away from Jamie and me.

I signal back and forth between them. "You two need to quit acting like you're Noah's age and get along."

Archer walks away without replying and helps a customer.

Sadness crosses Georgia's face as she scoops up her hardly eaten salad. "I'm out of here. I'll finish my food somewhere that's asshole-free."

"You don't have to go." I set down the glass and then scrub a hand over my forehead.

She and Archer have been arguing for years, and no one knows why. Eventually, it has to end because it's giving me a goddamn headache.

Just as I'm about to lock them in a room to work on whatever the fuck their issue is, Silas's voice rings through the bar. "Hey, yo! We have that new vodka everyone is talking about!"

Silas comes into view with a heavy box in his hands. He groans as he drops it onto the bar next to Georgia.

"You mean, the vodka Lola told you to buy?" I ask.

"Obvi," Georgia replies for him with a snort. "He'd pierce his dick if Lola told him to."

Lola is one of Georgia's best friends who works for one of our liquor distributors. She tends to sucker Silas into purchasing whatever alcohol she's promoting.

"Bullshit," Silas says, shooting Georgia a glare before plucking the box cutter sticking out of his pocket and slicing the box open. He pulls out a bottle with a label I don't recognize and holds it up. "Now, who's up for testing this bad boy?"

"Hard pass. Lola already made me try it, and it's potent," Georgia says before wiggling her fingers in a wave, scooping up her things, and scurrying out of the bar.

"Over here!" a customer yells, swinging his arms in the air. "I'm up for taste testing anything!"

Silas hops over the bar and spins the bottle in his hand. "Any takers from someone who *works here*?"

The taste tester won't be Silas. He works in a bar yet doesn't drink.

Silas points at me with the bottle.

"Nope." I shake my head. "I'm about to head home."

He snags a shot glass and pours a shot. "Archer, my man! Looks like you're the winner!"

Archer grumbles curses under his breath, captures the glass, and swallows down the shot. "It's okay. Nothing to orgasm about." He hands the shot glass back to Silas with a shrug and walks away.

"That dude needs to get laid," Silas says, shaking his head.

"Lack of pussy isn't his problem," I comment.

Archer has his fair share of women. He comes from money, and even though he tries to hide it, women fawn over him as if it bleeds off him. The difference between Archer and other guys is that he doesn't broadcast his hookups. He's quiet and private, but given the shit that happened to his family, I don't blame him. He's rough around the edges, bulky, and broad-shouldered. He's a better fit for a bouncer than Finn, but Archer laughed in our faces and threatened to kick our asses when we suggested it.

Finn raises a brow.

"It's Archer being Archer," is my only explanation.

"Georgia probably put him in a bad mood. Anytime they're around each other, it's a negative-ass vibe. They need to bang and get it over with."

"Dude, what the fuck?" I seethe, shooting him a look of warning. "That's my sister."

He holds his hands up, palms facing me. "Oh shit, forgot about that."

I flip him off and smack him upside the head.

He jerks back. "Dude, what the fuck *to you*?"

"Oh shit, forgot it's painful when someone hits you." I signal to everyone behind the bar. "All of you assholes know my sister is off-limits."

That's been my rule since day one. Whenever a friend meets her, I make it clear he stays away from her. Georgia is grown and going to date, but I've worked with my friends long enough to know they're not the guys for her. They hook up with women,

women throw themselves at them, and none of them can hold a relationship without fucking it up.

Not happening on my watch.

They all know that, and they respect that.

We've never had an issue.

If that changes, that person will no longer be my friend.

And I'll kick the bastard's ass.

CHAPTER
ELEVEN

JAMIE

"You still mad at me?" Ashley asks, sliding into the booth across from me at our favorite smoothie joint.

I haven't talked to her in weeks. She and Jared went on an off-the-grid-to-find-myself vacation with no phones, no WiFi, and no Netflix. Not a good time, in my opinion. Since she's been gone, I haven't had a chance to tell her about the Cohen situation.

Ashley has been my best friend since third grade. We were the class nerds who spent our weekends doing homework and reading books while hanging out. We had a similar goal—to become doctors.

We were roommates in college and med school. She met Jared and moved out of our apartment and into his condo last year.

While I took a job in the ER, she took one as an OB/GYN. When she offered me a position at her practice, I declined. The ER holds my heart. It's stressful, but I love the unknown. People come to us at their most vulnerable times. I wanted to be a doctor to help people, and the ER is what makes me happy.

"Sure am," I answer, sipping on my açaí smoothie.

"Come on," she groans. "How was I supposed to know he was a D-bag who liked gangsters?"

"Jared knows what kind of guy he is."

She wrinkles her nose and rubs her bottom lip. "You see … Jared doesn't exactly speak to him."

"What the hell?" I shriek, tossing my straw wrapper at her. "You set me up with a guy *neither one of you* speaks to?"

Ashley takes a long drink before answering, "I know *about* him. Sometimes, I talk to his assistant when I visit Jared at the office. She said he was a winner, so I set you up." She throws her arm out before placing her hand over her heart. "What if someone gave me the opportunity to set you up with a Hemsworth brother? I wouldn't say no because I hadn't personally met him."

"Big difference," I mutter, shooting her a dirty look.

"Look, my goal is to find you love, and I'm doing the best I can over here. Not all of them can be winners. It's called a process of elimination."

"I'll find my own love, thank you very much." I sip on my drink. "No more blind dates from you."

"Where will you find dates then?" She pushes her fire-red hair away from her face and leans across the table. "Did you finally decide to take my advice and join Tinder?"

"Tinder sounds better than Ashley Finds Me a Date, so possibly," I lie.

"Look, give me another chance." She presses her hands together in a praying gesture. "I'll check attorneys off the list. Jared has plenty of frat brothers."

"Absolutely not. Frat boys are the worst."

I stupidly lost my virginity to a frat boy I was tutoring my sophomore year of college. He invited me to a party, and one thing led to another. A week later, he hired a new tutor, who I then caught giving him a blow job.

"Technically, they graduated and are no longer frat boys."

"Thank you, next," I sing out.

"No accountants, no former frat boys. Anyone else on your no-no list, you picky pain in the ass?"

"No one you suggest."

She pouts, and her response comes out in a whine, "You're no fun. Get married, so I can deliver an amazing maid of honor speech. I demand to take credit for you finding the love of your life."

I roll my eyes.

She perks up in her seat. "How about this? You let me apologize with margaritas tomorrow. You have to forgive someone who offers margs—*top-shelf* margs."

"As great as that sounds, can I take a rain check?"

"Why?" Amusement crosses her freckled face as her lips curl into a smile. "You find a boyfriend? Is that why you're turning down my fabulous list of men?"

"First off, it's far from fabulous." I squirm in the booth. "Don't kill me for not telling you this, but you have been MIA."

She tips her drink toward me. "Don't you dare say you got married, and I missed my maid of honor speech."

I prepare myself for her impending freak-out. "Cohen came to the ER with Noah."

"What?" she shrieks, catching the attention of the people around us. "Off the grid or not, I'm pissed you didn't send a letter, a raven, a tele—whatever the fuck they did before phones were invented—to tell me this!"

"He blew me off at first, but I gave him my card. A few days later, he called, asking for help because Noah was still sick, and it has kind of"—I search for the right explanation—"progressed from there." I snatch my smoothie and suck it down.

"You're bailing on me to hang out with Noah and his *daddy*?" she squeals, shimmying her shoulders from side to side. "I like it. I like it *a lot*."

"Gross." I scrunch up my nose. "Don't say it like that."

"Fine, to hang out with Noah and the guy you've wanted for years."

"Guy I've wanted for years?" My cheeks burn. "I haven't seen him in *years*."

"And?"

"And he was a total ass to me. He's not the guy who dated my sister. He's different."

"Obviously. Your sister fucked him over. That kind of betrayal will change a man."

I nod in agreement.

"Ask him out."

My eyes widen, and it's my turn to shriek and gain people's attention, "Are you nuts?"

"What will it hurt?" There's not a hint of sarcasm on her face.

I flick my hand toward the door. "Go away and get back to giving Pap smears."

"What will it hurt?" she repeats. Placing her elbows on the table, she rests her chin in her hand and stares at me dreamily. "I think you two would be super hot."

"Did you bump your head when you were doing that eat, pray, love shit? Not only is he my sister's ex but he's also the father of her child."

"Heather lost any right to him and Noah when she left him for that scumbag." She leans back and shrugs.

I play with my straw, and it squeaks as I move it in and out of the cup. "Still doesn't make it right. Heather didn't do anything to *me*."

She snorts. "She cut off all your Barbies' hair after claiming you were too old to play with them. She made fun of you like it was her job. Remember when she broke your grandmother's antique clock and blamed it on you?"

Struggling to sound defensive, I say, "Payback isn't sleeping with her ex, and that was childish stuff she did to *me*."

She sighs. "It sucks when your bestie is in love with someone but won't make her move."

"I don't love him," I say harshly, looking away from her.

"Don't bullshit me. You told me *yourself* you loved him."

When I glance back at her, my narrowed eyes meet her entertained ones. "I told you that my freshman year of high school when I didn't date, no guy paid attention to me, and he was always around. It was a stupid crush."

She tips her head to the side. "Look on the plus side, bestie. You won't have to endure any more of my blind dates."

"Cohen or no Cohen, I'm still not enduring any more of your blind dates. I'd rather have my period for a year straight."

"Make sure you make an appointment if that ever happens, okay?"

"I'm still not hiring you as my gyno."

"Lame." She checks her watch, frowns, and slides out of the booth. "Find out when I can meet the little guy, and if anything happens between you and Cohen, don't wait a damn month to tell me, okay? I don't care where I am. I want all the deets."

My throat tightens as my nerves go into overdrive.

I considered driving to Cohen's house to ask him this, but I don't have panties big enough to do that. So like the scaredy-cat I am, I call him.

"Hey," he answers.

Playing with my hand in front of me, I inspect my nails in an attempt to control my anxiety. "Do you have a minute to talk?"

"Sure," he drawls, curiosity in his tone. "What's up?"

"My parents want to meet Noah," I rush out before I lose my nerve.

My hold tightens around the phone, and I glance around the hospital cafeteria, wondering if I'll need Xanax by the time this call ends. This request can piss him off enough that he won't talk to me again.

"You told them?" he hisses, and my eyes slam shut at his tone.

It's a mixture of shock and anger.

As if I betrayed him.

My wish of him taking this lightly is not coming true.

"It was an accident." Tears prick at my eyes, regret sliding through me as my hands start to shake.

"An accident?" he slowly repeats, calling my bullshit.

"My mom called when I was babysitting Noah. I ignored her calls, but she kept calling. I was worried it was an emergency."

"Jamie," he warns.

"I didn't plan for her to find out. She heard Noah in the background and asked who he was."

"You couldn't tell her he was someone else?" The bullshit-calling is still evident in his voice.

"I suck at being put on the spot, and I suck even more at lying, which some would find a very honorable trait."

"You know what another honorable trait is?"

"Forgiveness?" I squeak out.

"Keeping your word that no one would find out."

"Cohen," I say his name like a statement.

"Jamie," he mocks in the same tone.

"I give you my word that they won't tell Noah who they are. Please give my parents this. Even if just for one day. My mom's birthday is this week, and it'd make her day."

"I don't care what'd make her day."

The call goes silent, and the anxiety feels so similar to when my mom called, asking who was in the background.

"I'll think about it," he finally states.

"That's all I'm asking for."

"No, you're asking for *a lot* more."

CHAPTER
TWELVE

COHEN

> Jamie: Bad news. I'm sick, and I can't pick up Noah. I'm so sorry.

I drop my pen on my desk and grab my phone to answer her text.

Jamie was supposed to pick up Noah from school today. She's done it a few times this month, and he loves his time with her. They go to the park or the movies, and she takes him to get cupcakes.

Man, my kid is easily won over with sugar.

> Me: It's cool. You need anything?

Do you need anything?
What the hell am I doing?
Nothing. This is normal. Not out of bounds.
Right?

I'd reply the same to my sister or one of my friends if they were sick.

> Jamie: I'm okay. Thank you for the offer, though.

> Me: Get some rest. I'll get Noah from school.

> Jamie. Thank you, Cohen.

I slide my phone into my pocket and glance over at Archer. "I have to go. I'll have Georgia come in and cover my shift for a few hours when she gets out of class." I rub my temples, already anticipating the backlash of hearing him bitch.

"Why?" Anger radiates off him, and he throws the paperwork we were discussing on my desk.

"Jamie is sick and can't pick up Noah from school."

"Find someone else to cover," he snarls, scratching the scruff on his cheek. "I'm not working with her."

"Look, whatever beef you two have, it doesn't need to be brought up here. You work here. She works here. Get the hell over it."

He glares at me. "As part owner, shouldn't I have a say in our employees?"

"Not when she's my sister."

"I'll call Silas."

"He's out of town."

"Whatever, man," he grumbles.

I take that as his acquiescence, and thirty minutes later, I'm in the school pick-up lane. The back door flies open, and Noah jumps into the back seat.

A frown takes over his face as he looks around. "Where's Jamie? I thought she was picking me up today."

I stare back at him in excitement. "She's not feeling well, so you get to hang out with good ol' Dad today."

"Ah, man," he mutters with a frown.

"What am I, chopped liver?"

"She was going to take me to the cupcake place."

I frown back at the disappointment on his face. "How about I take you to the cupcake place?"

He thrusts his arm into the air. "I'd love that! Can we get Jamie one too? She loves cupcakes, like me. It'll make her feel better."

Just as I'm about to say no, I take in the elation on his face.

No way can I say no to that face.

It's probably why I've been a sucker for most of Noah's requests throughout his life.

"Sure."

He dances in the back seat. "Can I pick it out? I know her favorite."

"Of course."

I text Georgia, asking for Jamie's address, before putting the car in drive. She's brought Noah there a few times to hang out at Jamie's place. She called it a change of scenery, but I call it Georgia being nosy and wanting to know where Jamie lives.

Sally's Sprinkles is a cupcake shop that sits on the corner of Main Street and Maple in our small town square.

I've been here a few times, but Noah and I tend to visit the frozen yogurt shop when we go out for dessert. When we walk in, my mouth waters at the sweet smell of baked goods wafting through the air. Noah wastes no time in skipping to the glass counter.

"Hi, Noah!" greets the woman wearing a frosting-stained apron.

"Hi, Sally!" He wiggles in place while debating his options.

My gaze pings back and forth between them. Other than giving her our cupcake choices, we've never talked to this woman before, let alone know her name.

I'm assuming she's the owner, hence Sally's Sprinkles.

It hits me that Noah has been here with Georgia and Jamie.

That must be how they know each other.

"No Jamie or Aunt Georgia?" Sally asks.

Noah shakes his head. "Aunt Georgia is at school, and Jamie is sick. We're going to bring her cupcakes to make her feel better!"

Sally's hand flies to her chest, a grin taking over her wrinkled face. "You're so sweet. She'll love that."

I kneel to Noah's level. "What'll it be, buddy?"

"Hmm ..." He puts his finger to the side of his mouth, deep in thought, before pointing at a dark chocolate one. "She'll love that one!"

"She most definitely will," the woman squeals. "Those are her favorite."

Noah tips his thumb toward me. "This is my dad."

"Oh, it's nice to meet you! I'm Sally." She wipes her hands on her apron and waves to me as I stand.

Noah peeks over to me. "Her son and Jamie used to be boyfriend and girlfriend," Noah explains as though he were the head of the gossip committee around here.

Raising a brow, I feel a surge of jealousy tightening around my throat. "Oh, really?"

What the ...?

I shouldn't care that Jamie had a boyfriend.

Sally nods repeatedly. "My Seth was heartbroken when they broke up, but med school was demanding." An exasperated breath leaves her. "If only they'd get back together now that she's out of school."

Fuck Seth.

He had something I want—something I can't have.

I'll never have.

I clap my hands and rub them together. "All right, Noah, have you decided which one you want?"

No more talk of Jamie's former boyfriend.

Noah nods, and we leave Sally's Sprinkles with a box of cupcakes.

CHAPTER
THIRTEEN

JAMIE

F*uck bees.*

No longer will I share any Save the Bees Facebook posts.

Sorry, Cheerios.

My bottom lip is the size of a toddler's fist.

All because one got into my can of LaCroix and stung me when I took a drink. The swelling has shrunk some, but it still appears I had a lip injection gone wrong.

I hated canceling on Noah, but there was no way I was going to go out in public looking like this. I'll buy him extra cupcakes and maybe an action figure the next time I see him.

Shuffling from my kitchen to the living room, I hold a bag of frozen strawberries to my mouth and plop down on the couch before snatching my phone. The bag drops on my lap when I see a text sent fifteen minutes ago.

> Cohen: Mind if we stop by? Noah has something for you.

I'm struggling to come up with an excuse when the doorbell rings. I snatch the strawberry bag, set it on the table, and tiptoe to the door. When I peek through the peephole, Noah and Cohen are standing on my porch, and there's a familiar pink box in Noah's hands.

"I hope she's home," Noah says. "Everyone knows you have to stay home when you're sick unless you have to go to the doctor. Isn't that what you tell me, Dad?"

"It sure is." Cohen knocks again before peering down at Noah, who now appears heartbroken. "Maybe she's napping. We'll leave the cupcakes here, and I'll text her to grab them when she can."

"But what if someone steals them?" Noah whines.

My stomach burns with shame. I pull in a jagged breath, open the door, and cover my mouth.

"Hi, guys," I say, my voice muffled under my hand.

Noah holds up the box, a proud smile on his face. "We brought you cupcakes to make you feel better."

I return the smile at the heartwarming gesture and am unclear if they can make out my words. "That's so sweet. Thank you." Not wanting to be rude, I wave them in with my free hand.

They don't move.

Cohen scratches his head and nods toward my mouth. "Is everything okay, Jamie?"

He has the hot dad vibe going on with his sweatshirt layered under a jean jacket, holey jeans, and Chuck Taylors.

I nod. "Mm-hmm."

"Why don't you uncover your mouth then?"

I don't.

"Jamie," he says my name like a warning.

I slowly remove my hand, waiting for the gasps and questions.

"Oh."

"Yeah, oh." I gulp.

"What happened to your mouth?" Noah blurts.

Cohen shoots him a *don't be rude* look before his attention returns to me. "Are you allergic to something? I can run and grab you some Benadryl."

"I took some already." My words are still muttered, my lips not making it easy to speak.

Turning, I do a once-over of my house when they walk in. It's clean, but since I've been lying around, whining about my lip, I haven't exactly picked up today. An empty yogurt container is on the living room table next to the bag of strawberries and a bottle of water. A shag blanket is nestled in the corner of my couch, and a lavender candle is burning, the relaxing scent wafting through the air in an attempt to calm me.

My townhome has an open floor plan, allowing you to see the living room and the kitchen past the peninsula island separating the two rooms. Cohen carefully takes the cupcake box from Noah and sets it on the kitchen table. Noah doesn't waste a moment before opening the box and snagging one.

He jumps up and down and comes dashing toward me. "Here! I picked it out just for you."

The blue frosting lining his mouth tells me he's already devoured one cupcake.

I rest my hand over my heart and set the cupcake on the counter. "I'll eat this in a bit, okay?"

Noah nods.

Cohen shoves his hands into his jacket pockets and leans back on his heels. "Sorry if we're intruding, but Noah insisted on seeing you and bringing you the cupcakes since he thought you were sick."

I signal to my jumbo lip. "This qualifies as sick. No way am I going out looking like this."

"Why?" He smirks. "They look cute."

I smack his shoulder as I pass him. "Shut up."

He chuckles.

Noah is at the table, shoving another cupcake into his mouth, and I start straightening up my mess.

"How'd you know where I lived?" I ask Cohen.

"Georgia."

Noah hops up from his chair and barrels toward the living room. "Let's watch cartoons!"

"We can get out of your hair," Cohen says when Noah flies past him into the living room.

"You've already seen my face, so there's no hiding it. I could actually use the company."

"I figured you'd be eating Cheetos and watching Netflix." He winks at me.

"I save those for my wild nights, remember?"

"Ah, yes. I see it's frozen fruit and yogurt day instead."

Noah makes himself comfortable in the yellow paisley print chair with the remote in his hand and starts flipping through channels.

"Noah," Cohen says in his dad voice, "you can't turn people's channels without asking them."

Noah frowns. "You let me turn channels all the time."

"*At home.* We're at *Jamie's* home."

"It's totally fine," I say. "Flip away."

Noah shrugs and stops at a cartoon.

I fall on one end of the couch, and Cohen takes the other.

He looks around the room. "I like your place. It suits you."

I drive a hand through my hair, realizing it's a hot mess, but all I can do now is roll with it. "I mean, I do live here."

"You know what I mean. It matches your personality."

I shift to face him. "What exactly is my personality?"

"Sophisticated but fun. Stylish but not too overboard or tacky."

"Hmm …" I tap my chin. "Has someone been reading Martha Stewart magazines?"

"Smart-ass," he grumbles, cracking a smile.

My townhouse does scream me. The two-bedroom home isn't large, which was number one on my wish list because less cleaning. My father had all my appliances updated, and I changed the deep brown cabinets to a clean white, making the place brighter. An electric fireplace—another item on my wish list—is under the TV.

All my furniture is white, and I've scattered color throughout the room with my décor—bright pillows, large candles on my coffee table, and two bookshelves lining a wall, filled with medical textbooks, paranormal romances, and thrillers.

"Speaking of homes, your crib definitely doesn't suit you. I was expecting a man cave," I say.

"It's the Martha Stewart magazines. She knows her shit."

I cock my head to the side. "Family man design is all the rage."

He points at himself. "Funny, because that's what I am, minus the whole cheesy dad T-shirts and tacky jokes."

"Uh, that cheesy dad joke was plenty tacky."

"Dad! It's my favorite!" Noah shouts, turning back to look at us while pointing at the TV where *Toy Story* is playing.

Cohen scoots in closer to me, bows his head, and whispers, "To be honest, the sequel is nowhere near as good as the first one."

I raise a brow. "Look at you, Mr. Cartoon Critic."

"What can I say?" He shrugs. "I know my shit."

"Dad!" Noah yells. Briefly peeking back at us, he furrows his brows. "We're not allowed to say that word."

"Shit—shoot, sorry," Cohen replies with a chuckle.

I elbow him. "You're in trouble now."

"Who would've known the hardest part of raising a kid was not cursing around them?" He shakes his head. "It's not like I work in a school where I regularly have a PG-rated vocabulary."

"Speaking of work, do you have to go in tonight?"

"Nope. Georgia and my friend Archer are covering for me."

I glance away, fake focusing on Buzz Lightyear, when I ask, "Which bar do you own?"

"Twisted Fox Bar." There's no mistrust in his tone. No sign he doesn't want me to know.

Buzz loses my attention while Cohen reclaims it.

"Really? You were voted one of the top bars in the state."

"Heck yeah, we were." Pride shines on his face.

Noah's gaze whips back to us. "Dad! Bad word!"

"I said *heck*," Cohen argues.

"My teacher, Mrs. Jones, said we're not allowed to say heck either."

"Jesus," Cohen mutters. "Mrs. Jones is on my nerves."

Noah responds, "Shh … this is my favorite part of the movie. You guys watch, okay?"

I nod, feeling like a kid in time-out, and talking toys are the only sound in the living room.

Noah is engrossed in the movie.

Cohen? Not so much.

Me? I couldn't care less about Woody.

Sorry, not sorry.

I steal glances at Cohen, and there's no missing the way his eyes flash to me every few minutes. We're not snuggling, this isn't romantic, but I never imagined I'd be on my couch with him, watching—*ignoring*—a movie. With each peek, I take in the differences in him from the past and how maturity has changed him.

Dark stubble covers his cheeks and the angular curve of his jaw.

The old Cohen had smooth cheeks and was cleaner-cut.

His laid-back clothes are different than when he went to clubs.

The man who was once the life of the party now makes cartoon character-shaped pancakes.

Heather never deserved him, his love, and she definitely doesn't deserve the man he is now.

How could you turn your back on them?

If only I'd been older.

If only he'd seen me as more than just his girlfriend's geeky sister.

If only he hadn't dated my sister.

But then again, I would've never known him.

Is that a good thing?

Did fate bring Cohen and me together?

Did it bring Noah into my life?

Shaking my head, I mentally slap myself for my stupidity.

Cohen will never be anything more to me than my sister's ex-boyfriend.

I'll never be anything but the little sister of his ex-girlfriend—albeit less annoying and geeky.

What made me fall in love with Cohen was how he treated me. He'd give Heather shit when I wanted to watch a movie with them and she'd scream at me to leave a room. My parents were lenient with them and allowed Heather to have sleepovers at his house even though they knew his mom was always MIA. I'm shocked Noah was their first pregnancy. They screwed like teenagers who'd just discovered sex.

I adored her relationship with Cohen.

Everyone knew it.

Everyone teased me about it.

Noah's snoring breaks me out of my thoughts. I stand, grab a blanket, and wrap it around him.

"We should get going." Cohen lifts to his feet. "He has school in the morning, and I need to make dinner. He won't be happy when he finds out dinner doesn't consist of pizza or cupcakes."

"What's on the menu then, chef?"

"Cheese quesadillas."

"Oh, yum."

"I'll have to make you some when you come over sometime."

I scrunch up my face. "It's so weird."

"What is?" He turns to look at me.

"You cooking, being responsible, being a *dad*."

"Hey now, I knew how to cook before I was a dad. People seem to forget I took care of Georgia before Noah. We couldn't eat fast food all the time. It was too expensive and bad for our health."

"Good point. I don't know why I ever doubted you."

His face falls at my words.

My voice lowers and softens. "I'm sorry, Cohen. From my parents and me, we wish everything had happened differently."

"I appreciate that. I grew up with your family. You knew I was the parent for Georgia when I was a teenager. I could take care of a baby in my twenties. I'm not fucking selfish, and it hurt."

My parents and I went to the hospital when Noah was born, assuming Heather would change her mind, but nope. That was when they asked Cohen to allow them to adopt Noah.

It was wrong.

We saw how over the moon Cohen was about becoming a father.

"Trust me, we hate how things went down. My mom recently asked for your number to apologize, but given how private you are, I didn't want to cross any lines." I hesitate, my stomach twists, and my head hurts, in fear I'll piss him off. "She also asked for a photo of him, which I haven't sent either. I'm following your rules here."

A pained expression passes over his features. "Your parents really want to meet him, huh?"

"You have no idea."

His shoulders straighten. "All right then."

"What?"

"They can meet him."

I perk up. "Really?"

"On the condition they don't tell Noah who they are. You're Georgia's friend, they're your parents, and you're just babysitting for me."

"I understand. I promise." I clasp my hands together and hold myself back from squealing. "Thank you so much."

His voice hardens. "Heather had better not be there."

"She's in Vegas and very rarely comes home. It's been over a year."

"Good." He runs his tongue over his lips before gesturing to mine. "Ice that."

I touch my lips because I'd forgotten about the swelling then salute him.

He collects Noah in his arms and sends me a polite wave, and then they leave. I snag a cupcake and shove half of it in my mouth.

I love this new Cohen.

How he's coming around and letting me in.

No longer is he being as cold and callous as he was at the hospital.

What's changed in him?

And what does it change with me?

CHAPTER
FOURTEEN

COHEN

My nerves have been on fire since Jamie picked up Noah today.

My stomach clenches when I ask myself why I agreed to let her parents meet Noah.

Sheila and Ted Gentry are good people and had been nothing but warm and welcoming since I met them. Even with their wealth and status, they weren't unhappy that their daughter brought home a boyfriend who came from a broken home and was living off the system. They helped my family and me, and even though it pissed me off, I knew their asking to adopt Noah came from a good place. They were willing to step up and parent Noah if no one else would.

I glance up at the sound of the front door opening and hear Noah blabbing about how long he held his breath underwater. I smile, knowing he must've gone swimming at her parents' house. Noah comes darting in, ready to tell me about his day, and just as I'm about to ask him a million questions, the sight of Jamie stops me.

Her face is blotchy, and she's struggling to hold back tears.

She's seconds away from a breakdown.

I stride to the fridge, pull out a pudding cup, snatch a spoon, and hold them out to Noah. "Go eat this in the living room, and we'll be in there in a minute."

"Really?" His eyes widen as if I grew another head. "I can eat it on the couch?"

"Just this once."

I pat him on the head, and he grabs the goods before dashing into the living room.

She's practically shaking when I step closer.

"Jamie," I say, "what's wrong?"

"Please, Cohen." A single tear slides down her cheek. "Don't hate me."

Those aren't good words to hear.

Especially after where they've been.

I stare at her, trying not to jump to conclusions, and wait for her to continue.

She doesn't, but the sobs come.

"Jamie," I say, "you're scaring me here."

She opens her mouth, shuts it, and then slowly opens it again. "I took Noah to my parents' house, like we agreed."

I nod and stay silent.

"I told him they were my parents, like we agreed."

"Good."

"Everything was going fine." Her voice, her jaw, her hands— they're all shaking. "We were swimming and then ..."

"And then what?"

Her gaze drops to the wood floor. "Heather showed up."

A storm rolls through me, an anger I've never experienced, and the urge to throw something consumes me.

I don't.

I don't because Noah is in the next room.

"The fuck?" I hiss. "You promised me, Jamie."

It's done.

She's done.

It'll break Noah's heart but no more Jamie.

I stepped out of my comfort zone and did this for her.

And it was all a fucking lie.

"I know," she cries out, keeping her voice low. "No one knew she was coming. It was out of the blue—"

"Bull-fucking-shit," I snarl. "Maybe *you* didn't know, but your parents did." *Out of the blue, my ass.* "Heather lives in a different state, and you want me to believe she was just in the neighborhood?"

Her green eyes are pained, anguished, as she gapes at me. "My parents were as shocked as I was. She came to surprise my mother for her birthday. We tried to hide Noah. Trust me, we don't want to mess up seeing him, nor did we want her to say something that'd confuse him."

"Did she see him?"

She nods. "She did."

I grind my teeth. "Did she talk to him?"

The thought of her telling Noah who she is sends a bitter taste in my throat.

The thought of my son's head being fucked with is a stab to the heart.

"At first"—she stops to level her breathing—"I told her he was a kid I was babysitting, but then Noah introduced himself."

"Did she tell him anything?"

"No."

My anger falls a level.

"She stormed out of the house as soon as she found out who he was because she didn't want her husband to know Noah was there. You have nothing to worry about with Heather. I promise you. She was mad that he was there." Every muscle in her body is tense. "I'm sorry. I really am."

I pace in front of her. "This is what I was scared of."

"I'm sorry," she mutters again.

Jamie doesn't deserve this anger.

This hurt.

The respect and the compassion I have for her calm me.

I run my hands through my hair, taking the last of my anger

out on the strands before blowing out a long breath. "It's not your fault."

She frantically rubs her arms up and down.

"That asshole wasn't around my son, was he?"

"No," she rushes out. "He was chain-smoking outside, and I hurried and got Noah out of there. They were driving to his family reunion." She steps forward and rests her hand on my chest. "I give you my word, Cohen. Nothing has changed for her. She's no threat to you ... to Noah."

I rest my hand over hers, the warmth of her skin underneath mine settling me. "I trust you, Jamie." My hands move to her shoulders, and I squeeze them before slowly massaging them for a moment. "Relax."

Her eyes are watery when I finally step back, my arms falling to my sides before I raise one to cup her jaw in my hand.

"It's okay," I whisper. "I trust you."

She bows her head. "Thank you."

Time to make light of this situation.

My dad mind shoots straight to how I help Noah with his tears.

"Looks like someone might need a quesadilla," I say, my tone teasing.

She laughs, wiping her eyes. "You mean, looks like someone needs some tequila?"

Turning on my heel, I reach into the tallest cabinet above the fridge and extract a bottle of tequila I save for moments like this.

Moments when I need to clear my head.

I pluck two shot glasses from another cabinet, fill them to the rim with tequila, and hand one to her. "To us not giving a shit about Heather."

She picks it up without hesitation. "To us not giving a shit about Heather."

There's a *clink* as our glasses hit together, and the tequila burns as it seeps down my throat.

Fuck.

It's been a minute since I've drunk this shit.

Blowing out a breath, I wipe my lips with the back of my arm and groan. "Tell me that helped."

Instead of answering, she pours another and shoots it down. "Now, *that one* helped."

I chuckle and rub my hands together. "Now, how about the quesadilla?"

"A quesadilla sounds amazing."

Without thinking—because I'm an idiot—I kiss her forehead. "Everything is good. Don't worry about it."

Her mouth drops open, and Noah, with perfect timing, comes stomping into the kitchen.

"Pudding cup is gone!" He holds it up. "But my belly is still hungry."

I snatch the tequila and shove it back into the cabinet while Jamie places the shot glasses into the dishwasher. With how flustered we are, I'm shocked one of us didn't drop anything.

"How about a quesadilla?" I ask Noah, raising my voice and forcing it to be as playful as possible.

At least, I'm hoping it sounds that way.

"Woohoo!" Noah shouts. "I love quesadillas!"

I gesture for Jamie to sit down, and she does. Noah starts rambling about school and random shit while I get to work. Jamie listens to Noah, engaging in his conversation as if she were being told the world's secrets while I drag out the quesadilla essentials. My mind is on the kiss as I warm the flour tortillas in a skillet.

It was a friendly peck, I tell myself while topping one with cheese.

One I'd give Georgia or one of her friends if they were upset, I think while flipping it over.

I remove the quesadilla from the skillet, drop it on a plate, and start on another.

That's it.

Innocent.

I've convinced myself our relationship is nothing but platonic when I drop the plates in front of them and grab the salsa, and then we dig in.

I believe Jamie.

I saw the pain in her eyes, the honesty in her words, and the fear.

No way is she capable of faking that.

She never even had to tell me.

That's why, while we clean up, I invite her to Noah's basketball game.

"Noah is going to kick some ass today," Finn says, sliding down the bleachers in the YMCA gymnasium until he's sitting next to me.

"Hush," Grace, Georgia's friend, warns behind him, slapping his shoulder. "There are kids around. Use your PG voice."

Finn groans, throwing his head back. "Just because you use your PG voice at all times doesn't mean I have to."

Georgia, who's sitting next to Grace, smacks the back of his head. "She's an elementary school teacher, dimwit. She has to use her PG voice."

"And I'm a bouncer at a bar. I don't." He rubs the back of his head. "And you're brutal, Georgia."

Most of the gang is here for Noah's basketball game. We erupt in cheers when he runs onto the court with his team, wearing his red uniform and matching tennis shoes. I love the support we have.

Georgia will be at our side, no matter what. She calls us The Three Musketeers. After our father left and our mother fell victim to addiction, I was there to pick up the slack. I was her big brother, and if my parents weren't going to care for her, then I was. I fed her, made sure she was at school every day, helped her with her homework, and provided anything she needed.

Lola and Grace are always a help to us and love Noah to death.

Silas, Finn, and Archer are the same.

Maliki, one of my best friends, is here too. He owns Down Home Pub, a bar in the next county. It's nice we can visit each other's bars, and we've never felt a sense of competition.

We all have fun together.

During the summers, we regularly have cookouts at my house.

"Hi," Jamie whispers, squeezing into the spot on the other side of me. "I tried to get out of the hospital as fast as I could."

I glance over at her with a smile. "You're good. The game hasn't started yet."

The woman behind Jamie taps her shoulder, and we both peek back at her.

"Hi. You're Noah's mom, right?" She points at Jamie. "It's nice to finally meet you." She presses her hand to her chest. "I'm Mary, the teacher's assistant in Noah's class."

Jamie's face pales while I nearly fall off the bleachers.

"Oh, no," Jamie stutters, "I'm not his mom."

Mary blinks. "That's what he said when you picked him up from school last week." Her head tilts to the side. "You're a doctor, right?"

Jamie nods.

Thank fuck no one else is paying attention to us.

My heart batters against my chest. I wish it'd fall out, and I could give it to my son, so he'd have more. I believed I had it all figured out, playing the role of both parents.

I was wrong.

Just as they say a daughter needs her father, a son wants his mother.

Hell, I want that for him.

The memory of the first time he asked me why he didn't have a mom slams into me. He was four, and I hadn't been prepared for it. I froze, words not coming, and it took me a moment to get my shit together.

I knew whatever I said would break his heart.

She didn't want you, was what I wanted to say.

That way, Noah would never track her down.

It's what my mother had told me and Georgia about our father, and I gave no fucks about finding him.

He hadn't wanted me, so I didn't want him.

Sure, it'd crushed me when she told me, but it made me stronger. I never held out hope that he'd return one day, and I was thankful she'd fed me the truth.

Would my son feel the same way?

Would he appreciate the truth, or would it break him?

Those were my worries.

The truth had shattered Georgia. For years, she wondered where he was and why he didn't want her. Eventually, she tracked him down with the hope that he regretted leaving us.

He didn't.

He had two other children.

Two other children he was a dad to.

A real dad to them.

She'd left with a larger hole in her heart.

She finally had to come to terms with not being wanted.

Who will Noah be—me or Georgia?

Wanting the person or not giving a shit?

In the end, I told him the truth.

There were mixed reactions.

His therapist said I was wrong.

Georgia said she understood.

I'd prepared the little guy's heart, so it'd be stronger.

Maybe it was wrong.

Maybe we weren't so much alike, and the pain from the absence of a parent was harder for him than me. It could be different because he lost a mother, not a father. I had plenty of friends with fathers not in the picture. Mothers not in the picture were less common.

I have a feeling if Noah ever seeks out Heather, it'll be the same as what happened with Georgia.

"Maybe there was some confusion. I'm not—" Jamie stops and gives Mary a warm smile. "It's nice to meet you." She whips around, setting her eyes on the court, her shoulders tense.

Not as tense as mine, but pretty damn close.

These are the moments I feel like a failure.

I don't regret Noah, but I regret who his mother is.

Never in the time we'd been together—nearly a decade—did I think Heather would turn her back on us like she did.

Her actions have made me question any type of relationship.

I haven't been celibate, having my fair share of hookups, but that's it. I'm too weak to give them what they want. My heart is too untrusting after giving my all to someone for so long, only to get shit on.

My guard is up for both of us.

So I fuck a little here and there, but I always go home to Noah.

Noah sends us a wave from the court before they start the game.

"He looks adorable in his uniform," Jamie says, leaning into me.

"Grace tried to bedazzle it," Finn comments.

"It would've been cute," Grace argues.

"Sorry, babe, but no."

Finn gets smacked in the back of the head again, this time by Grace, and he chuckles.

Our circle is strange—a heap of sexual tension.

Grace and Finn flirt like no other, and they're opposites. She's the sweet schoolteacher while Finn is far from innocent. He's been through hell and back, and he refuses to ask Grace out, in fear he'll rub his tainted life on her pristine one.

Sexual tension bleeds off Lola and Silas. Everyone is waiting for the day they bang. They share the same personality—sarcastic assholes who date around and avoid commitment.

That leaves Archer, Georgia, and me as the odd ones out.

Archer isn't a dater.

Georgia is too busy enjoying life for a boyfriend—or so she says.

And I have my issues.

"Go, Noah!" Georgia cheers.

Pride punches me while I watch him play. It's entertaining since most of the kids don't know what the hell they're doing, but Noah is having a blast.

Since the kids are just learning the game, there isn't a winner.

"Jamie, you're going out for tacos with us," Georgia insists after the game.

Everyone's attention whips to her in expectation, and her eyes avert to the bleachers that are clearing out.

One thing I appreciate is how they're not acting strange around Jamie, as if it were normal that she's here even though they all know the situation.

"Come on," Noah says, moving to her side and jumping up and down.

She shoots me a questioning look.

"Yeah, come on," I say, throwing my arm back to gesture toward the doors.

"At least you have decent taste in tacos," I tell Jamie.

She's sitting next to me at the best taco joint in town.

Granted, La Mesa is the *only* taco place in town.

The food is to die for, and Noah loves their nachos and cinnamon churros. We eat here a few times a month with the gang since there's enough room for everyone and an arcade in the back for the kids to play games.

Jamie points at me with her fork. "At least, *you* have decent taste in tacos."

"How about we agree we *both* have decent taste in tacos?"

"Fine, but I ordered first, so you copied me."

I chuckle, turning in my chair, and rest my elbow on the table while focusing on her. "I order the same thing every time!"

"As do I."

"Mm-hmm."

"Ask Ashley."

"You two still best friends?"

She nods. "Yep, and she'll confirm I'm a creature of habit. Shredded chicken tacos have always been my go-to." She bites into her lower lip. "I do get their quesadillas sometimes too. They're delish."

I throw my head back. "Can we both agree my quesadillas are more *delish*?"

Everyone around us is having their own conversations, and Noah is in the arcade, playing with Georgia, while Jamie and I are wrapped in our own little world.

"You have a major hard-on about your quesadillas, huh?"

"They're my specialty." I wink at her.

"Dad!" Noah comes barreling toward us and snags a churro from his plate. "Can I hang out at Jamie's tonight?"

Like when Georgia asked Jamie to come to dinner, everyone's attention darts to her. The table falls silent.

And also like when Georgia asked her, she appears uncomfortable as she shifts in her chair.

Noah pouts out his lower lip. "Pretty, pretty please?"

Not only has he put Jamie on the spot, but he's put me on the spot too.

"Buddy," I chime in, "we don't know if Jamie has plans tonight."

"I mean, I have the night off," Jamie rushes out, her eyes directed at me. "I don't have any plans and would love the company."

"Yay!" Noah dances in place with the churro in his hand. "We can eat cupcakes and watch cartoons and play games."

"*You sure it's okay?*" I mouth to her.

She nods with a smile before mouthing, "*If it's okay with you?*"

I glance back at Noah, who's chomping on his churro. "All right, you can stay over there, but you have to promise to behave."

"I will!" Noah chirps.

Silas slaps the table. "Looks like we're having guys' night!"

"Are we doing Twisted Fox or Down Home?" Maliki asks.

We tend to have guys' night at one of our bars. When one of us needs a break from our workplace, we go to the other's.

"Twisted Fox," Finn says. "That way, we can try to talk Archer into joining us."

"Why does it only have to be guys' night?" Georgia asks. "I nominate it to be guys' and girls' night."

Georgia lives up to the little sister role through and through. Even as a grown-up, she crashes my parties and always has to be in the know. Not that I mind. I love that she enjoys spending time with us, and that way, I can also keep an eye on her.

"It can't be a guys' and girls' night because Archer will act like we have the plague if you're there," Finn says.

"Archer can kiss my ass," she fires back.

"It's okay. We'll have a girls' night," Lola says, a sly smile spreading along her bright red lips. "At Twisted Fox."

Georgia laughs, reaches across the table, and high-fives her.

"It'd be nice if you stopped stalking us, ladies," Silas comments, smirking.

Georgia turns her attention to Finn. "Prepare for men to hit on Grace at our girls' night since you want nothing to do with us, and you can't cockblock her."

Grace's cheeks redden as she hisses Georgia's name.

"Nobody is hitting on any of you," Finn snaps.

Lola rolls her eyes. "Someone had better hit on me."

Silas flips her off.

I lean in to whisper in Jamie's ear, goose bumps crawling up her neck as I get closer. "Seriously, if you have plans, I can be the bad guy and tell Noah no."

She massages her hand over her neck, as if attempting to erase her reaction to me. "No plans, seriously. Go have fun."

I don't remember the last time I had a guys' night.

Sure, every so often, I have drinks with the guys before heading home, but nothing like this.

Whiskey—a rarity for me—is in my glass. I tend to stick to beer when I drink.

Noah is in good hands tonight, and I need to drink away my thoughts of the woman whose hands he's in.

My relationship with Jamie is changing. She's becoming like family to us.

Noah is falling in love with her.

And me?

When she's around, my heart clenches—and also battles with my brain.

It's right, my heart says.

It's wrong, my brain chimes in.

Finn, Silas, Maliki, and I are huddled around a table in the corner of the bar, shooting the shit. I called in our part-time bartender to cover for Archer tonight, and we've been trying to drag him away from the bar for an hour, but he's reluctant.

"How's the bar going?" I ask Maliki.

He shrugs, circling his hand around the neck of his beer bottle. "Same shit, different day."

At one time, Maliki and I had planned to open a bar together, but when his father nearly lost their family bar, he moved home and took over. Before opening Twisted Fox, I checked with him to make sure he was cool with it. We aren't direct competition, but I didn't want to step on anyone's toes.

He was fucking ecstatic for me.

And wanted to kick my ass for doubting if he would be.

"Oh, wow, fancy seeing you jerks here," Georgia says, coming into view.

Lola and Grace are behind her with drinks in their hands. They set their drinks down, then drag another table and stools next to our table, and join us.

"Isn't the little sister supposed to quit being annoying to the big brother when she gets older?" Finn asks.

Georgia narrows her eyes on him. "Shut up. Don't act like you don't love it when Grace is around."

Grace's cheeks redden, and she twirls a strawberry-blond strand of hair around her finger. "Are ... you okay with us interrupting?"

"You know I don't care," I say, jerking my head toward the guys. "Neither do they. They just like giving you a hard time."

"*Almost* all of you don't care," Lola chimes in, her attention moving to Archer, who's talking to the bartender.

"Which is why Georgia needs to go sit in the corner by herself when Archer comes over," Finn states.

"Archer isn't a child, so you need to stop worrying about how he feels." Georgia shrugs. "I'm cooler than him anyway."

"That is true," Silas says. "She's nowhere near as grumpy as Archer."

"Archer is only grumpy when Georgia is around," Finn argues. "Cause and motherfucking effect."

Georgia rolls her eyes. "He'll get over it."

"Will either of you ever explain why you hate each other?" Silas asks.

Grace's and Lola's eyes nervously shoot to Georgia.

"Our personalities clash," Georgia answers before downing drink.

People stop at our table to say hi and offer to buy us drinks. We might have some pain-in-the-ass customers, but I love the majority of our clientele. Archer remains behind the bar, slinging drinks while also eyeing us, and I'm clueless whether he'll join us now since Georgia is here.

He can get the fuck over that.

"Have you decided what we're doing for Noah's birthday?" Georgia asks.

"He's narrowed it down to a snow resort, a water park, or Chuck E. Cheese," I answer.

"Dear Lord, please don't let it be Chuck E. Cheese," Silas says with a shudder.

"Why?" Lola asks. "Don't all your nineteen-year-old girlfriends love Chuck E. Cheese?"

"Piss off," he grumbles, and they both crack up in laughter.

Swear to God, they need to fuck and get it out of the way.

Same with Grace and Finn.

Scratch that. It'll only create more problems if my friends start fucking Georgia's friends.

Thank fuck none of them have a thing for Georgia.

We'd have problems.

I love my friends, but that's against bro code.

It's crossing the line.

Just like me thinking about touching Heather's sister is crossing the motherfucking line.

So why do I want to?

As I sit here drinking, why is she on my mind?

"Look who's finally joining us," Georgia says, wiping away my thoughts.

Archer is standing at the table, a Jack and Coke in his hand and a glare on his face. Seconds later, he turns around and storms away.

Georgia jumps up from her stool. "Oh, my God!"

She scurries behind Archer, grabbing his elbow, and he swings back to look at her. They exchange words, him tipping his head down as they talk to each other, until he runs his hand through his hair. He nods, and when they return, Archer slides a stool next to me and sits.

We drink.

We laugh.

We have a good-ass time.

Three hours later, I grab my phone to text Sylvia and inform her I'm on my way home. My hand freezes at the realization that she isn't babysitting.

It's the first night Noah has stayed somewhere other than my home or Georgia's.

I'm letting Jamie in.

And I hope to God she doesn't rupture our hearts.

CHAPTER
FIFTEEN

JAMIE

My phone rings at the same time I crawl into bed.

To say the day has been exhausting is an understatement. I worked a double before Noah's game and went to dinner, and then Noah and I watched movies when we got home. Noah crashed on my couch a few hours later, and I carried him to my guest bedroom. He whined as I tucked him in the same way Cohen had the night Noah was sick.

When I grab my phone, I see Cohen is calling.

He called to check in on Noah a few hours ago and told him good night.

Is he that paranoid that he's calling again?

No way am I waking up Noah.

"Hello?" I answer, stuffing a pillow behind my head and making myself comfortable.

"Hey, Jamie," he says, his voice sounding off. "How's my guy doing?"

What's *off* about his voice is the slight slur with each word.

"The better question is how are *you* doing?" I reply with a laugh.

"What do you mean?"

"Come on. You're drunk as a skunk."

He chuckles. "You know, I've never understood what that saying means, and I hear it a lot at my job."

"Yeah, me neither." I stretch out my legs and fight back a yawn, not wanting him to end the call because he thinks I'm tired. "Did you have fun at your guys' night?"

"Actually, I did."

"That's good."

"It's been a while since I've detoured from my two-beer rule."

"Two-beer rule?"

"Georgia has been swamped with work and school, so Noah has been with Sylvia more. I get nervous he'll need something or that he'll get hurt. Not that Sylvia is a bad babysitter. I'm just a nervous-ass dad. So if I grab a drink, it's two beers."

"But tonight?" My heart races as I cross my ankles and then uncross them.

"Tonight, I know he's in good hands."

Biting away the urge to squeal, I grab the fluffy pillow next to me and place it against my smile.

"I'm sorry for being such a dick to you at first." An exasperated breath leaves him. "My trust in people is shit."

I drag the pillow away, still frazzled. "I get it. I'd be protective too."

"I love that you understand. That you get me." A light *hmm* leaves him. "It's hot."

I force a nervous laugh and wait for him to tell me he's kidding.

He doesn't.

All he does is wait for me to say something.

"Wow," I drawl. "You really are drunk as a skunk."

"Guilty as charged."

"Do you need a ride home?"

"I'm home. Silas was the DD. He's having issues with his girlfriend and crashing on the couch. She doesn't like when he has guys' nights."

"Lola? Did the girls not crash your party?"

I don't see Lola being that overprotective of Silas, but if I had a boyfriend that hot, I'd probably want to keep an eye on him too.

"Silas wishes Lola were his girlfriend. Hell, we all do."

"But he flirted with Lola all day."

"Lola won't date Silas, so he has Helena. None of us are exactly sure what Helena is to him—girlfriend, fuck buddy, definitely a pain in his ass, and she's a nightmare. His dumbass let her move into his place last month. So when they fight, he crashes at one of our places to avoid her."

"That sounds like a mess."

"Guys like us"—his voice turns strained—"we're not built for relationships anymore."

"You're not built for a relationship because of Heather?"

"Because of Heather," he whispers.

"One bad relationship, and you're done?"

"One bad relationship?" he scoffs. "Jamie, I got fucked over big time."

For a moment, I'm at a loss for words. I don't want to bad-mouth my sister, but no way am I sticking up for her actions. She did fuck him over big time.

"What about you?" he asks, snapping me away from my thoughts. "You dating anyone? Word is, the Sprinkles heir held your heart."

Oh, my God.

"The Sprinkles heir?" I bite back a laugh.

"Sally Sprinkles's son."

"How do you know about Seth?"

"Noah. My kid is quite the gossiper."

I'd say so.

How did this conversation go from him to me?

"I dated Seth when I was in med school," I explain, my heart roaring in my chest. "I was too busy for a relationship, so we didn't do much of the dating life. It was mostly us, you know, hanging out."

"You mean, fucking?"

My cheeks turn a bright red, and I'm happy he can't see me. "I'm so not answering that."

"Why not?" he groans. "You throw me any question, and I'll answer it."

"No, because you're … you."

"Heather said you eavesdropped on her talking to her friends about us having sex when you were younger and even listened to us *you know* a few times."

"Gross. I *overheard* Heather talking about your sex life because the girl has a big mouth. Yes, I also heard you banging from her bedroom since we *shared a wall*." I make a gagging noise. "Trust me, you and my sister never made sex sound hot. She sounded like a dying bird."

"And what did I sound like?"

I shut my eyes and remember the vomity memory.

He didn't sound like a dying bird.

He moaned Heather's name.

Vomit.

Told her she felt good.

Gag me.

Once.

That was the only time I heard them.

After that, I used my allowance and invested in some quality sound-canceling headphones.

"How long has it been since *you* had sex?"

My mouth falls open as my skin tingles. "I'm most definitely never, ever having that conversation with you." I pause and add another, "Never," for extra measure.

He laughs. "Oh, come on. Give a drunk man some entertainment."

"I'm sure you have someone in your Contacts you can call for entertainment."

"What if I don't want someone else's entertainment? What if I want *yours*?"

The hell?

What has suddenly changed with him?

"You're drunk," I say sternly. "You need to get some rest."

"Is that doctor's orders?"

"That is the doctor's orders."

"Dr. Jamie is no fun."

"Never said I was fun."

"Noah says you are."

"Noah says I'm fun because I play with him, give him candy, and buy him pizza."

"Sounds pretty damn fun to me. Let's be fun together."

"Okay, now, this is *really* when I say good night."

There's a brief silence, and when he speaks, all humor has ceased, "Why couldn't you have been older?" There's pain in his voice. "Why couldn't I have chosen the other sister?"

His pain causes me to release an anguished sigh. "Cohen—"

"Seriously, Jamie," he cuts me off. "The fact that I'm thinking about you is … I don't know … messed up? But I can't help it."

"You need to get some sleep." I release a drawn-out breath. "Good night, Cohen."

"Good night, Jamie," he whispers. "Sleep tight."

Does Cohen remember last night?

That's my first thought when I wake up.

It's what runs through my mind as I make Noah French toast.

Cohen's words have consumed me.

"Why couldn't I have chosen the other sister?"

If only I'd been older.

The problem is, all we have are what-ifs.

It's like a never-ending story.

Crossing any lines between us would be some Jerry Springer shit.

And Jesus, it'd confuse the hell out of Noah.

He's already telling people I'm his mom.

My gaze moves to the rug rat as he drowns his French toast in syrup. My heart sinks. It has to be hard for him not to have a mother. Anger toward Heather plows through me.

How could she do that to him?

To both of the boys who deserve so much more than being abandoned.

I'm in the kitchen cleaning up when Cohen texts me.

> Cohen: Is it cool if I pick up Noah around noon?

Nervousness and anticipation zip through my veins.

A shift is happening between us.

I shut the dishwasher, scurry to my bathroom, and fluff my hair out with my hands while staring in the mirror.

Why am I stressing?

Why am I trying to impress him?

With a groan, I pull my hair into a ponytail.

No looking cute for him.

Bad Jamie.

Hopefully, he sticks with that same rule and shows up, looking like a hungover mess.

My yoga pants stay on, and I pull a loose sweatshirt over my head.

I pour myself another cup of coffee and join Noah in the living room where he's watching cartoons. The urge to find out why he said I was his mom is on the tip of my tongue, but I don't have the courage to ask.

It's not my place.

Plus, I don't want to embarrass or confuse Noah.

I suck down the rest of my coffee at the knock on the door. When I open it, my wish that Cohen would look like a hungover mess isn't granted.

No, he looks hot—as per usual.

He leans against the doorframe, a smile on his lips. "Hey. How'd everything go?"

"Great," I say, my voice too chipper, too unlike me. *Until you drunk-dialed me and sent me for a tailspin.*

I scurry backward before walking to the kitchen. He shuts the door behind him and joins me. I look like I crawled out of the hole I'd wanted him to crawl from since I slept like shit after his little mindfuck phone call.

"How much sugar did he talk you into?"

I laugh. "Not much. The churro gave him enough of a sugar high."

We hear Noah's footsteps before he comes into view.

He runs to Cohen and hugs his legs, grinning up at him. "Hi, Dad! I missed you!"

Cohen returns the hug with a tight squeeze, happiness in his eyes. "Hey, buddy. I missed you way more."

"How was your night?" I ask after Noah runs back to the living room to finish his show.

If Cohen remembers our call, his face doesn't give it away.

"Good. I had the first relaxing night in my bar than I think I've ever had."

"Did the whole crew show up?"

He raises a brow. "The whole crew?"

"Yeah, your squad."

"Squad? Who am I, Taylor Swift?"

"Wow, you know Taylor Swift has a squad?"

"Noah digs her." He smirks. "He's a Swiftie, so it's hard for me not to be one too."

"Who would've thought that behind all that hard-ass persona, you get down to 'Shake It Off'?"

He holds his hands out, palms facing me. "Whoa, whoa. Settle down there. I don't get down to it. I *tolerate* it."

"My show is over now!" Noah says, running back into the kitchen. "I'm hungry."

"I was going to make some lunch," I tell Cohen. "Want some?"

He tilts his head to the side. "What's on the menu?"

"Your options are grilled cheese, pizza rolls, or turkey sandwiches."

"Ah, such delicacies."

I shrug. "Shush, or you'll starve."

"What are pizza rolls?" Noah cuts in.

"The best food ever." I whip my attention to Cohen, mustering the most serious look on my face I can manage. "He's never had pizza rolls? What kind of monster are you?"

"As a doctor, should *you* be eating pizza rolls?"

I playfully bite my lip before swatting at him. "Listen, pizza rolls and coffee are my main food groups."

Noah taps Cohen's leg, looking up at him. "What's the difference between pizza and pizza rolls?"

"Pizza rolls are like bite-sized pizza," I explain, preheating the toaster oven, opening the freezer, and pulling out the bag of pizza rolls.

"Ooh, sounds yummy!" Noah says, holding up both hands and separating his fingers. "Can I have this many of them?"

Cohen pats Noah on the back. "Sure. Go have a seat at the table."

Noah hops to the table while singing the theme song of the cartoon that was playing.

I cut the bag open and drop the pizza rolls on aluminum foil while waiting for the toaster oven to heat. "These will probably help with your hangover," I comment, patting Cohen's stomach when I pass him.

"Dad, what's a hangover?" Noah asks.

Cohen chuckles. "One lesson you'll learn is that he picks up on everything you say." His gaze pings to Noah. "It's what adults say when they aren't feeling well."

"Cool! I want to be an adult and have a hangover."

"You can't say that until you're an adult," Cohen scolds, his tone still gentle.

Cohen leans against the counter next to me. "Who says I have a hangover?"

I drop a pizza roll on the floor, and he picks it up.

"I mean, you were with your friends, so it was an assumption." I dramatically gesture to his face. "Your face also looks like it was run over by a car."

"Run over by a car?" He throws the pizza roll across the kitchen, and it lands in the trash can. *Show-off.* "Thank you for the nice compliment."

"Always happy to serve them." I slide away from him. "Do you want something to drink? Water to wash down the Advil?"

"I'll take a water, no Advil." He signals toward the pizza rolls. "And be sure to throw me some of those in there for the hungover dude."

"Nope, none for the haters." I still add more.

"Pizza rolls were my jam when I was twenty and ate like a kid in college with no priorities involving a healthy diet."

I elbow his stomach, and he lets out a, "Humph."

While the pizza rolls bake, Noah tells Cohen about all the fun he had here last night, and as they talk, I make our plates.

We sit at the table like one cute, dysfunctional, will-never-happen family.

"These are delicious," Noah says, licking sauce off his fingers. "I want to have them every single day, okay, Dad?"

"Yeah, not happening." Cohen pops the last one in his mouth.

Noah's attention shoots to me as a mischievous look comes across his face. "Jamie will let me come over and eat them whenever I want."

I laugh and poke his shoulder. "Not if I eat them all first."

He hugs his belly while cracking up in giggles.

Noah is munching on a cookie he bribed out of me when Cohen stands to help me clean the kitchen.

"Can we talk about what happened yesterday?" he asks, close into my space.

"Sure," I drawl, uncertain of which situation he's referring to. "I don't know why Noah told people you're his mom, but I'll talk to him about it."

"Oh, right." I sigh. "My guess is, he doesn't want to be the odd one out."

"Mine too." His face falls. "It sucks because I can't do anything to fix it. Any other issues, I find a way." He runs his hands through his hair. "When he has school events, I'm the only one there for him—Georgia, too, sometimes—and I see the look in his eyes when he watches his friends with their mothers. He wants that, and fuck, I want that for him."

I work to keep my voice as soothing as possible. "I know it's hard, and I wish Heather would get her head out of her ass."

He recoils, stumbling back a step, and his stare turns cold. "Heather will never be Noah's mother. She has no place in our lives, period, Jamie."

I shuffle my feet on the floor. I opened the box, so I might as well explore some. "You've never wondered …?" I abruptly stop, questioning if I'm about to make the right move before asking, "What if she returns and wants to know Noah?"

"Nope." His voice is rough. "She signed over her rights and isn't shit to him. It'll stay that way." He shakes his head, torment on his face. "It's bad enough she saw him at your parents', and her behavior further proves my point. Hell, she didn't even want to see Noah. She was afraid her fucking boyfriend—"

"Husband," I interrupt.

"Husband," he grinds out. "She doesn't deserve any of that boy's love." He jerks his head toward Noah.

"I understand." I offer him a comforting smile—or at least, I hope it appears that way.

My question has changed the mood of the room.

No more pizza roll jokes.

Talk of Heather has ruined that.

His shoulders slump. "I wish I'd chosen a better mother for him."

"Why couldn't I have chosen the other sister?"

My head spins, and I step closer, rubbing his shoulders. "Hey, don't be too hard on yourself. He's lucky to have such a great father."

"That'll never fill the need for a mother's love. Obviously, look at what he told his teacher."

"Eventually, you'll find a woman who can be that figure for him." *And I'll hate her.*

"We have Georgia"—his eyes lower, sorrowful but with a hint of hope in them, and then they meet mine—"and you."

CHAPTER
SIXTEEN

COHEN

S ilas claps me on my back while passing me behind the bar.
"Don't make any plans tomorrow night."

"Why?" I ask.

"We have a double date."

"No, we don't."

"Yes, we do." He throws his head back and groans. "Helena's cousin is in town."

"That's a big *hell no*."

"Why?"

"Helena's cousin is annoying as fuck, and Helena is crazy as fuck. Not people I want to spend my night with. No offense to you, man."

"Oh, come on. She liked you last time she was here."

"Hook her up with Archer."

He scoffs. "Archer doesn't have the patience for her. He said, 'Fuck no,' before I even finished my sentence."

"Neither do I, so fuck no. Ask Finn."

"He's working."

"I'm sure you have another friend."

"Come on," he pleads. "One night. All you have to do is sit at the table with us, drink, laugh a few times, *maybe* let her kiss your dick."

I shake my head, shuddering. "Nope."

"What about kiss your cheek?"

"Also a no."

"You didn't have a problem with her before."

"Oh, you mean, the first time I met her when she drunkenly tried to drop to her knees underneath the table here and blow me?"

He points at me with his lollipop. "See, she liked you!" He presses his hands together in a begging motion. "A few hours. That's all I'm asking. Hell, you don't even have to listen to her. Just nod and agree with whatever she says."

"I don't have a babysitter." That's always my get-out-of-jail card.

"Georgia and Lola already agreed to babysit." A shit-eating smirk covers his face. "I bought them tickets to one of those ice-skating shows."

"You already found a babysitter for me, you jackass?"

He releases a booming laugh. "I knew you'd use that excuse."

I narrow my eyes at him.

"Do it for me, man."

"Fine," I grumble. "But you're taking one of my shifts this weekend."

He snaps his fingers and points at me. "You're the best."

"I know; I know."

He turns to look at me and walks backward. "Who knows? Maybe you two will hit it off this time."

"The odds of my dick falling off are higher." I blow out a noisy breath. "I'm not staying out late, either."

"Okay, old man."

"You sure are dressed like shit for a date," Georgia comments, falling onto the couch when she walks into the living room.

"You can't see how excited I am?" I give her a cold stare. "Thanks for throwing me under the bus."

"Pardon you. He asked Lola, and I'm only along for the ride." She grins. "Who's the lucky woman you're dressing homeless for?"

I look at the floor as I mutter the answer, "Helena's cousin."

"Silas's Helena?"

I nod.

"Ew, sorry." She perks up when I glance back at her. "Maybe you'll get laid."

I dramatically fake dry-heaving. "Don't ever talk about me getting laid again."

"Oh, come on." She props her feet on the coffee table. "We're adults here. You don't think I know how Noah was made?"

Noah comes rushing out of his bedroom, saving me from this dreaded conversation, wearing one of my hats, a T-shirt, and dinosaur socks over his jeans that hit the knees. "I'm ready!"

At least Silas was smart enough to have us "double date" at the bar.

I slipped Archer twenty bucks to come over and say he needed me to do something in the office.

That was twenty minutes ago, and his ass still hasn't made his way over here.

The smart-ass grins he's shooting my way confirms he's fucking with me.

I'm giving him ten more minutes before I tell Becca to kiss his dick.

It's not that Becca isn't attractive.

She's gorgeous.

Thick blond hair, nice *fake* breasts, and a body fit for men's magazines.

She's smart.

The problem is, we don't click.

There's no spark.

Our lives are too different.

She's twenty-one and in the stage of her life wrapped around partying and having a good time. There's nothing wrong with that. That was my scene before I had Noah. My priorities have changed, and even though she insists she loves kids, dating a man with a child is harder than she thinks.

The woman is always second in line.

"And that's why I stopped drinking raspberry vodka," Becca says, cutting me away from my thoughts and stopping my glare pinned at Archer.

I tilt my head and phony smile. "I'm not a fan, either."

She laughs before releasing a sigh. "You weren't listening to a word I said."

"Sorry." I scrub a hand over my face. "My brain is scrambled right now. I've had a long day."

She takes a drink, her red lips wrapping around the straw. "I get it. This is your workplace. We should've gone somewhere else. Helena yelled at Silas when he came here, but I told her it was cool." She shrugs. "It's a fun place." She taps my shoulder. "But get out of work mode and into fun mode."

"I'm working on it." I grind my teeth while Archer acts like he hasn't noticed my signals to save me.

"Maybe tomorrow we can go to dinner?" Becca asks.

I frown. "I don't have a babysitter tomorrow."

She caresses my arm. "You can bring Noah. I'd love to meet him."

"I'd love to meet him."

I hate when chicks say that.

Noah isn't meeting anyone until we've had at least five dates. I refuse to bring new women in and out of his life.

Maggie, one of our waitresses, stops at the table. "Cohen, Archer said he needs you."

About damn time.

I slide off my stool and shoot Becca an apologetic glance. "I'll be back."

"Mmkay." She grabs her drink and takes a long draw, shimmying her shoulders from side to side.

I shove Archer when I make it behind the bar. "Took you long enough, asshole."

"What?" He smirks. "You looked like you were having a blast."

I narrow my eyes at him.

"Not to mention, Silas outbid you. He paid me fifty to wait longer to bail you out."

"You sneaky bastards."

He laughs. "I would've done it for thirty. Now, since I bailed you out, why don't you bring another keg up here, will ya? Might as well make yourself useful."

CHAPTER
SEVENTEEN

JAMIE

I FaceTime Cohen's phone a few times a week and talk to
Noah.

It's become the highlight of my day.

I get home, shower, throw my hair into a messy bun, and hit
Cohen's name.

My face shows on my screen as it rings a few times before it's
answered.

I nearly drop the phone, and my mouth goes slack when the
woman comes into view.

A drop-dead gorgeous woman.

"Hello?" she answers.

A deep tinge of insecurity wracks through me as I notice how
different we are. Her hair is down in loose waves, her eyeliner is
winged with a precision I could never master, and her low-cut
top shows more cleavage than any of my push-up bras can
manage.

"Is, uh"—I play with my messy bun, an attempt to make it
look not so sloppy—"Cohen there?"

"Why?" She puckers her lips. "Who are you?"

"A friend." I'm gripping the phone so tight that I'm waiting
for it to crumble in my hand.

"What kind of friend?"

"Is Noah around? I called to talk to him."

"Why do you want to talk to his son?" Something hits her, and she lowers her voice, scooting in closer to the phone's camera. "Oh, my God. Are you the baby mama?"

"What? No. Can you just tell them Jamie called, please?"

"Not if *Jamie* doesn't tell me who she is."

"Who's that?" Another girl comes into view before a dirty look forms on her face, and a snarl leaves her.

Oh, this is the mean one. Definitely.

"Why are you calling Cohen?" the mean one asks.

"Whoa, whoa." Silas is the next person I see.

It's like they're passing me around in a game.

"Oh, hey, Jamie," he says with a smile.

"Um, who is Jamie?" Mean Barbie snaps.

"There it is," Cohen says in the distance. "I thought I'd lost my phone."

There's a moment of silence.

"Wait. Becca, what are you doing on my phone?"

"Um ..." *Becca* bites into her lower lip. "It rang, and I didn't want you to miss a call."

"It's Jamie!" Silas informs him.

I still and hover my finger over the End button.

"Oh shit. Hey, Jamie," Cohen says, jerking his phone out of Becca's hand.

"I'm getting another call," I say before hanging up.

It's a slap in the face.

Another reminder.

I cannot fall for Cohen.

He'll never be mine.

CHAPTER
EIGHTEEN

COHEN

"Where's Noah?" Maliki asks, standing next to me while I season the burgers on the grill in front of me.

We're in my backyard, having a barbeque. It's something I try to do a few times a month when the weather is nice. I invite everyone. We eat a shit-ton of food, play cornhole, and hang out. Our lives can be shitstorms sometimes, so it's nice to catch up.

There's nothing better than enjoying a beer with your friends and playing some yard games.

That sounds way more honky-tonk than it is, I swear.

"He's with Jamie," I say, flipping a burger.

Jamie and I have returned to our avoidance game since the Becca incident. I tried calling her on my way home to apologize, but she hit the *fuck you* button. She hasn't FaceTimed us since, and it's sucked. We started looking forward to her calls. She'd tell us hospital stories or embarrassing memories of me when I was a dumbass teenager, and Noah would burst into laughter. Sometimes, she'd even read him bedtime stories.

Shame hits me whenever I think about what happened.

I took that away from him.

"Oh, he's with Jamie, huh?" Maliki says, covering his smirk with the neck of his beer when he takes a drink.

"Don't give me that look."

He situates his hat, drawing it further down his forehead, hiding his eyes. "What look?"

"How about we talk about your little girlfriend instead?" I grab my beer and suck it down.

"Nice subject change, jackass."

I shrug. "I like her, and you seem happy."

"We're friends. She needed somewhere to stay. The end."

"It'll be a good story you tell your kids one day about how you met their mom because you were kicking her out of your bar."

"Funny," he grumbles, handing me a plate, and I start loading it with the cooked burgers.

Maliki brought his *roommate,* Sierra, with him. He and Sierra have been playing a cat-and-mouse game for years. It started when she kept sneaking into his bar, underage, and he kept kicking her out. When she turned twenty-one, they became friends, some shit happened in a relationship she was in, and now, she's living with him. The way they look at each other and how his arm was wrapped around her shoulders in ownership as they strolled through my backyard scream that they're more than friends.

Just as I'm about to tell him I'm offended that he's lying to me, Georgia yells, "Hey, Jamie!"

Even though I've been expecting her to drop off Noah, adrenaline speeds through my chest at the sound of her name. I turn around at the same time Noah slams into me, nearly knocking me over. My brow arches as he waves something in the air.

"Jamie bought me an iPod!" he announces.

An iPod?

The hell?

Noah doesn't need a damn iPod at his age.

Not wanting to rain on his parade, I shoot him a smile, and we head over to Jamie, who's talking to Grace, Lola, and Sierra.

"An iPod?" I ask when I reach her. "You spoil him too much."

Even though I know the true intentions of the iPod.

Jamie laughs; it is fake and fraudulent, and it pisses me off. "It's for selfish reasons, so we can FaceTime."

I frown—mine not fake. "You always FaceTime him on my phone. It's never been a problem."

She's gone back to communicating through Georgia again as though we're playing fucking telephone on the playground, which has resulted in dozens of questions from my nosy sister. I planned to bring up the FaceTime call Becca answered to Jamie today, but with all the attention on us, it isn't the time.

It'll have to wait until I can catch Jamie again when she's not avoiding me.

Her face is blank when she replies, "You're busy sometimes."

I wince before checking myself, deciding to go a different angle with this. Maybe I can get her to stay and corner her later, make her talk to me.

"We have plenty of food." I sweep my arm out to gesture to the table loaded with burgers, hot dogs, chips, and every other barbeque food you can think of. "Stay."

Hang out.

Let me explain myself.

Don't be pissed at me.

"Thanks for the offer, but I can't." She kneels and hugs Noah. "Make sure you call me, okay?"

Noah hugs her back and salutes her. "You got it!"

She kisses the top of his head and waves good-bye to everyone, not giving me one more glance.

"She is pissed at you," Georgia sings when Jamie is out of earshot.

"She's not pissed at me," I say, imitating her high-pitched voice.

"Why's she pissed at you?" Grace asks.

"She FaceTimed Cohen to talk to Noah the other day, and

some chick answered, asking Jamie twenty-one questions about who she was." Georgia rolls her eyes and glares at me. "That's why she bought the iPod."

I'm well aware.

"I need to stop telling you stuff," I mutter before shaking my head, grabbing Noah, and throwing him over my shoulder.

Noah shrills in laughter, clasping his arms around my neck, and I take off, running across the yard.

I drop him to his feet when we reach Silas and Finn, who are playing cornhole. Noah shows off his iPod to Finn while I shove Silas's shoulder.

"I can't believe I was dumb enough to let you set me up on that date," I hiss to him. "Jamie hates me now."

"Oh, so that's my fault, huh?" he asks.

"Damn straight."

"Maybe it is my bad, but it's *your* bad for not talking to her about it. *Your* bad for not telling her about the hard-on you have for her."

I roll my eyes and shake my head before playing a round of cornhole with Noah and the guys, hoping it'll take my mind off Jamie.

CHAPTER NINETEEN

JAMIE

"Don't forget. We're going out for Kelsey's birthday," Ashley reminds me from across the table.

We're having lunch at the deli across from the street from the hospital. It's her lunch break, and my shift just ended. I can't wait to go home and take a nice long bath. As much as I love work taking my mind off my issues, I need to clear my head. The call with Cohen's date *Becca* has been on my mind since it happened, and I can't seem to shake the jealousy that consumes me anytime I think about it.

Cohen isn't mine.

He never will be.

I went to the Apple store and bought Noah an iPod to make sure an interrupted by a gorgeous girl phone call didn't happen again.

"Dinner, right?" I ask.

Kelsey is our friend from med school, and every year, we go out for our birthdays.

"Nope. She switched it up this year, and we're going where her boyfriend wants." She rolls her eyes and fakes enthusiasm. "Yay!"

"Where's she having it now?"

Ashley bites back a grin. "He likes sports."

"Okay ..."

"He likes watching sports at *sports bars*."

I glare at her, knowing where she's going with this. "A sports bar not around here, and where I don't know the owner, correct?"

She shakes her head, her grin now in full effect.

I've kept her updated on all things Noah and Cohen. She even met Noah once and had dinner with us.

"Oh, darn." I smack my knee. "I forgot I have plans."

"You do have plans." This time, she tries to hide her smile while biting into her straw. Doesn't work. "Going to Twisted Fox and hanging out with yours truly are your plans."

"I had a super-long shift today." I fake a yawn.

"You had a super-short shift today."

"How do you know?"

She grabs her phone, unlocks the screen, and shows it to me. "Remember when I texted you last week, asking if you had the night off, and you said this? Not to mention, you just got off work."

I glare at our text message thread where I told her I was most definitely open tonight.

Damn texts get you caught every time.

It makes it really hard to lie in today's day and age.

"I agreed to go to dinner, not a bar."

"You've never had a problem with going to a bar before, Miss Loves Her Wine."

"The problem isn't going to a bar. It's going to a bar owned by a man I have issues with." I shoot her a *so there* look.

"Since when and why do you have issues with Cute-Boy Cohen?"

"A.) Quit calling him that, creep, and B.) since I called his phone and some cranky chick answered, questioning me like I was the mistress calling *her* husband."

"You don't have to talk to him then. I'm asking ..." She

pauses and holds up a finger, her face turning serious. "No, I'm *telling* you that you're coming."

"Fine, only because I know you'll show up at my house and annoy me until I agree."

"Damn straight, I will."

"I seriously need to rethink this friendship."

"You love me. Make sure you dress cute."

Finn gives me a head nod when he notices me walking into Twisted Fox. "Yo, Jamie. I didn't know you were coming tonight."

Neither did I until a few hours ago.

"Hey." I wave. "It's my friend's birthday, and this is where she wanted to come."

Tell that to Cohen, so he doesn't think I'm randomly showing up and being all stalkerish.

Ashley snags my hand, and I follow her through the packed bar, looking around while also maneuvering through the crowd. The place is nice, and even though it has a hometown-bar vibe, it's updated, fun, and hipster-friendly. It for sure brings in plenty of business.

I've heard great things about Twisted Fox, and I'm happy for Cohen.

Kelsey stands on her stool, waving her hands in the air, and motions for us to come to the table where she and her boyfriend are sitting. She jumps off her stool and gives us each a hug, and I hand over her gift.

"This place is a madhouse," Ashley says as we sit down next to each other.

"Okay, bouncer dude is hot," Kelsey's friend Carrie says, falling down on the stool next to Kelsey, puckering her lips and focusing her attention on me. "He seemed to know you. Is he single?"

Ashley and I groan at the same time.

Carrie isn't my friend, and I dread when she goes out with us. She calls every damn guy we see hot. Waiters, bartenders, random guys walking down the street, women's husbands.

I've witnessed her get bitch-slapped for it once.

Fun times.

It's not that Finn isn't attractive with his light brown hair, muscles, and cocky smile. It's that he isn't Cohen—tall, his face handsomely rough. Even though they both sport scruff on their face, I love how dark Cohen's is. How well it matches his eyes.

After graduation, Kelsey took a job working for a plastic surgeon and is now dating said plastic surgeon. Carrie asked for a discount on a nose job—after calling him hot, of course.

Before I get the chance to answer her, Georgia comes skipping to our table, a bright smile aimed at me.

"Look who it is! What can I get you, babe?" she asks. "We have some amazing cocktail specials tonight, and to be honest, the one I named after myself is *delish*."

I laugh, grateful she's not making this awkward. "I'll take a Georgia then."

"Good choice." She winks at me and takes the table's orders.

Ashley and Kelsey order the Georgia too.

I hope it's not too strong. Wine and margaritas are the drinks to my heart, and I haven't wandered into territories of anything stronger. The last thing I want to do is get drunk and make a fool of myself in front of Cohen again.

Georgia shoves her pencil behind her ear and through her braided hair and tells us she'll be back in a snap. She takes the long route on her way to the bar, dodging Archer, and gives Silas her order.

"There's Cohen," Ashley shrieks, suggestively elbowing me.

"Who's Cohen?" Kelsey asks.

"He's the owner," Ashley answers.

Ashley points at him, and that's when I finally gain the nerve to look in his direction.

I lose my breath. He's behind the bar and in deep conversation with Archer. He's wearing a bright blue V-neck shirt with the bar's logo on the right side of the chest and jeans—a bottle opener sticking out of a pocket.

The sound of a woman yelling his name steals his attention, and he walks to the end of the bar to talk to her. I can't take my eyes off them as she leans across it, whispers something, and laughs. Cohen nods, retreats a few steps, then starts making a drink. When he hands it to her, she blows him a kiss.

"Cohen is good people," Heath, Kelsey's boyfriend, says.

"He's hot," Carrie says, licking her lips.

Just as I'm about to shove her off the stool and tell her to back off, Georgia returns with our drinks and does the job for me.

"He's off-limits," she says, handing the glasses and beers to us.

"Your boyfriend?" Carrie asks, raising a drawn-on brow.

"My brother."

"What about the other bartender?" Carrie signals to Archer.

Like with the other guys, I don't blame her attraction to him. Archer is built like a football player with broad shoulders and an expansive chest, and unlike the other guys who are clean-cut— shorter hair, light on the scruff—Archer's hair hits the base of his shoulders, and his facial hair is on the heavier side.

Apparently, Twisted Fox doesn't only deliver in drinks and bar food; it also always delivers in hot-as-hell eye candy. If they sold a yearly calendar, it'd have its fair share of sales.

Georgia throws Carrie a death glare. "He's also off-limits. Don't speak to him and don't look at him, or I'll break your fingers." She gives her a tight smile, and the table goes quiet. She perks up as if she didn't just go Cujo on Carrie. "Anything else I can get you guys?"

We do a mixture of shaking our heads and telling her no.

"That girl will scratch your eyes out if you talk to that bartender," Kelsey warns Carrie. "Find another guy to hit on because I don't want her to spit in my drink or have my birthday ruined by you getting beaten up. I love you, but I will not be stepping in."

Carrie rolls her eyes. "Whatever. There's more fresh meat around here."

I sip on my Georgia and engage in conversation as the TVs roar around us. People cheer, groan, and argue at game calls. My gaze flashes to Cohen every few seconds, and even though I've tried to stop it, no one is as intriguing as him.

He's in his zone.

Jealousy wraps around my heart anytime a woman talks to him.

Maybe this is what hurt Heather, what ruined their relationship—Cohen working in bars. She hated his job, and if there's anything I can understand about Heather, it's that. Seeing girls flirt with him sends a wave of insecurity through me as I compare myself to each one of them.

Heather did attempt to work at a bar with him but couldn't handle it. She got into a fistfight with another waitress. My sister isn't a fan of working, and I blame my parents for that. While I focused on studying, Heather focused on partying and Cohen. When she wasn't with Cohen, who worked, she was with her friends, talking about him.

There was a time my sister was obsessed with the gorgeous man behind the bar.

A time he was obsessed with her.

A time I had the biggest crush on him.

I know the moment Georgia tells Cohen I'm here when they turn in my direction. When his eyes hit mine, I glance away, acting as if he hasn't been my main focus of entertainment. I rest my hands in my lap, innocently looking around the place in an attempt not to appear to be the stalker that I apparently am.

After my third Georgia—two of them I hadn't ordered, but Georgia kept dropping them in front of me—I'm in need of a restroom break. I scope out the sign on the wall signaling toward them and head in that direction. Since there's only one way, no matter what I do, unless I climb the walls, I have to pass Cohen.

"Jamie," Cohen calls out, waving me over to the bar.

I halt, not wanting to be rude, and walk toward him. I force my best shocked expression while timidly waving at him. "Oh, hey."

An awkward silence passes between us.

We've briefly spoken since the barbeque, and hell, even that wasn't much of a conversation.

He gestures to the bottles of liquor lining the shelves behind him. "What can I get you?"

I play with my hands in front of me, a slight buzz zipping through my blood. "Your sister has already loaded me up on Georgias."

"Oh hell, be careful. Those babies will sneak up on you."

I nod in agreement. "Pretty sure I tasted the alcohol bleeding through my veins with every sip."

"Cohen!" a waitress yells, stalking our way. "I need your help."

"Archer or Georgia will take care of anything you need." He shoots me a sympathetic smile before walking around the bar and following the waitress.

Perfect timing.

No weird convos with him.

Just my luck.

I don't bother asking Archer for anything, but I pay a glance at him before continuing my journey to the restroom. That's when I see Carrie flirting with him.

So much for her looking for fresh meat.

Georgia leans over the bar, snags a piece of ice, and throws it at them. It hits Archer's cheek, and he whips around, glaring at her.

Whoa.

We're all definitely missing something there.

I need to ask Georgia what's up with her and Archer.

"I'm waiting on drinks, asshole!" Georgia shouts.

"Make them. You know how," he says dismissively.

Her hands park on her waist. "I thought you didn't want me behind the bar?"

Archer ignores her.

"All right then." She throws her pen down, jumps over the bar, and starts grabbing an alcohol bottle.

He swings around and storms toward Georgia before attempting to pull the bottle from her hand. "Chill out."

She jerks away from him. "Screw you."

I'm probably the only one paying enough attention to notice her voice breaking in the end and the defeat on her face.

Archer tips his head down and whispers in her ear, but no anger leaves her face. It only mixes with hurt, and she slams the bottle onto the bar before walking away from him. Archer's head hangs low for a moment before he gains control of himself. Carrie perks up but then frowns when he walks to the other side of the bar and yells for Silas to switch sides with him.

Maybe I should come here more.

This shit is better than Netflix.

I scurry to the restroom, check my appearance, noticing the flush in my cheeks, and on my way back to our table, a man steps in front of me.

"Hey, baby," he slurs, his breath smelling like stale beer and chicken wings. "Can I buy you a drink?"

I bite into my lip, reading his shirt, and cringe.

It says *Orgasm Donor*.

His black hair is gelled back, and *too much* is happening with his cologne.

"No, thank you," I say as politely as I can.

His shoulders square up. "Why?"

"I have a full drink at my table."

He leans in closer, causing me to stumble back and smack into someone. She gives me a dirty look and shrugs away from me.

"How about I join you?"

"Table is full, too, actually." My throat constricts, the bar swallowing me up and feeling ten times smaller than it did minutes ago.

When I move to step around him, he blocks me.

"I've been watching you all night. There's plenty of room for me to slide in and get to know you, darling."

I clench my fists, my nails biting into my palms. "I have a boyfriend."

He makes a show of eyeing the bar. "I don't see a boyfriend here."

Jesus Christ, dude, take a freaking hint.

Fed up, I decide to take the blunt route.

"Look, I'm not interested."

His stare turns icy. "Why the fuck not?"

I tense when an arm wraps around my waist, but as soon as I hear his voice, I settle against him.

"Hey, baby," he says loudly, nearly in jackass's face.

"Cohen," the man stutters, his gaze shooting back and forth between Cohen and me. "You're her boyfriend?"

Cohen drags me in closer to him, my backside hitting his thigh. "Yes, so leave her the fuck alone. Don't even look at her."

"Shit, sorry, man. No disrespect."

"You need to apologize to her, not me."

"Sorry," the guy says, wide-eyed, before scurrying away from us.

Cohen's arm doesn't drop from my waist when I turn to face him.

"Thank you," I whisper.

He gives my hip a gentle squeeze. "I got you."

When I turn around and head back to the table, I'm shocked that he stays behind me.

"I'm on break," he explains, taking Ashley's abandoned stool.

Her boyfriend showed up, and they've practically been sucking face all night.

"Are you having a good time?" Cohen asks, shifting to face me.

I nod. "It's been forever since I've gone out."

"And you decided to come here? I'm honored." He places his hand over his heart and bows his head.

I sweep my hand toward Kelsey, who's standing between her boyfriend's legs as they whisper sweet nothings to each other. "It's her birthday."

"Ah, so you didn't come here for me?"

I laugh. "She's my cover. I'm actually here because I'm obsessed with you. I've been peeking through your windows at night, but I'm taking my stalker-ship to the next level and creeping on you at work."

"Finally! The truth comes out." He rests his elbow on the table, placing his chin on his knuckles, and looks pleased as he stares at me. "Have you been here before?"

I shake my head. "Twisted Fox virgin over here."

"I'm happy I was here when you popped that cherry, but I am disappointed you haven't been here before."

"I didn't want it to look too weird, me showing up here after finding out you owned it."

"It wouldn't have been weird." He chews on his lower lip, and his gaze clings to mine. "I owe you an apology for what happened with Becca."

"What do you mean?" I reach across the table, steal Ashley's half-full Georgia, and suck it down. "I have no idea what you're talking about."

He lifts his head to level his eyes on me. "Don't bullshit me."

"There's honestly no need to apologize."

"I also want to apologize for whatever drunken shit I said the night I called when you had Noah."

I glance around the table in search of another drink to swipe. All the glasses are empty around me, leaving me with nothing to chug down to give me the liquid courage I suddenly need.

"Now, I *really* have no idea what you're talking about," I finally say, my eyes darting to the table next to us.

He chuckles. "I saw in my call log that I called you that night and *vaguely* remember what was said."

"New subject." I hold up my empty glass. "This was so good! I'm going to need another if you want to talk about awkward conversations that will only make this conversation as awkward as they were."

"You sure you don't want to talk about it?"

"I'm absolutely positive I would rather talk about anything else in the world but that."

"Amuse me." He leans back and crosses his arms. "Tell me how big of an idiot I made of myself."

"You didn't make an idiot of yourself."

"Does that mean I made myself sound cool?"

I slap his shoulder. "You definitely sound like a dad. *Made myself sound cool?* I can't believe I used to crush on you."

He cracks a smile. "You're not giving me much to work with here, babe."

Babe.

He called me babe.

Good thing there's a dim light in the bar, or he might notice the heat creeping up my cheeks.

"It was an"—I search for the right word—"entertaining conversation."

You asked why you couldn't have chosen the other sister.

There's no way I'm going the honesty route.

"You admitted to loving Hawaiian pizza," I say, a smile playing at my lips.

"I call bullshit on that." He smirks.

"I am going to kill your bartender," Georgia snaps, storming toward our table. "Like, legit kill him—or at least slice and dice his balls."

Saved by the little sister.

She halts when her eyes focus on us—our bodies facing each other, close enough that our shoulders slightly brush when we move, and we're in our own little world, half-whispering in the corner.

"I'm definitely interrupting something. You two get back to … whatever." She stops to snap her fingers. "And tomorrow, you can bail me out of jail for coworker homicide." She whips around and stomps away.

"Heather did always call Georgia a cockblocker," Cohen says with a shake of his head.

"Ah, I bet." I heard her complain about how much time Cohen spent taking care of Georgia all the time.

"Georgia didn't like Heather."

"Not too many people do around here."

"Georgia likes you, though."

"She hardly knows me."

He fixes his stare on me. "Georgia reads people well, and with that, she's guarded with who she lets in. Sure, she was concerned the first time you came over, but after that, she's had nothing but good things to say about you. According to her, she likes *your vibe.*"

Georgia saying she likes *my vibe* doesn't surprise me.

She talks and dresses like a nineties hippie.

"Too bad it took you so long to like *my vibe.*" I cringe after the words leave my lips. "That was so lame. I did not mean for it to come out that way." I point at the empty glass. "Blame it on the Georgias."

"It wasn't *your vibe* I didn't like. It was concern." He rubs the back of his neck, a hint of defensiveness in his tone. "Your sister, she fucked me up, and I saw her as the root of your family. The further away from her life, the better." His hand brushes mine. "No offense."

"None taken," I squeak out. "I understand."

"That's why you were always my favorite."

"Oh, cut the shit." My eyes harden as a spike of jealousy darts through me, and there's no stopping the change in my tone. Maybe it's the liquor or him saying *favorite* or that I want to return to the friendly, flirty conversation we were having before this. "I wasn't your favorite when you were screwing my sister. *She* was."

He dips his head down, his peppermint breath hitting my cheek at the same time his lips brush against my ear. "Did I love your sister, Jamie?" He pulls back, not fazed that he's nearly giving me a heart attack with his lips, his proximity, this conversation. "Absolutely. We had our issues, and at times, I knew she wasn't the best person. What I also knew was, she was by my side through everything when I was growing up. My mom issues, my fucked-up family life, all of it."

I set my attention on the straw in the empty cup and play with it. "She was."

Heather was once a decent person who was head over heels in love with Cohen.

I stay quiet, unsure of how to reply.

"What about you?" he asks. "I remember you had a terrible date and had a thing with Sprinkles boy, but anyone else in the picture?"

"Nope," I quip, biting into the straw.

"Really? Come on."

"My job is my orgasm." *Oh God, my response is too similar to Orgasm Donor dude's shirt.* I shudder.

"Kinky." He grins. "Mine too."

I hold up my hand. "Can we stop talking about orgasms? I have a big mouth when I drink, and I tend to make an idiot out of myself." I throw my head back and laugh. "At least I'm not trying to make out with you this time."

"Unfortunately."

"Please, you were a terrible kisser."

He chuckles. "I like Tipsy Jamie."

That only makes one of us.

"Tipsy Jamie makes a fool of herself."

"Tipsy Jamie is more open."

I cross my legs. "Drunk Cohen is also more open when he calls me."

He clicks his tongue and points to me. "Tipsy Jamie won't tell me what Drunk Cohen said."

"Tipsy Jamie is officially going to stop referring to herself in the third person. Drunk Cohen should follow her lead."

"All right, you crazy kids," Ashley says, hopping off her stool and pulling the bottom of her dress down as Jared stands behind her. "Time for me to go." Her attention whips to me, a smirk playing at her lips. "Are you going to hang out here and call an Uber later, or do you want a ride home?"

I peek a glance at Cohen, whose eyes are crestfallen while he waits for me to answer her. He doesn't want this night to end as much as I don't.

"I'll call an Uber," leaves my mouth at the same time, "I can give you a ride home," comes from Cohen.

Ashley grins. "You heard the man." She kisses my cheek. "Smoothies tomorrow, okay?"

"If you aren't hungover."

She laughs and uses the same tone as she did before. "Hungover smoothies tomorrow, okay?"

I point at the bar after she scurries away, my attention on Cohen. "Do you need to get back to work?"

He shakes his head. "I'm off for the rest of the night. I was about to head out, but then I saw you and thought I'd stop and chat."

"You're not on break?"

"It was an excuse to sit down and talk to you since you'd been avoiding me."

"As I've said many a time, I was not avoiding you."

"You bought Noah an iPod."

I throw my arms up. "What kid doesn't want an iPod?"

"You bought it to *avoid* calling me."

"I didn't want what had happened with Blondie to happen again. It wouldn't look good if one of your girls caught me calling."

His face contorts in disgust. "Whoa, Becca is not my girl."

I flick my hand through the air. "You know what I mean."

His voice turns serious. "I forgot my phone on the table while hanging out with her and some friends. I hadn't wanted to go out with her, but Silas begged me."

I can't stop myself from snorting. "I'm so sure he had to beg you to go out with a hot girl."

"I have nothing to hide. She shouldn't have answered my phone, and for that, I'm sorry." He bumps his shoulder against mine. "You can start calling us again whenever."

"I actually FaceTimed Noah earlier." After getting the heads-up from Georgia that Cohen was at work.

He frowns. "Don't you miss seeing this face too?"

I pout out my lower lip. "Are you feeling left out, Mr. Fox?"

"A little bit, yes. Here I thought, I was a good time."

"I'll think about calling your phone next time."

"Oh, you'll *think* about it? That's so kind of you."

I playfully flip my hair over my shoulder. "I'm super nice."

"And gorgeous."

I wince, and he catches me before I stumble off the stool.

My response comes out in a stutter, "What?"

How dare he pull that out on me.

When I'm sitting on a stool and tipsy nonetheless.

He draws in a long breath before scrubbing a hand over his face. "Shit, sorry."

"Uh ..." I do another once-over, searching for a drink, wishing Georgia would randomly drop one in front of me like she has been doing all night.

Of course she stops now.

"Not sorry that I said that because you do look amazing. I'm sorry I shocked the shit out of you." His hand cups his chin before he caresses it, staring at me, waiting for my response.

"Thank you," is all I can muster out.

It's not that I don't believe Cohen, that I doubt he's attracted to me. It's that I hate that he is. I hate that I'm attracted to him. It'd make our relationship much easier if he weren't.

Cohen's phone ringing interrupts this super-awkward, weird talk.

He fishes his phone from his pocket, and a smile fills his face when he shows me the screen. "It's Noah." He answers the call, moving the screen back to face him, "Hey, buddy!"

"Hi, Dad," Noah replies on FaceTime.

Cohen's stool squeaks as he drags himself closer to me. "Look who's here with me." He tilts the screen, so we're both in front of it.

Noah's face is so close to the camera that I can see up his nostrils, and a few seconds later, he drags it away, his eyes wide.

"Hi, Jamie!" He looks back and forth between Cohen and me in suspicion. "Where are you guys? On a date?"

"We're just hanging out," Cohen answers while I chew on my cheek uneasily. "I'm about to come home, okay? I'll be there before bedtime to tuck you in."

"Is Jamie coming over too?"

Cohen shakes his head, and apparently, I no longer know how to speak. "No, Jamie is going home to her house."

"Ah, man," he groans. "I think she should come over too."

Cohen's voice lowers. "Maybe another time."

"All right." He grins. "Will you ask her what I asked you to?" Noah looks all secretive while Cohen looks nervous.

"I'll ask her tonight," Cohen says with a head nod.

"I'll see you when you get home." He waves at us. "Bye, Jamie!"

I return the wave and find my voice. "Good night, honey."

Cohen hangs up, and I grab my purse from the back of the stool.

"Looks like it's our curfew," I say, laughing as I stand.

"The kid does make the rules." He taps his knuckles against

the table. "Let me tell Archer and Georgia I'm heading out. Be right back."

I play with the strap of my bag. "Are you sure you don't want me to take an Uber?"

"You're not getting an Uber." His tone is flat, and he walks away.

I grab my phone when it beeps with a text.

Ashley: OMG! I'm obsessed with you two being all snuggly in the corner.

Me: Stop.

Ashley: It was cute!

"You ready?" Cohen asks, returning a few minutes later.

I slide my phone into my bag. "Whenever you are."

CHAPTER
TWENTY

COHEN

J amie looks gorgeous.

Breathtaking.

As soon as she walked in, she had my full attention. I did my best to hold back from staring at her the entire night and *finally* acted like I noticed her when Georgia pointed at her table, telling me my future girlfriend was there.

I didn't plan to venture to her table before leaving, but when I saw that jackass hitting on her, there was no stopping me.

My hand rests on the arch of her back as I lead her through the bar to the employee entrance. She's quiet as we make our way toward the Jeep, and I open the door for her before slipping into the driver's side.

She tucks her bag into her lap. "Thank you for the ride home."

"I got you," I answer, looking over at her before reversing out of my spot. "Anytime, and come back to the bar *anytime*."

"I'll remember that."

I drum my fingers against the steering wheel. "Are you busy next weekend?"

"Not that I'm aware of."

"It's Noah's birthday."

"Oh, yes. He's told me all the things he wants."

"That's my son." I hesitate, the question I'm supposed to ask Jamie at the tip of my tongue. *Is this a bad idea?* "We're going to Ski North. It's a few hours from here."

"Ah, Ski North. The place where they have fake snow and forced us to go on field trips."

"He asked me to invite you."

There. I did it.

What Noah had asked.

Granted, it'll be more difficult than just asking.

She's quiet for a moment. "I mean, sure. That'd be fun."

Here comes the problem.

"I checked the cabin availability since we made reservations already, and unfortunately, there isn't anything open."

She frowns, and when we stop at a stoplight, there's a *why are you telling me this then* expression on her face. "Oh."

"We have a two-bedroom. If you're up for it, you can stay with us. I'll crash on the couch, and you can have my bedroom."

"No, I don't want you to do that."

"I thought you knew I'm a fucking gentleman. Come on. Noah wants you to come, and it's his birthday. Georgia and her friends will be there too."

Does it sound like I'm begging too much?

"Let me check that I won't be on call."

"And if you aren't, you're game?"

"I'm game."

I grin.

"I do want to make it clear that I am *not* skiing or doing anything of any physical sort. My workouts are yoga, work, and Pilates. Not extreme sports."

"Skiing isn't an extreme sport."

"It is in my book. You can break your bones."

"You won't have to ski. You can watch us."

I pull up in front of her townhouse and put the Jeep in park. She unbuckles her seat belt. "Thank you for the ride."

"Thank you for the company tonight."

She lets out a long breath. "Can I tell you something?"

"Shoot."

"The night you called me drunk, you asked why you couldn't have chosen the other sister."

My eyes widen as I stare at her underneath the streetlight.

Shit. That's what I remember saying, but I didn't want to bring it up in case I'd imagined it.

That thought has hit me too many times, and I wasn't sure if it'd left my mouth.

"That doesn't surprise me," I say, my mouth turning dry. "I was drunk, and my drunk ass likes to be honest."

"You can't." She frantically shakes her head. "You can't say things like that, Cohen."

"I can't be honest?"

There's sadness in her eyes. "Because you did choose her."

"It was a lot more complicated than that. You were so much younger than I was, and I met you while I was *dating her.*"

"I also wasn't pretty then."

"Excuse me?"

"Not tooting my own horn here, but I'm not the geeky kid I used to be."

"Are you shitting me? Why do you keep thinking you were geeky? Because you were smart?" I snort before releasing a harsh breath. *Will she quit with the* I'm not good enough *attitude?* "You had goals, which I love about you." Another harsh breath leaves me. "My feelings, our situation, are complex. It crosses lines even though we technically haven't *crossed any lines.* I'm trying my hardest not to ruin this … to ruin your relationship with my son because of our … feelings."

"So am I."

"We're teetering very close to that line."

"What are you saying? Where are you going with this?" She laughs, and there's an edge in her voice. "Forget it. I should've never brought it up. Stupid Georgia drinks. Tell her I'm never drinking those things again."

I turn, facing her, and move a strand of hair away from her face.

She shuts her eyes. "Can we act like I never brought it up?"

Hell no.

We shouldn't throw it under the bus, but I don't know what else to do.

"Sure," I say, "we can."

I never knew I was such a good liar.

CHAPTER
TWENTY-ONE

JAMIE

I zip my suitcase shut.

Cohen offered for me to ride with him and Noah.

Since I didn't want to drive by myself, I took it.

Here we go again.

Crossing another line.

Cohen said he'd take the couch, so it's not like we're sharing a bed.

Ski North is a ski resort a few hours away from town that offers skiing, tubing, and other activities I know nothing about. They're open year-round, and they use artificial snow when there isn't any. I'm not an outdoorsy person, and when we traveled here for school field trips, I would hang out in the ski lodge —which will also happen on this trip.

Noah rambles nonstop the first two hours of the ride, telling us how excited he is to play in the snow.

Eventually, exhausted from his excitement, he passes out.

"I love my son to death," Cohen says, stealing a glance at Noah, "but damn, silence can be a great thing sometimes."

"Silence can be boring," I reply.

"That why you work in the ER? You like chaos all the time?"

I shrug. "I like staying busy. It keeps me out of my head."

"Same, but it's so much better when it's quiet, so your head can rest a moment." He clicks his tongue against the roof of his mouth. "You like chaos. What else is different about Jamie Gentry now?"

"I thought you liked silence? Let's try that the rest of the ride."

He laughs. "Consider this our road game. We can make it chaotic if you want?"

I shift in my seat to glare at him.

"All right, you dated the Sprinkles heir—"

"Stop calling him that," I cut in, playfully shoving him.

"Have you dated anyone else? Doughnut Doug's son?"

"I am so strangling you in your sleep tonight."

"Don't make me scared to sleep on the couch." He peeks back at Noah. "We have an hour. You entertain me. I'll entertain you."

"That sounds way more suggestive than it should."

He lifts his chin. "Okay, Dr. Mind in the Gutter."

I decide to give in. If he asks questions, then I get to ask questions. Although I'm not sure if I want to know anything pertaining to his dating life. Maybe I'll get deeper, ask him his darkest secrets, what he thinks about when he jacks off at night, stuff that will make him squirm, as he enjoys doing to me.

"Fine, I've dated some, but it was hard in med school. I thought I'd make up for it after graduating, but dating seems to be at the bottom of my to-do list." I jokingly punch his arm and decide against asking him make-him-squirm questions. It'd open a door, but he'd do the same—or worse. "What about you?"

"I've dated some, not much." There's no squirming on his part.

I suck.

"Dated women who like answering your phone." As much as I hate talking about the call, I'm also mean, as I love hearing him say she means nothing to him.

"I have not dated, am not dating, nor will I ever date Becca," he grinds out, the subject irritating him.

"She sure made it seem like you were."

"She was jealous."

"Jealous?" I poke my chest and squint at him. "Jealous of what?"

"Of the gorgeous woman who called my phone."

His answer should make me smile, giddy, but it does the opposite.

"Don't say that," I mutter.

"What?"

"A gorgeous woman?" I roll my eyes, possibly seeming bitchy, but from what I've witnessed, Cohen has his fair share of *gorgeous* women who don't sport scrubs and Cheeto cheese on their lips instead of pink lipstick.

"I'm confused about how Becca looked makes you any less gorgeous."

I snort.

"Wait." He lowers his voice. "Do you seriously not believe I'm attracted to you?"

Just as I'm about to answer—well, just as I'm *thinking* of an answer—Noah saves me.

"I have to potty," he whines. "Really, really bad."

Cohen sends me one last puzzled look. "Looks like a pit stop is in order."

"Nope, not happening," I say. "Over my dead body, which will happen. My body will be dead if I do this."

As soon as we arrived at Ski North, nobody wanted to go along with my brilliant plan of getting *settled* before hitting the slopes—or not hitting the slopes and grabbing some hot chocolate from the ski lodge.

Everyone *but* me wanted to be outdoorsy.

Ew.

We loaded our bags into the cabin, and we're now in the store thingy place where you rent shit to go down hills and break limbs.

"I promise, it's super easy," Grace says, patting my shoulder.

"Yeah, kids do it all the time," Georgia pipes in.

"It'll be fun," Cohen says, joining the peer-pressure party.

"Breaking bones is not fun," I grumble.

He chuckles. "You won't break any bones."

"I told you that I don't do extreme sports. I do yoga. It's safe and calming. Snow and velocity are not calming."

He gestures to Noah and then Grace's niece, Raven, suiting up. "The *kids* are doing it."

"*All the kids are doing it,*" I mock. "You're like the cute kid in class, asking me to do PCP."

He leans in, his lips going to my ear, and he's chuckling again through his words. "And you said I'm dramatic as fuck."

I groan when he pulls away. "Being a doctor has taught me to take extra precautions. I've witnessed too many accidents from people with better coordination than me, a girl who never picked up the skill of jumping rope."

Cohen holds out his hand. "I'll bet you fifty bucks you won't fall—or at least, you won't break something."

"Why would you make that bet? I can easily fall right now and win that fifty."

"Because I know you won't, and you like to play fair."

I frown. "Fifty bucks isn't worth a broken bone."

He throws his head back. "We'll put you on the beginner hill with the kids."

"No thanks on seeing elementary students ski better than me." I glance around. "Maybe I'll try the snow-tubing thing. The chances of me not smacking into a tree in a tube might be better odds."

"Actually, it's not."

I groan.

"What if I hold your hand?"

"That sounds more dangerous."

"Come on, Jamie!" Noah says.

"You got this!" Georgia adds.

I feel like such a fun-sucking loser.

"All right"—I throw my arms out and then allow them to slump to my sides—"I'll do it."

"I told you it was a bad idea," I grumble, shooting Cohen a death glare.

I should've never gone down that hill—beginner or not.

Just like I said, skiing is not a good time. You slide down a snowy hill with no helmet—or if you're like me, you *tumble* down a snowy hill with no helmet. I'm not sure what went wrong, but I lost my footing and tripped.

It went downhill from there—literally.

"Wrong. You said you'd break something," Cohen argues, handing me a Ziploc bag filled with ice and wrapped in a paper towel. "All your bones are in place."

"But my ankle is as swollen as the tree I hit."

Not swollen or painful enough to go to the hospital.

It just sucks.

Not to mention, it was embarrassing.

More humiliating than me trying to drunkenly make out with Cohen forever ago.

Kids—yes, kids—were staring at me, a few of them stopping gracefully on their skis to help me after my fall. I was tempted to go home, but Noah came running over to me, giving me a big hug, so I decided to stay.

"The swelling will go down," he says. "We'll try again tomorrow. I wonder if they make ski training wheels."

I roll my eyes and place the ice on my ankle. "You're smoking crack if you think I'm hanging out on Murder Hill again."

"What will you do then? Become a snow-lodge bunny?"

"Damn straight."

We're in the cabin, and thankfully, I dropped my bag into the bedroom upstairs before my accident. It's a decent-sized cabin with a large kitchen and a living room, and it's decorated how you'd expect a ski cabin to be—an antler chandelier, pillows, blankets, beds, curtains with bears on them, and a comfy plaid couch.

He jerks his head toward the staircase. "Do you need a piggy-back ride to your room?"

I shoot him a dirty look.

He turns around and bends down, showing me his back. "Come on. Hop on."

Noah is sleeping. He exhausted themselves skiing today. Tomorrow, they're going out again

"Ugh, fine." I slide the ice bag into the pocket of my pants, and he assists me onto his back.

"Piggyback might not be the best idea." He snaps his fingers before placing me back to my feet. "Stand."

"What?" I stare at him, unblinking.

He waits for me to do as he said.

I sit, clasp my hand around his shoulder, and lift myself, using his body as leverage. As soon as my feet graze the floor, he picks me up in his arms, wedding-style, and I gasp.

"This is going to be much easier."

I clasp my arms around his neck, tucking myself into his body, and the aroma of his aftershave relaxes me. I love it. It's masculine with a hint of menthol and officially my favorite smell. I'd love to wake up with my sheets smelling like him.

Just as soon as it seems he's lifted me into his arms, he's up the stairs and carefully depositing me on the bed.

"I'll be in the living room if you need me," he says, walking backward and stopping in the doorway. "Yell before your unco-ordinated ass comes down in the morning. I can't have you falling down the stairs." He taps his knuckles against the door. "Open or shut?"

"Shut, please," I croak out.

"Good night, Jamie."

I love the way he says that to me.

There's always a burn of gentleness in his tone.

"Good night, Cohen." I shut my eyes, inhaling a deep breath, and just as I'm opening them, he's closing the door.

After my skiing tragedy, I asked Georgia to grab my pajamas and toothbrush from my suitcase. We went into the restroom, where she helped me change, rolling the bottom of my flannel pants up to give my ankle room to be its new swollen self, and I brushed my teeth.

I fluff my pillow a few times before snuggling into bed, whiffing Cohen's aftershave that somehow rubbed onto my skin while wishing he were lying next to me.

I set my iPad to the side when Cohen sits next to me on the couch in the ski lodge.

I've been hanging out here all day in my snow-bunny outfit to match the feel of the place. If I'm not skiing, I might as well look cute in my chunky white sweater and black velvet leggings.

I brought snow boots, too, but swollen ankle.

We had a birthday lunch for Noah, and then everyone, except me, went skiing.

"What are you doing?" I ask.

Just as I came prepared to look hot on this trip, Cohen did too. Although I'm not sure if that was his reasoning behind his puffy black vest bunched over a gray sweatshirt.

"Figured you could use the company." He hands me a mug. "Hot chocolate?"

I take a sip before pushing my arm out, holding the mug

away from me and scrunching up my face. "Jesus." My voice lowers. "Did you spike the hot chocolate?"

A sly smile passes over his lips. "I might have added a few drops of Fireball in there."

"This'd better not be an attempt to get me drunk and back on that hill."

"Negative. You can't even ski sober, let alone drunk."

"Rude."

I wrap both hands around the mug and take a slow sip. Good thing my grasp is tight because my body goes into freak-out mode when he sets his mug down and grabs my foot to examine my ankle.

"The swelling has gone down."

I stare down at it. "Thank God."

I shiver, my blood tingling, when he starts massaging my ankle, his abrasive fingers gently stroking my skin.

"At least you can say you've skied before."

It takes me a minute to gain control of my voice, and his touch is soothing, relaxing my body. "I'm never telling anyone about that ski nightmare."

"Jamie has never skied—got it."

"You don't have to hang out with me," I say. "You can hang out with Noah."

"I got ditched for a hot tub and air hockey at the girls' cabin. Noah is loving hanging out with Grace's niece." He rests my ankle in his lap, his hand not leaving it, and relaxes. "Thank you for coming."

"Thank you for inviting me."

"And I'm sorry you got hurt."

I laugh. "I'm blaming you for that one, Mr. You Won't Get Hurt. Next time, we're doing something safer that doesn't involve coordination."

He gestures to my ankle. "You want to head back to the cabin and put some more ice on this?"

I nod, biting into my lip.

Thankfully, I packed a pair of Birkenstocks and have been wearing them since last night. He grabs them from the floor and slips one onto my hurt foot, and I slide my other foot into the shoe after he helps me up.

Our arms are looped together so he can help stabilize me while we walk to the cabin. He settles me onto the couch when we make it inside, lifts my body so I'm lying down across it, and asks if I need anything.

I shake my head. "Look at you. You'd make a pretty good doctor yourself."

He straightens his vest collar. "Yeah, I know."

I roll my eyes. "Dr. Cocky."

I chew on my nails when he lifts my feet, plops down on the couch, and situates my foot onto his lap just as he did in the lodge.

This feels so personal, especially since we're alone. The only other times we've not had Noah around are the night at the bar and when he took me home.

When he turns on the TV, it's on a channel with an image of a burning fireplace.

A cheaper way to give it that cozy, warm cabin feeling.

He holds up the remote. "Anything you prefer to watch?"

I gesture to the TV. "This is my favorite show, actually."

"Finally, I meet someone who shares the same taste as I do." He releases a heavy breath. "If you ask me, I'd say this fireplace channel gives this place a romantic feel."

I stiffen against the couch, hoping he doesn't notice how tense my leg is, and snort. "Romance is the last type of *feel* we need at the moment."

His fingers move up my ankle, casually making small circles along my skin. "Good point."

My heart rages against my chest as the air in the room grows thinner, and though the fireplace isn't real, it suddenly seems warmer. My mouth opens and then shuts as a somber silence happens.

"Fuck it," he grumbles, shifting to face me. "Jamie, what the hell are we doing?"

The question sends a throb through my head … and my heart. It's not a simple *what are we doing* question.

The answer isn't a simple, *Why, Cohen, we're sitting on the couch in front of a faux fireplace.*

Nor is it, *We're waiting for Noah to return, so we can act like we were never alone together.*

The answer he's looking for, the one I'm so terrified of giving, is something along the lines of, *I have no idea, but the way my heart grows wild when you're around or as you touch just my feet, I want more. We both want more, but we have to stop it. Shut it the hell down.*

It's a disaster waiting to happen.

A disaster, from the heated look and the need in his eyes, that will happen.

Unless I pull away.

Unless one of us comes to our senses.

And as much as I crave his touch, I'm terrified.

Fucking terrified.

Do I need to stay away from Cohen to stay away from heartbreak?

If something happens with Cohen, it's not only our hearts that would be shredded.

It'd also gash so many others'—Noah's and my parents'. They'd never look at me the same.

"Quit overthinking it," Cohen grinds out. "Tell me what you want."

His eyes are on mine as if he's begging for an answer, a confirmation that what's riding through him is also riding through me.

He grumbles, "Fuck it again," and my breath hitches when he moves.

I shut my eyes, expecting him to drop my foot and leave. They fly open when I feel a weight over my body. Cohen has one hand resting on the back of the couch while the other moves to cup my face as he settles above me.

His eyes meet mine.

No bullshitting him allowed.

This is when I turn stupid.

When I decide not to answer him with words but with my lips.

I wet them before tilting my head forward and brushing them against his.

He hesitates, shocked, but then crashes his onto mine.

Our kiss turns deeper, and I moan when his tongue slides along the crease of my lips. I open, allowing him entry, and he tastes like Fireball and chocolate as our tongues meet.

Cinnamon has never tasted so delicious.

He groans into my mouth, raw and rough, and I part my thighs in invitation, and he slides between them. I groan, soft and shuddering, when he jerks his hips forward, and the buckle of his jeans brushes against my core over my leggings. They're thin, as are my lace panties, and the friction ignites a fire through me.

"Oh my God," I whimper, bucking my hips, silently begging for more.

What he gives is better.

My pulse races when he pulls away, our breathing ragged, and his gaze captures mine while he levels himself on his knees before unzipping his vest.

It's not the hot chocolate intoxicating me.

It's him.

The vest drops off his shoulders and lands on the floor. I bend forward to drag off his sweatshirt next. Waves of lust coil through me as my hand lands on his six-pack and then drifts up his muscular chest. My eyes drop to his waist, eyeing his hard-as-a-rock erection through his pants.

"I want you, Jamie," he says, his voice thick.

Desire runs through my veins as we frantically start moving. It's not easy—with my hurt ankle, the narrow couch, and through the thick layers of clothes.

Damn ski-lodge clothes.

Why do you need to be so layered, heavy, and complicated?

Our breathing is heavy, and when he pulls away, his pants are unbuckled, his shirt is gone, and my bra strap is hanging loose over my shoulder. My tongue darts out, and I lick my lips again while waiting for his next move. His strong hand slides up my leg, between my thighs, and he cups me through my leggings. Skillfully, he rubs the base of his thumb against my clit. I gyrate my hips, grinding against his touch, and frown when he stops. That frown turns upside down when he moves his hand and shoves it inside my leggings.

"Open wider for me, baby," he groans. "Give me more room to play with you."

I do as I was told, my body shaking, and one of my legs falls off the couch. He draws back as he starts jerking my leggings and panties down my body, careful of my ankle, and tosses them onto the floor.

My heart rate skyrockets at the realization that I'm bare in front of Cohen—in only a bra, no panties—and he sweeps his gaze up and down my body, drinking me in.

"I'll keep saying it until you believe me," he whispers. "You're goddamn beautiful." He slides a single finger along my slit, skimming it up and down. "You're soaked for me."

Back and forth, he moves.

Like a torturous asshole.

A gorgeous, torturous asshole.

"Cohen," I hiss, "I need more."

My back arches, coming off the couch, when he shoves two thick fingers inside me. I squeal, squirming underneath him, while he strokes me, his eyes on his fingers.

"Take off your pants," I croak, meeting his thrusts. "Fuck me, Cohen."

His gaze flicks up to meet mine. "You want me to fuck you, Jamie?"

Just as soon as the words leave his mouth, Noah's voice

screams through the cabin, "Dad! I want a hot tub for my birthday!"

Cohen's fingers are out of me in seconds, and he jumps off the couch, scrambling for our clothes. I sit there, my hand on my chest, and my head is spinning. He slings my leggings to me, and there's no way I'm getting them on.

"The blanket," I yelp, pointing at a throw on a chair.

He tosses it along with my sweater to me at the same time he slips his shirt over his head.

Noah comes crashing into the room. "I want a hot tub for my birthday!"

Even though we're covered and most likely in the clear, my heart hasn't calmed. Cohen slides a hand down his shirt, smoothing it out, as I tighten the blanket around my waist.

How am I going to get these leggings back on without Noah seeing?

As if he can read my mind, Cohen tells Noah it's time to brush his teeth.

My ankle throbs when I stand, and while keeping the blanket tight around me, I dash up the stairs, ignoring my ankle pain.

Cohen peeks his head into the doorway of my bedroom at the same time I pull my sweats up my waist, his eyes refusing to meet mine. "Can you watch him for a minute?"

"Yeah." I rub my arms. "Sure."

He nods in thanks, and I see his back as he rushes out of the cabin.

CHAPTER
TWENTY-TWO

COHEN

W*hat the fuck was I thinking?*

I scrub a hand over my face and instantly regret it when the scent of Jamie hits my nostrils.

The scent of her pussy.

My fingers were inside her.

She was wet for me, and hell, I wanted to fuck her more than I'd wanted anything.

I storm toward the bar in the ski lodge. As I trek in, I see Archer sitting alone at the bar.

As much as I love my friends and that they came along with me, I'm happy no one else is here.

Archer glances at me, raising his brow when I slump down on the chair next to him. "Damn, dude, you definitely look like you need a drink. A motherfucking strong one."

Stupidly, I rub my hand over my face again. I slide Archer's glass over, grab the napkin that was underneath it, and wipe my hands. "I need a few of them."

He signals to the bartender and orders us a round of Jack and Cokes before giving me his full attention. "What happened? You and Jamie finally fuck?"

I flinch. *Am I that easy to read?*

"Is that a yes?"

I don't answer him.

I need the booze before I can give him story time.

The bartender drops my drink in front of me, and I mutter a quick, "Thanks."

"How was it?" Archer pushes.

"We didn't fuck."

"Something happened, though." It's not a question. It's a statement. "How was it?"

"Fucking wrong. That's what it was."

"Wrong because there was no connection or wrong because of who she is to you?"

I knock back my drink in seconds, slam the glass onto the bar like the assholes do at my bar—the ones I want to kick out—and order another.

"Wrong because of who she is to you, I take it."

"She's my son's aunt. Hell, he doesn't even know she's his aunt. She's my ex's sister. Her family attempted to take my son away from me, and now, I'm fucked. If Noah loses her, it'll break his goddamn heart. All because of my stupidity."

Archer doesn't ask *what* happened.

He isn't like that.

He won't make snide remarks or jokes.

"What are the reasons it could be right between you two?"

"Nothing."

"Yet you still hooked up."

I give him a hard stare.

He shrugs, grabbing his drink and taking a sip. "You're attracted to her. There's something there. Go for it."

"Attraction doesn't always mean it's a good idea."

He tips his glass my way. "True."

His phone rings, and my attention hits it before he has a chance to silence the call.

"Why's my sister calling you?"

He shoves the phone into his pocket. "Who knows? Probably to yell at me or ask me about work."

"I didn't know you had each other's numbers."

"We work together." It's his turn to finish his drink off in one swig. "Look, you're my friend. The situation you're in is weird, and I don't blame you for not crossing a line. I can't tell you what to do." He pokes my shoulder. "Only you know how far you want to take it, how much you want her, how fucking broken you'll be if you lose her. Whatever your choice, just remember, it's on you. Either way, I'll support you, but in the end, I hope whatever you choose makes you happy."

His phone rings in his pocket again, and he ignores me, his face stressed.

The bartender serves our next round, and this time, we knock them back at the same time, as if my stress has rubbed off on him.

That, or he was already that way, and like me, that's why he escaped to the bar.

Archer stays at the bar, not looking at his phone, not watching TV, just thinking, when I decide to head back to the cabin.

He mutters a, "Good-bye," along with a, "Good luck."

"The end," I hear as I walk up the stairs.

I peek into the door of Noah's room to find Jamie parked on the edge of the bed with a book in her hand.

Noah's eyes are sleepy and his smile lopsided when he notices me. "Hi, Dad! Jamie read me my bedtime story tonight. She said I should wait for you, but I told her I was tired and that you could do it tomorrow."

Guilt floods me.

I should've been here.

Not drinking away the regret of finger-fucking Jamie.

I nod to the book when Jamie timidly looks back at me. "It's his favorite."

She bows her head, her cheeks blushing. "That's what he said."

"Bedtime," I say as the room grows silent.

Noah nods. "Night, Daddy! Night, Jamie!"

Jamie scrambles off the bed, cringing when her foot with the hurt ankle hits the floor, and pain or not, she manages to get as far away from me as possible. I walk farther into the room to kiss Noah's forehead and tuck him in tight.

We leave the room, and when I shut the door, she presses her back against it, catching her breath.

"Jamie," I whisper, turning to face her.

She shakes her head. "Nope. I'm not having this conversation."

"We need to—"

"My ankle is swollen, and my mind is confused." She looks up at me with fear and confusion swimming in her eyes. "And I need a shot of whatever the hell you were drinking."

I massage the area between my brows with my thumb. "I fucked things up."

She sighs. "It was bound to happen."

I nod in agreement.

"I need to get some sleep."

When she goes to hobble around me, I capture her elbow. "Jamie—"

"What happened, happened. We were drinking spiked hot chocolate. We can blame it on that."

I tip my head down and lower my voice in case Noah turns nosy. "We had, like, two sips."

"Two sips too many, obviously."

"Why can't I get you out of my head?"

Her lip trembles, and she slumps against the wall behind her. "Why can't I get you out of mine?" She rakes her hand through her hair before pulling it. "I wish our situation were different."

I solemnly nod. "Me, too, but do you think it's that wrong?"

"I honestly don't know what to think anymore. When this started, when you walked into that hospital room, my entire world changed. Even when I pleaded to see Noah, I never thought this"—she signals back and forth between us—"would happen. I didn't foresee that storm, and now, I don't know what the fuck to do with it."

"You think I did?" I grind out.

"Neither one of us did." She blows out a tired breath. "This is the wrong time, the wrong place, to have this conversation."

I nod. "Agreed."

I assist her to her bedroom, stopping at her doorway this time—as if we are worried that, if I go any further, we'll end up in her bed.

"Good night, Jamie."

"Night, Cohen."

I trek down the stairs and make my pallet on the couch.

I don't sleep.

All I do is lie there and think.

I'm so fucked.

"Don't forget," Noah shouts from the back seat, rocking from side to side. Kid had too much root beer at lunch. "I'm spending the night with Aunt Georgia tonight!"

Every year for his birthday, Georgia and he have a sleepover where she spoils him rotten with sugar and fun before he passes out in exhaustion.

They go to the movies and dinner, and he always looks forward to it.

"I didn't forget, buddy," I reply.

To say this morning was awkward is an understatement. Good thing my child loves to talk because it's what saved me from engaging in too much conversation with Jamie. We woke up, packed our shit, said good-bye to everyone, and left. We stopped for a quick lunch through the drive-through, and I let Noah listen to his Kidz Bop shit, knowing damn well I'd have a headache from it later.

Since Jamie's car is at my house, I go straight to mine.

She doesn't utter a word as I do.

Jamie sits in the living room while I pack Noah's overnight back—vetoing him wearing his swim trunks with cowboy boots and a sweatband around his head.

Where the hell did he even get a sweatband?

When we're done, Georgia and Jamie are in the living room, talking about Georgia's classes. As soon as Georgia and Noah are out the door, I decide to jump right in before either I chicken out or Jamie leaves.

If I hesitate, it might never happen.

The question has been on the tip of my tongue since it slid into her mouth last night.

"Jamie," I say, sprawling out on the couch with my legs spread, "why'd you kiss me?"

She stares at me with reluctance in her eyes. "I wanted to show you my skills have improved since high school." The smirk fighting at her lips tells me she's damn proud of her answer.

Those were probably the words on her mind since we pulled away last night.

"Definitely have improved," I reply, and my dick stirs at the memory of how soft her lips were and how responsive she was to my touch. "Now, tell me the *real* reason you kissed me."

She hesitates, opening her mouth and then closing it before shutting her eyes and blowing out a long breath. "I kissed you because I've never felt this way about anyone, and out of all people, it has to be you."

I spread my palm over my chest. "That sure makes a man feel good."

"You know what I mean," she says with a sigh. "The guy

who's definitely, one hundred percent, without a doubt off-limits to me is you—the one I definitely, one hundred percent wish weren't."

"Why am I one hundred percent, all the rest of the shit you said off-limits to you?"

She winces. "You need me to answer that question? I never thought you were one hundred percent clueless."

"There are a million reasons it could be. What's the *main* reason you don't want me to touch you again? You don't want my mouth back on yours?"

Is it because of Noah?

Heather?

Because you think I'll break your heart?

All of the above?

"You chose her." Her response is merely a whisper, and I'm surprised I made out the words.

My chest squeezes tight. "Why do you keep saying that? I didn't choose her over you. You were younger than me—*much* younger—and I met you because I was dating Heather." I throw my arms out. "There was never a lineup, an ultimatum, that said, *Choose Heather or choose Jamie.* At that time, you were my girlfriend's little sister—too young, and no offense, but too immature. And I'm not going to lie to your face; yes, I was in love with another woman. I *believed* I was in love with another woman."

Her face twists in pain.

My heart does the same.

My words have struck a nerve.

Hell, they have with me, and I was the one saying them.

I continue before she smacks me in the face and leaves, "Did my thoughts sometimes change as you got older? Was there ever a doubt in my mind after you shoved me into that bathroom and kissed me? Yes. That night, the urge to pin you against the wall, to teach you how to kiss so I could keep kissing you, burned through me, but I didn't. I couldn't. You weren't mine—"

"And you weren't mine," she shrieks, unshackling the hurt and anger my words created.

"I wasn't yours," I repeat with a bowed head before tilting it up, my eyes set on her, hoping she can read the honesty in them. "I was a different man then. And I'm not spouting this bullshit because Heather is no longer around, and I see you as a second choice." I slap my hand over my heart. "I let you in, Jamie, even when I'd sworn the door would never open again. I did that, not with the intention or the *thought* of the feelings emerging, because you're the kindest fucking soul I know. I opened myself up because you're beautiful, inside and out. I tried to keep my distance by not being around when you saw Noah, but that didn't work." My heart hammers against my chest. "I fucking crave you, Jamie. As much as I want to stop it, I can't."

Her jaw drops as she gawks at me, and I stand in front of her.

"This is it. Me handing my heart to you, giving you the decision to stay here, kiss me again, or tell me to go fuck myself. It's your call, and if you leave, I'll never bring this up again. I won't take Noah away from you. We can speak in passing and remain friends."

I kneel on one knee, our eyes on the same level, and hers are glossy as they stare at me.

"It's time we set this straight, and by setting it straight, I'm letting you make the decision. You have more to lose than I do. Me? I'm one hundred percent in. There's no question that the feelings I have for you are much more than platonic. You make the call."

CHAPTER TWENTY-THREE

JAMIE

"*I* *fucking crave you.*"

"*One hundred percent in.*"

"*You make the call.*"

Like the night I came over when Noah was sick, this moment will change everything.

Our lives.

Our relationship.

Our hearts.

What makes you a stronger person?

To hold your happiness, so others won't lose theirs?

To break your own heart?

If I say yes, I'd be choosing him over Heather.

He stares at me in expectation, waiting for an answer—if I'll break our hearts or dive into something I've wanted for years.

My brain scrambles with indecision.

I'm not someone who makes rash decisions.

If my feelings weren't this strong for Cohen, if being with him didn't set my heart on fire and it was only sexual attraction, I'd already be out the door.

I'm not out the door because I don't want to lose him.

To lose what's happening between us.

"Cohen …" I search his face for any apprehension. There's none. "Will you break my heart if I do this?"

"No," he replies with no hesitation, and his hands stretch over my thighs. "I know the pain of your heart being shattered, and I'd never put you through that. Never." He gently squeezes my thighs. "That's why I'm stopping myself from kissing you, from pinning you onto the couch and touching you. Don't think there isn't fear on my end. You can break my heart just as much as I can break yours. And to be honest, while doing my best not to sound like a pussy, I'm not sure how I'll recover from yours with how deep I'm starting to care for you."

Honesty is in his eyes.

I reach out, splaying my hand over his chest, feeling his heart beating madly.

As my answer, as I make a decision that will spin my world on its axis, I lean forward and press my lips to his.

"Thank God," he breathes against my mouth, tasting like fresh mint, and he cups his hand around my neck, deepening our kiss.

His hand moves from my thigh to circle my waist, and he pulls us up. As he gets to his feet, I wrap my legs around his waist, a struggle at first with my swollen ankle. He cups my ass, keeping a tight hold on me. We devour each other, and no questions are asked when he walks us to his bedroom and kicks the door shut behind us. With me in his arms, he flips on the light before gently laying me down on his bed.

It's my first time in his bedroom.

Black bedding. Black furniture. Deep gray walls.

More masculine than the rest of the house. Definitely Cohen.

Chills run down my spine. The weight of his body over mine is perfection. Our movements are slow, our touches soft, unfaltering.

Unlike last night, there's no uncertainty with us.

I want this.

He wants this.

We need this.

My legs tremble, and his hands are chilly as they strip me of my shirt. He tosses my shoes over his shoulder and slides my pants down, goose bumps following his every touch. His breathing is labored when he draws back and levels himself by pressing his palm against the mattress. My breathing matches his as he drinks in my half-naked body.

"Perfection," he whispers, reaching out with his free hand and skimming the base of his knuckles against my cheek. "So damn beautiful."

He gently squeezes my chin, and the air becomes heavy as he moves down my body. With each inch he drops, the harder my breathing drags. I'm close to a heart attack when his head aligns with my black hipster panties—not exactly the sexiest panties, but he shows no complaints while dragging them down my legs. As soon as they're flung to the side, he pushes my thighs apart, situates himself between them, and starts torturing me.

His facial hair is rough around my thighs, and his tongue teasingly strokes my slit once.

"Holy shit," I gasp, hearing a light chuckle from him.

"You like that?" he questions, peeking up at me, his brows raised.

"Definitely like that," I whisper.

He nods, delivers a smirk on his lips, and mercilessly drives his tongue inside me. I lose count of how many moans escape me when he dips his fingers inside me, moving his tongue to gently suck on my clit, and I moan, losing myself.

My eyes shut, and I'm close.

Close to Cohen giving me the best orgasm I've ever had.

Sure, I've done this before but never like this, never with a man who seems to already know what sets me off.

And he does know because as soon as I'm on the brink, he shoves another finger inside me.

"Mmm, you're about to come for me," is all I hear before I let go.

I arch my back.

Lose a breath.

The need for more sets me on fire.

His mouth meets mine, his kiss hard and deep, and I taste myself on his tongue. My head spins as I lift forward, clutch the bottom of his shirt, and drag it over his head, flinging it across the room.

"I want to see your cock," I say, boldness taking over me.

He pulls back, allowing me room to rise, and his hips are aligned with my eyes. His erection strains against his jeans, and my mouth waters.

That's from me.

I did that.

I'm aching for him.

Soaked for him.

With shaking hands, I unbuckle him. The slow movements are long gone. We're back to our frantic touching as I shove his pants and boxer briefs down his waist. His cock springs free, so hard and inches away from my mouth, and his head falls back when I suck on the tip of him.

"Fuck, Jamie," he groans.

I shift, angling myself to take the full length of him inside my mouth. His hand reaches down, cupping my head, and he pushes more of his dick inside.

I might have a big mouth for shit-talking, but a mouth for taking in a cock as large as Cohen's isn't one of my traits apparently.

I gag for a moment, and he pulls back, his cock falling off my lips.

"Shit, sorry," he whispers. "I didn't mean to get carried away."

"It's fine," I say, my eyes watering. "It's been a while, and you're huge. I'll probably need to practice that a few times before I become a skilled head-giver—"

I'm cut off by him pushing me down on the bed and hovering over me.

"We can practice that skill later. I'm sure your pussy can handle my cock just fine."

My eyes widen.

That might take some adjusting as well.

He kicks off his shoes and starts undressing while I focus on his hard cock—its size and how amazing it'll feel inside me. My attention moves from his dick at the sound of a drawer opening. He withdraws a condom, tears it open with his teeth, and slides it on.

I hold in a breath, hoping my vagina won't be as difficult as my mouth in the whole Taking in Cohen's Cock game, and he positions himself at my entrance.

He levels his hand on my stomach. "Breathe, baby."

I nod, biting into my lip, and do as I was told.

"You good?"

"I'm good."

His hands grip my thighs as he pushes himself inside me. My lip twinges as I bite into it, Cohen's size stretching me, and I relish in how perfectly he fills me.

"Fuck, Jamie, you're tight," he hisses, and when his eyes meet mine, they're intense—a look I've never seen before.

"You good, baby?" he asks, his hips raised but not moving.

I nod. "I'm perfect. This is perfect."

With my words, his hands move from my thighs to my ass, and he tilts my hips up before giving me one hard starting thrust.

Then another.

And another.

He grips my waist in ownership as he pumps in and out of me. "How do you want me to fuck you, Jamie?"

"Oh my God, just like that," I whimper, rocking my hips in sync with his.

I'm drunk on him—his touch, the filthy words flying from his mouth, and his cock.

Our hips slap together.

Our moans are loud.

The sound and smell of sex are in the air.

My arm reaches back, and I clench the sheets when he drops my waist, his sweaty chest hitting mine. He pumps his hips forward, the headboard now beating against the wall as he fucks me.

"Tell me you're close," he says, reaching up and squeezing my breast.

"I'm close."

His mouth crashes onto mine.

I come apart first and nearly break a nail as I take my orgasm out on his sheets.

My eyes fly open when his pace quickens, and his face squeezes before he groans my name.

Damn, he's hot when he comes.

"How are we going to explain this to Noah?" I ask Cohen.

After another round of sex, we raided the kitchen for snacks.

Who knew screwing could work up such an appetite?

After I scolded him for buying sugar-free fruit snacks, he lifted me onto the counter, fucked me, and told me to shut my mouth. I then proceeded to tell him his pudding selections were trash, to which he then ate me out on the kitchen table.

We're back in his bed, and I pop a pathetic excuse for a fruit snack into my mouth while waiting for his answer.

Beggars can't be choosers.

I'm going to need to up Cohen's snack game if he wants another sleepover with me.

"Whatever we tell him, guarantee he'll be one happy-ass kid. He loves you."

Do you love me?

My stomach clenches.

I should've asked more questions before I allowed him to screw me senseless and nearly choke me to death with his cock.

He squeezes my thigh. "What's going on in that complicated mind of yours, babe?"

Deciding honesty is best, I turn to face him. "Do you love me?"

He gags on his fruit snack, his hand groping his throat, before clearing it as the snack goes down. "Do I love you?"

I nod. "Yes."

"Did I not make myself clear in the living room?"

"You said you *craved* me." I pull the sheet up my naked chest. This talk feels more intimate than us actually being intimate.

"That, I definitely do."

He leans forward to brush his lips against mine. I taste the fruit snacks, minus the sugar, and he gives me one last simple peck before drawing back.

I lick my lips, savoring the taste of him. "But you didn't say that exactly. Didn't say those three words."

"Neither did you," he deadpans.

Are we ready for that yet?

How is it easier for us to have sex than to say I love you?

Why is it harder to give yourself away emotionally than physically?

He clears his throat. "Should we save that conversation for another day?"

I nod.

He rolls on top of me, using his legs to separate mine, and laces our fingers together, holding them over my head. "I don't want to scare you away." He licks a line up my neck before trailing his mouth back down with soft kisses.

I tilt my head, giving him better access to do with me what he pleases, and wiggle my hips at the feel of his erection sliding against my leg.

"What I feel for you, I've never felt for anyone else," he whispers into my ear before shifting.

I grab his chin, no longer caring about the words, and press my mouth against his.

Sex now.

Anxiety-inducing talks later.

CHAPTER
TWENTY-FOUR

COHEN

I 've never heard a ringtone more annoying.

It's loud.

Some classical music-sounding shit.

And it's ringing over and over again.

Jamie slides out of bed and starts hopping around the room on her good foot, scrambling through the clothes tossed around the bedroom.

"Where the hell is it?" she mutters, tossing a shirt behind her, and she finds the phone underneath it. "Hello?" Her eyes widen as she listens to whoever is on the other line, and she shrieks, "What?" seconds later.

I sit up at the shock in her voice.

"Let me call you back, and I'll be there."

She hangs up the phone, and her search turns frantic as she finds her clothes. Her hands shake as she slips her panties up her legs.

"Jamie," I drawl, panic pulling up my throat. "Are you going to tell me what's going on?"

Her shoulders droop. "Heather is in the hospital."

I freeze, my eyes wide.

"She's in the ICU in Vegas. My parents are booking me a flight now. I'm sorry, Cohen, but I have to go."

I run a hand over my face, taking in her words. "What happened?"

"I have no idea. My mom is a hot mess. I could barely make out her words. She didn't provide much info, except that I needed to meet them at the airport."

"Keep me updated, okay?"

She nods.

I rise, ready to slip out of bed and kiss her good-bye, but she rushes out of the bedroom before I can stop her.

CHAPTER
TWENTY-FIVE

JAMIE

I'm a shit person.

A pathetic excuse for a sister.

While Heather was being rushed to the hospital, I was having sex with her ex-boyfriend.

Not that I knew it was happening, but still.

The Most Terrible Person in the World award goes to yours truly.

I couldn't look at Cohen when I ended the phone call in his bedroom. I have no idea what his face looked like when I broke the news about Heather. I was scared to see it, so I stormed out, not giving him another word.

I drive home and start packing a bag, and thirty minutes later, my mom texts me with flight information. Luckily, she managed to snag us direct flights to Vegas with our flight departing in only two hours. My father is the psychologist of one of their hotshot pilots, so that has its perks.

"Is everything okay, honey?" my mom asks when I find them in the airport terminal. "You look exhausted. Did you not get enough sleep last night?"

I am exhausted. I was fucking my sister's ex all night.

"I slept fine, Mom," I answer. It's not a lie. I did sleep perfectly in Cohen's arms.

She gestures to my leg in concern. "Why are you limping? Did something happen to your ankle?"

"I think I sprained it." I shrug. "It's no big deal."

The issue—why I look like a raggedy bitch—was the wake-up call I received.

My beautiful mother, whose chestnut-colored hair is usually pulled back into the perfect bun, resembles a different person. Her eyes are red and puffy, tears linger around her eyes, and she's close to another breakdown.

I wrap my arms around her, squeezing her tight, hoping to soak away some of her pain. I hug my father next, worry laced on his face, but he's handling it better than my mother.

We sit down, and I hold my mom's hand until our flight is called. While we load into our first-class seats, I still feel Cohen's hands on me.

I still smell him on me.

The words he whispered in my ear as he thrust inside me ring through my mind.

He's texted a few times, but out of guilt, I shut off my phone.

I slap my eye mask over my face and fall asleep.

Guilt and shame make you one tired bitch.

As soon as our flight lands, we throw our bags into a cab and go straight to the hospital. Dragging our luggage through the waiting area, my mother charges toward the nurses' station, crying as she repeats my sister's name until a doctor comes out.

"She's in bad shape," the trauma surgeon explained after introducing himself.

As a doctor, I know the severity of those words.

Whatever this bad shape is, it'll break my parents.

"What happened?" my father asks.

The doctor lowers his tone and jerks his head toward a corner in the waiting room. "It seems to be a domestic dispute that ended violently."

"Domestic dispute?" my mother shrieks. "Are you saying that Joey hurt her?"

Before the doctor can answer, a woman approaches us. "Are you Heather's parents?"

"Yes," my father answers, stern-like.

"He beat her up. He beat her up really bad," the woman says. "And then he shot her."

Either she's clueless to how terrible her delivery is, or she doesn't care.

A sob escapes my mother. "What?"

"Your daughter suffered a gunshot wound," the doctor says, shooting the stranger an irritated look. "The bullet hit her thigh, and luckily, it didn't rupture any veins or arteries. It went straight through, leaving no dangerous shrapnel. Your daughter is very lucky the bullet hit where it did."

"So ... she's ..." My mom's voice shakes before she continues, "She's not going to die?"

"She's not going to die," the doctor confirms. "She'll just need time to heal."

"Can we see her?" my father asks.

The doctor nods. "Of course."

With our luggage in tow, we—including the random chick—follow the doctor through the emergency room and up an elevator, and we land in the ICU wing of the hospital. The door to Heather's room is open, and my mother wastes no time in dashing into it, rushing to Heather's side.

I gasp as I circle the bed, and she comes into view.

Her eyes are black and blue, IVs are pumping fluid into her, a breathing tube is in her mouth, and she's hooked up to beeping monitors.

My stomach churns with guilt.

I really am a shitty fucking person.

"Sweetie," my mom sobs, grabbing her hand. Then she brushes her other hand along Heather's forehead. "My sweet daughter."

My father joins her, wrapping my mother into a hug as she lets loose into his shoulder. I'm frozen in place, the need to comfort my mother barreling through me, but I let my father do the job. As a doctor, I'm used to seeing grief, tears, family members breaking down, but it's different when it's your family.

"We treated the injury, and the surgery was successful," the surgeon explains. "We're keeping an eye on her, but recovery is very promising."

"Thank you," my father says, giving him an appreciative smile.

The surgeon leaves, and the stranger steps to my side.

"I'm Pat," she says, "Heather's neighbor and the one who called your parents."

"Thank you," my father says. "We don't know what we would've done had you not called us. We might not have found out about this."

"You're welcome."

They introduce themselves—my mother, Regina, and my father, Jack—and then I do the same.

Pat explains that her apartment is next to Joey and Heather's, and hearing them argue wasn't anything new. She also says that him putting his hands on her wasn't new either, but it was the first time she heard a gunshot. She immediately called the police, and they were there in minutes. They arrested Joey and rushed Heather to the hospital.

"You have my phone number if you need anything," Pat says when she's finished. "Can I come check on her tomorrow?"

My father tells her, "Yes," and thanks her again before she leaves.

I pull a chair up for my mother, softly asking her to sit down, and then do the same with my father. Taking the one in the corner of the room, I sit and stare at my sister. The room is quiet, the beeps of the machines the only sounds, and I don't bother turning my phone on.

I sit there.

I think.

I question my actions.

And I hate myself.

Four hours later, the breathing tube has been removed.

Her recovery is quickly improving.

"Gentry girls are strong," my father claims.

We stare at Heather and wait for her eyes to open.

When they do, my mother jumps for joy and calls out for the doctors, and they rush into the room.

"Sweetie," my mother says, tears swelling in her eyes—tears that haven't stopped since we entered the room. "I'm so happy you're okay. We're here, honey."

"What happened?" my father asks. He's a man who gets straight to the point, no matter what.

"Joey beat the shit out of me," Heather snaps.

I wince, my mother flinches, and my father tilts his head to the side at her harsh tone.

Whoa.

I was not expecting that.

She definitely woke up on the wrong side of the hospital bed.

Why's she so angry?

Her eyes cut to me. "I don't want to hear any shit either. None of that *I told you so* bullshit."

What the hell?

"Never!" my mother says. "We're here for you, honey. No one, even you, knew Joey would do something like this."

I did.

Dude's a fucking psycho.

"Good." Heather's eyes cut to me in disdain. "I don't want to hear anyone's judgmental bullshit. I'm stressed, and I don't know what to do."

I look around the room.

I've never had a patient wake up this angry, especially after surviving a gunshot wound.

"Don't know what to do?" my father asks. "You're coming home. That's what you're going to do."

"I need to talk to Joey first before I do anything drastic."

I shut my eyes, inhaling a deep breath, and wait for my mother's freak-out.

"Talk to him?" she screeches. "You need to stay away from him."

"Pat said they arrested him. The jerk is in jail," my father says.

"He'll bond out," Heather says. "He always does."

"What do you mean, *always does*?" my dad asks, pushing his glasses up his chubby nose. "How many times has he been arrested for this?"

"I need to talk to him," Heather says, ignoring my father's question.

"He could've killed you!" my father yells, gesturing to her in the bed. "He did this to you, and you want to *talk to him*?"

"Jack," my mom whispers.

"No, don't *Jack* me," he seethes. "This has gone on for too long, Heather. It's time to dump the trash and come home."

"He's my husband."

"Leave him," I finally say from my corner. "Divorce him."

Heather rolls her eyes. "Of course that's your almighty input, Jamie."

I look away, choosing to ignore her.

"Honey, you need to close this chapter of your life and come home," my mother says.

Heather shakes her head, her voice cracking. "I've burned too many bridges there. That's why I've stayed here for so long."

My mother grabs her hand. "You haven't burned any bridges. We all love you."

"I hurt Cohen … I gave away my son. I can't go back there and see him. What if I run into him with another woman? I'll die, Mom. I'll die!" She glances at me. "Does he have another woman?"

I shrug. "I don't know."

Her eyes narrow. "Don't you see him all the time since you see Noah?"

I cringe when she says his name.

She's never said it before.

Never acknowledged him.

Now, she wants to know about his life?

I shrug again. "We talk sometimes."

"Move home. Maybe you can reconcile with him," my mother says in an attempt to give Heather hope. "Apologize. It's been years."

She sighs. "I don't know."

"You were perfect together. You're older now. Maybe you can mend what you broke."

"Excuse me." I stand. "I need to make a few calls and get some fresh air."

I inhale deep breaths when I step out of the hospital, take a seat on a bench, and pull out my phone. Hesitation runs through me as I power it on and stare at his name.

I have to do this.

I'm a grown-up.

I've never been one to run from my problems.

"Hey," Cohen answers after one ring as if he's been waiting by his phone. There's an edge of relief in his voice. "How's everything going? What happened?"

My head throbs. "Her husband shot her."

"Holy shit. Are you serious?"

"I am."

"Is she …?"

"She's going to be okay."

"Good, good." He blows out a long breath. "Are you staying there? When are you coming home?"

"We're going to stay in a nearby hotel for the next few days while she recovers."

"Will you call me when you can talk?"

"Yes."

"Thank you."

"Tell Noah I miss him."

We say good-bye, and I sit on the bench, contemplating my life choices for thirty minutes before going back inside.

"Let's hope your sister finally leaves that jerk," my mom says, throwing down a fry and scraping her hands together, removing the salt.

Visiting hours ended twenty minutes ago, and we stopped for a quick burger before going to the hotel. My mother offered to stay the night with Heather in her room, but Heather declined, claiming she wanted to rest in peace.

"She'd better," my dad says, dipping his fry in ketchup. "She might be a thirty-year-old woman, but I'm going to put my foot down on this."

My father, an award-winning psychologist, is used to people taking his advice. Well, everyone except my sister. He's smart, a great father, a straight shooter, but he doesn't take any bullshit. I grew up proud that my father was a doctor, and there were tears in his eyes when I graduated from medical school.

My mother taught high school English for years before retiring last month. She and my father have the perfect marriage, the perfect balance of sweet and strict. They've made it thirty-five years, and I only anticipate they'll make it another thirty, happily married.

My mother pats his arm. "She's scared, honey. She knows life won't be the same as it once was when she was home, and Anchor Ridge is only twenty minutes out of town. She'll see Cohen, and if he doesn't accept her apology, it'll break her every time."

Not as much as she broke him.

"Will it?" I chime in. "She made it clear she didn't give two damns about Noah when he was at your house."

If my parents think Cohen will take her back, they're setting her up for failure.

A surge of panic hits me.

What if she does come home and begs for Cohen back?

What if she wants them to become one big, happy family?

I can't see Cohen reconciling with her, but I also couldn't see her leaving them years ago.

You never know what's going through people's minds.

"Jamie," my mom says, breaking me away from my thoughts.

"Huh?" I blink at her.

"I asked if you thought Cohen would be open to talking to her."

"Do you want the truth?"

She nods.

"No."

Her face falls. "Cohen doesn't seem like a man who holds grudges."

I give them a *really* look.

"It took him *years* to allow us to see Noah. Do you think he'll let Heather walk back into their lives? And we don't even know if that's what she'll do. She's flaky—"

"Your sister was shot. Have some compassion," my mother says. "You're a doctor. You know the pain people suffer through these situations."

"I'm not trying to be mean. All I'm saying is, let's see what happens, and when the time comes, I'll talk to Cohen."

We have more to talk about than just that.

On the way to our hotel, I call my work and explain Heather's situation, apologizing and swearing to make sure my shifts will be covered. The hospital is understanding, telling me not to worry, but I still do. I tell my parents good night, kiss my mother on the cheek, and am exhausted by the time I walk into my room.

I collapse onto the bed face-first, yell into my pillow, and breathe when lifting myself up.

I needed that.

I get ready for bed and wait until after Noah's bedtime before calling Cohen.

"Hey," he answers, his voice sleepy.

"So ..." I drawl, searching for words.

"This feels a little off," he says for me.

"Just a little."

"Do you regret it?"

My heart quickens at his question. "I don't know," I whisper around a tight throat.

"How do you not know?"

I give him honesty because it's what I'd want from him. "I'm scared, Cohen."

"Why?"

I rub my temples, hoping to release some tension, but it doesn't help. "This seems like a slap in the face, Karma, for what we did."

"What happened to Heather was not your fault," he grinds out.

All my frustrations, my lack of sleep, my exhaustion rise. "You dated her for years. Years!"

"What the hell? We're back to that?" he seethes. "I told you not to take that step with me unless you were certain it was what you wanted, unless you were certain that I didn't give a shit about my past with Heather."

Hurt clenches my heart as memories hit me.

Memories of him and her.

Of their love.

Why is this happening?

"You had a baby with her," I say, sobs approaching. "Even if that love isn't there any longer, it once was, and I slept with you." I lower my voice as if I'm telling a secret. *Hell, everything we're saying is practically a secret.* "If my family finds out, especially after this, they'll hate me."

"Heather moved on and found someone else. I moved on and found you. That's how breakups work. The moment she turned her back on us was the moment any love I'd had for her was gone."

"How would you feel if the man she moved on with was your brother?"

"I don't have a brother."

"Hypothetically!"

"Fuck hypotheticals."

"You'd be pissed."

"Different circumstances, Jamie. Different fucking circumstances."

My heart breaks as I gather the strength to do what I don't want to but what needs to be done. "Last night was a bad idea. Can we act like it never happened and go back to normal?"

I hate myself for this.

For throwing away last night.

For making it seem like it was nothing to me.

A ragged breath leaves him. "Wow, be just like her."

"What ... what do you mean?"

"Turn your back on us because shit gets a little complicated."

"This is different." I sniffle, pulling in a few breaths to stop myself from breaking down. "I'm not turning my back on anyone."

"You want to go back to us avoiding each other? Done."

He ends the call.

CHAPTER
TWENTY-SIX

COHEN

I slept on the couch last night.

As soon as I got into bed, my sheets smelled like Jamie.

I ripped them off, stomped to the laundry room like Noah does during his tantrums, and threw them in the washer.

My mind is dead.

My heart is dead.

This isn't a situation you can easily ask advice on.

It's different. Unconventional. Confusing.

I'm not a heartless bastard. I feel bad for Heather, but that doesn't mean I'll forgive her.

That I'll give her a pass for her absence and let her hop back into our lives.

She was the heartless one when she walked out.

Noah bounces in his seat after finishing his oatmeal. "Can I FaceTime Jamie?"

I stop rinsing out his orange juice glass. "I don't know if that's a good idea right now. She's out of town."

I haven't talked to Jamie since I hung up on her.

Noah slides off his seat and disappears from the kitchen. I snatch his bowl and am on my way to the sink when I hear the FaceTime ringtone blasting through the living room. I peek around the corner to find Noah with his iPod in his hand, smiling as he stares into the screen.

He waves into the camera when the call is answered. "Hi! I called to see Jamie."

"Jamie ran to the restroom, but I can talk to you for a moment. Do you remember me?"

I throw the bowl into the sink, hearing it shatter, and I rush into the living room. I snatch the iPod from him as if he'd been watching porn and end the call.

Noah frowns, reaching out to take the iPod from me, but I pull away. "Why'd you hang up?"

"That wasn't Jamie," I answer, nearly out of breath.

"I know," he chirps. "It was her sister. I met her when I went swimming."

The iPod rings, and a selfie of Jamie and Noah pops up on the screen.

I decline the call.

"We'll call Jamie later, okay?" I say.

"But why?"

"How about I take you to get some frozen yogurt?"

That changes his mind, and ten minutes later, we're in the car.

"You look like hell," Archer says. "What happened?"

"I'm fucked." I swipe my beer from the bar and take a long swig.

It's after hours, and I typically don't stay late, but I need a beer, time to clear my head. Georgia is watching Noah, and I instructed her not to let him talk to Jamie. I hid his iPod in the glove compartment of the Jeep. I'm not taking any chances of him seeing Heather again.

"Fucked in a good way or a bad way?"

"Jamie and I hooked up—*again*. Only this time, we actually

fucked."

He only nods, giving me his full attention, and waits for me to continue.

"The next morning, she got a call that her sister—*my ex*—was admitted into the hospital."

"Oh shit, what happened?"

"Her husband had shot her."

"Damn. Wasn't expecting you to say that." He pours himself a whiskey straight and carries the bottle with him as he sits down next to me. "Have you talked to Jamie?"

"She and her parents went to Vegas, where Heather is." I drag my hand through my hair. "I should've kept my hands to myself. I messed this up for Noah. If Jamie disappears from his life, it'll kill him."

"Jamie doesn't seem like the type to run away from Noah because shit didn't work out between you two."

I pull at the wrapper on my beer. "Never say never. Heather didn't seem like the type to walk out on her family, but she did, leaving my son without a mother. I don't put anything past anyone anymore."

I sound like a whiny asshole, but I'm lost.

Lost with no one to talk to.

Sure, Georgia is always there for me, but this goes beyond a chat with my little sister.

Archer claps me on the shoulder. "I'm here for you, man. If you need time off, I got you. I'd say I'm good for advice, but you know I'm shit at this. Silas, Finn, hell, even Georgia are better options for a heart-to-heart than I am."

I grab the bottle and drink straight from it. "Bullshit. You say that to scare people off. There's a heart buried in that cold chest of yours."

"Words of wisdom or not, I have your back."

"When will I see Jamie again?" Noah asks, his lower lip sticking out while I tuck him into bed.

It's the fifth time he's asked that tonight. That's not counting the times he's asked to FaceTime her.

"I told you, she's out of town," I answer for the fifth time.

We haven't spoken since I ended our call her first night in Vegas. I've debated on calling her back, but I decide against it every time.

She hasn't reached out either.

Maybe it's for the best.

Maybe Noah will forget about her.

Doubt it.

I can't forget about her.

"When she gets back, can we go on another trip together?"

I tap his forehead. "Hey now, you know that was your birthday trip. You have to wait until your next one, silly goose."

He giggles as I tickle him, hoping it'll take his mind off Jamie.

It doesn't.

"Can Jamie come too?"

"We'll see."

"Can we turn Jamie into my mom?"

I freeze, my hand covering my mouth, and my heart breaks for my son. "No, we can't."

Just like I was straight-up with him about Heather, I need to do the same with Jamie.

No false promises for my son.

"Why not?" he whines.

"Jamie is our friend." I pat his bed. "That's it."

"Can't she be my friend *and* my mom? Ricky's mom isn't his real mom. His real mom died, and then his daddy married another woman. Ricky calls her mom now. He says kids get new moms and dads all the time. Can I do that too?" He sighs. "Let me ask Jamie. She'll say yes. I'll FaceTime her tomorrow."

The iPod is going in the trash.

It's getting burned.

No way is Noah going near it again.

I squeeze his side. "You can't ask her that. Jamie is just our friend. I'm not marrying her."

"Will I have another mommy like Ricky someday?" His voice breaks at the end, and the hurt on his face kills me.

I smile gently. "Yes. Someday."

I'll give him hope on that.

I can't stay a single man forever.

He perks back up. "It'd be so cool. Ricky's new mom makes him peanut butter and jelly sandwiches in the shape of dinosaurs! Dinosaurs, Dad!"

I'm going to kick Ricky's dad's ass if his kid doesn't stop telling mine stories.

I've never been a crier, but goddamn it, I'm close to losing my shit.

That can't happen in front of him.

My stomach twists at the same time as my eyes water.

"You need to get some sleep."

He nods. "Night, night. Love you, Dad."

"I love you too."

I cover my face when I reach my bedroom and gain control of myself.

Then I get on Amazon and search for fucking dinosaur cutouts for sandwiches.

CHAPTER TWENTY-SEVEN

JAMIE

"Your sister is coming home and moving in with you."

We're in the hotel's restaurant having dinner, and I wince and stare at my mom, waiting for her to tell me she's kidding.

She doesn't, and I take that as my cue to chug my wine.

"I'm sorry, what?" I ask, setting the empty glass down.

"Heather agreed to divorce Joey and move home."

My mother's face lights up in happiness, and I feel bad that I'm about to burst that bubble.

"Mom, that's not a good idea."

"Heather doesn't want to be thirty, living with her parents—"

"Thirty and living with her sister is better?"

"Jesus, have some compassion. She was shot!"

That's all I'm going to hear about for years.

Anytime Heather wants something from me, they'll throw that in my face.

She recovered quickly, and we found out the bullet had barely grazed her. She's in pain but walking with the assistance of crutches.

We've been here for a week, and I'm going home tomorrow.

Apparently, Heather is coming home with me.

I'm not trying to be a bitch, but my parents have more patience with her than I do, and the old Heather—the heartless Heather—is returning with each day we visit.

"I have plenty of compassion for her, but you know we don't get along," I say. "She'd do much better with you and Dad helping her get her life in order."

A wrinkle forms on my mother's forehead as she scrunches up her face. "I already told her yes. She's not asking for much, Jamie. Give her this. Give *your father and me* this."

"Mom—"

"We already told her yes."

"You can't approve someone to move into *my home* without asking me."

My mom delivers a skeptic look. "We didn't think it'd be an issue." She sighs. "Heather also plans to reach out to Cohen about Noah. She thought staying with you would be a great way to ease him into it, make him feel more comfortable."

"That's not a good idea." *I refuse to be used as a stepping stool for Heather.*

My mom pats my hand. "Heather is finally growing up, sweetie."

I pick at my chicken. "That's nice, given she's in her thirties."

"Not everyone is as responsible as you," my dad inputs, staring down at me over his newspaper. It's not an insult; it's a compliment.

"You need to quit bailing her out," I argue. "Let her move home—*move in with you.* She doesn't always have to get her way."

"No one is bailing her out, honey," my mom continues. "She's moving home and needs a helping hand."

"Will she get a job? Sit around my place all day? What's the plan here?"

"She plans to work, yes."

I stay quiet.

"This isn't a yes or no thing," my father finally chimes in.

"Do this for your sister. Give it a month, and we'll find her an apartment."

"Fine." I stand from the table. "I need to pack my bags."

I leave the restaurant and take the elevator to my room. I fish my phone from my pocket, curses flying in the process, and go to my call log. That's when I notice a FaceTime call from Noah from a few days ago.

It's not a missed call, and I haven't talked to them since Cohen hung up on me.

I FaceTime Noah first.

No answer.

With a nervous breath, I FaceTime Cohen next.

Declined.

Seconds later, he calls through with a normal voice call.

"You want to tell me why Heather answered a FaceTime call with Noah the other day?" is what he says after I answer.

Whoa.

It's a smack in the face.

Heather never told me that.

Sure, I left my phone in her room a few times when I ran to the restroom or the vending machines, and I let her borrow it to make calls.

I grab my suitcase and start packing. "I had no idea that happened. I'm sorry, Cohen."

"Not to be a dick, but I don't want you FaceTiming Noah until you're home and she's not around."

Oh no.

Cohen will take this worse than I did.

I bite into my lip. "I need to tell you something."

"What's up?"

"Heather is moving home."

"Goddammit," he hisses. "Tell her to stay away from us. We live in a different town, so it shouldn't be an issue."

Wait, there's more.

"She's moving in with me." I hold my breath, waiting for a reaction I know won't be pretty.

"Oh, is she?"

"I had no choice in the matter. I tried to say no, but my parents insisted and put me on a guilt trip."

"I get it. Heather has a way of always getting what she wants," he scoffs. "I'm not trying to sound like an asshole, but I'm frustrated."

I plop down on my bed next to my suitcase. "I don't want this to stop me from seeing Noah."

"No way am I letting him around her."

"What if he comes over when she's gone?" *It's not like the three of us can hang out now without it being weird anyway.* I chew on my nails while waiting for his answer.

"She can pop up at any time."

I chomp into one extra hard and spit it out, taking my Heather anger out on my manicure. "Looks like I'll go back to doing visits at your house with Georgia."

"We've really fucked this up, haven't we? You were right. We shouldn't have crossed that line. It was a mistake."

A mistake.

God, it hurts when he says that.

Did it stab a knife through his heart the same way when I said them to him?

"Is that Jamie?" I hear Noah ask in the background.

"Yes," Cohen answers. "Would you like to talk to her?"

Seconds later, Noah speaks through the speaker, "Hi, Jamie!"

"Hi, honey," I say, his voice relaxing me.

"Can I come over and hang out? Can we get cupcakes?"

I laugh. "I'm actually out of town right now, but what about when I get back?"

"Yes! Can Dad come too?" The call goes quiet for a moment, and I can hear low whispers. "Dad said I need to get ready for bed. Good night!"

"Good night," I whisper with a twinge of loneliness.

I miss them.

I wait for Cohen to take over the call, but he hangs up.

"Honey, I'm home!"

A stiffness forms in my jaw.

My head aches, and I roll my eyes before anyone comes into view.

Heather crutches herself into my house like she already owns it with my parents behind her. She does a once-over of the place. "Kinda small." Her eyes flash to me. "Tell me my bedroom is a decent size."

My attention snaps to my mother, and she mouths, "*Be patient,*" to me.

"Mom will show you your bedroom," I reply flatly from the couch.

Her hand flicks in the air as she follows my mom to the guest bedroom. I washed all the bedding, set up the features on the smart TV, and added a few candles, hoping to at least make it homey for her.

Also hoping she'll find her bedroom comfortable enough to spend all her time in there.

"Are you sure Jamie won't let me have the master?" I hear Heather ask.

My father sits down in a chair, concern etched into his forehead when he looks at me. "Thank you, Jamie. I know this will be hard, and I'll try to get her out of here as soon as I can, but this is for your mother."

I nod. "The faster, the better." I groan when I hear Heather complaining about the size of her TV next. I lean forward and lower my voice. "Her apartment was a hellhole compared to my house. What's her deal?"

My father lifts his arms and then drops them back onto the armrests in frustration. "I know just as much as you do."

"Can I have some money to get clothes until Pat mails mine?" Heather asks when they return to the living room.

"What about borrowing some from your sister?" my dad asks, shooting me an apologetic look.

Heather pays a glance at me before scrunching up her nose. "Jamie and I don't exactly have the same style."

I glance from the scrubs I'm wearing to her tight jeans, low-cut top, and crutches. While she was in the hospital, she complained that her crutches would ruin her outfits.

Definitely a different style.

Not that I'm judging her style, but I don't like the way she's judging mine.

Heather sits on the arm of a chair—an expensive chair that doesn't carry a sturdy arm—and I grit my teeth to stop myself from yelling at her.

"I'll also need toiletries and a phone. Joey paid all our bills and shut mine off."

My dad pulls himself up from the chair with a groan. "I need to run to my office. Your mother will take you out for things tomorrow, and until then, you can borrow Jamie's phone when needed."

Another apologetic look from him is shot my way.

The look I shoot his way is annoyed.

I hug them good-bye and kiss their cheeks before they leave.

Heather doesn't.

She mutters a good-bye, heads to the kitchen, and rummages through my fridge. "A little help in here please."

When I walk into the kitchen, she has a Coke in her hand, and there's a bag of chips and a bottle of wine on the counter.

My favorite wine.

"Pour that into a glass and carry those for me, will ya?" she asks, heading back into the living room without waiting for my response.

I roll my eyes, release a breath, and open the wine bottle. When I return with the glass of wine and chips, she's on the couch. I take a seat in a chair and cringe as she loudly starts chomping on the chips while double-fisting her drinks as if the Coke is the chaser to the wine.

I sit up straight and focus on the news playing on the TV.

"Can I use your phone?"

I peek at Heather, taking in her expectant expression. "Sure. Do you need to make a call?"

Since the FaceTime call with Noah, I'm reluctant to let her use my phone.

Crumbs fall onto her shirt and the chair as she talks with chips in her mouth, "I want to check Facebook."

I stand. "You can use my laptop."

She shakes her head, more chomping. "I also want to call Pat. I heard asshole Joey already has a new girlfriend."

How tragic.

"Should you care about that?" I ask, grabbing my laptop that's charging on an end table.

"He was my husband," she snaps. "Obviously, I should. You'd know that if you had a husband."

I roll my eyes, fighting back the urge to fling the phone at her head.

She wiggles her fingers. "I also need to call Mom to ask when she's picking me up tomorrow."

I hesitate a moment before handing her my phone. As she takes it, my eyes stay on her hand, and I feel like a cheating spouse as she uses her greasy chip fingers to scroll down the screen.

Please, Cohen, don't call or text.

It might be wrong, being all secretive, but what else am I supposed to do?

Heather calls Pat and spends thirty minutes interrogating her about Joey's every move.

"Can you do me a favor?" she asks me, my phone in her hand after she ends her Joey drama.

"Depends on what it is," I answer, not catering to her like my parents do.

"Talk to Cohen for me."

"For what?" I play dumb.

"I want to see Noah."

"That isn't going to happen."

"Why not?" she snarls.

"Cohen hates you, for one."

"We can talk and work things out. He always loved our make-up sex." She shimmies her shoulders. "I'm sure I could still do a good job. He loved it when I did this thing with my tongue—"

I cut her off, "I'd rather not hear about that."

She sighs. "We had our ups and downs—"

I interrupt her again, "Downs? You left your family."

She narrows her green eyes at me and swipes her straight brown hair off her shoulder. "Whose side are you on? I'm your sister. He's nothing to you."

"That's enough." I hold out my hand. "Give me my phone back. I have shit to do."

"Am I right? Is he nothing to you?" She eyes me skeptically. "You don't seem very open to the idea of me seeing Cohen. Is it because you want to be the only woman in their lives? You want to be Noah's mother. You want *my* life?"

I clench my fist, holding myself back from pouring that wine over her head. "That's not your life. Never was. Never will be."

She sets all her kitchen shit on the floor, relaxes in her chair, and plays with my phone, bouncing it from one hand to the other. "Wow, your little high school crush hasn't stopped, has it? You know you're not Cohen's type, right?"

"I'm not doing this with you," I grind out.

"Why? Have you slept with him?" She scoffs when my eyes widen. "You have, haven't you?"

"You don't know what you're talking about." I jump to my feet. "Give me my phone."

She smiles when it beeps with a text. "Oh, looky here. A message from Cohen." She reads it out loud. "*Let me know when you want to come over, and we can talk.*" She taps one finger against her mouth while she starts to scroll through something on my phone. "Hmm ... look at all these text messages."

I stand in front of her and hold out my hand. "Give me my phone." When she goes to stuff it under her armpit, I'm faster from her and snatch it from her hold. "You need to go to Mom and Dad's. I don't want you staying here."

"Why? Do you want me gone so you can keep fucking the father of my child?" A giggle leaves her. "How do you like my sloppy seconds? You probably couldn't wait to have him, could you?" She thrusts her finger into her chest. "Remember, he was mine first. He chose me first."

The string to my patience snaps. "I was too young for him then."

"You think that's it. Your age? You've always wanted my life, my looks." She peeks over her shoulder in a suggestive, smug way. "My friends, my boyfriends, my *sex life*. You think because you're a doctor, because the braces are gone, because you're *somewhat* attractive that Cohen will want anything to do with you?" She snorts. "You're pathetic. Out of all the guys out there, you ho yourself out to him."

I grab my keys and purse. "I'm leaving."

"Run away from facing the facts that Cohen will never want anything to do with you beyond sex."

I lean down and get in her face. "I'm running away from slapping you in the face. After what you've gone through, I want to be a decent person and not do that."

Her face is still, her eyes buggy, and she doesn't talk shit again until I pull away to leave. "Now, you have morals? You can't hit me but have no problem fucking my man?"

"He's not your man!" I scream. "He stopped being *your man* when you left him for *another* man. He's not yours. He doesn't want you. Get over it and move on—like you did when you left him and his newborn."

"*Our* newborn."

"Says the woman who signed over her rights."

With that, I turn around and leave, slamming the door behind me.

"Mom, I want her out," I cry into the phone.

I managed to hold the tears in until I got to my car. I broke down and cried, slamming my hand against the steering wheel while fighting to forget Heather's insults.

"What?" my mother asks.

"Heather," I burst out. "I want her out of my house before I put her belongings on the curb."

"Honey, I asked you to be patient with her. She went through something traumatic."

I clench my jaw and fist at the same time, inhaling the scream I want to release.

If I have to hear my mother use that as her excuse one more time, I'll lose it.

I don't blame my mother. It's not her being mean. She has a heart, one that's too big at times, and has missed my sister. She cried for months after she left.

"I understand and hate what happened to her, but we didn't even last one night before our first fight. We can't live together."

She clears her throat. "Does this have anything to do with you and Cohen having a romantic relationship?"

"What?" I croak out.

"Heather called a few minutes ago—"

"She called? How did *she call*? She doesn't have a phone."

"I'm not one for technology, but she said she was calling me on her iPad."

I grind my teeth.

She only wanted my phone to look through my shit.

To play games with me.

"She said you admitted to sleeping with Cohen?" She drags out a low breath. "Jamie, how could you do that to her? To our family?"

"I never admitted *anything* to her!" I scream.

"Is she lying?"

"I have to go. I love you."

"Jamie—"

"I have to go, Mom!"

I hang up and start my car, and with tears in my eyes, I go to him.

Not Ashley.

Not my parents.

Cohen.

CHAPTER
TWENTY-EIGHT

COHEN

J amie is standing in my doorway with tears running down her cheeks.

She runs into my arms, and I slam the door shut behind us.

"Baby," I whisper, "what happened?"

She sobs into my shoulder. "They know."

My stomach falls. "Know what?"

"That we slept together."

I freeze before gaining control of myself and rub her back. "How?"

"Heather had my phone when you texted, and she looked through our messages. I don't know. I guess she put two and two together," she says into my shoulder, some of the words muffled. "I didn't admit it, but she called my parents and told them what I did."

She breaks down harder, and I pull her away, holding her at arm's length, wiping away her tears with my thumb.

"My mom believed her! She believed her before even asking me."

My throat is tight, and I cup her face in my hands. "I'm so sorry. This is all my fault."

She sniffles, gaining some control of herself, and glances around. "Where's Noah?" She shakes her head. "I can't believe I came over like this."

"He's with Georgia. He's missed you, and we're trying to take his mind off it."

Her lower lip trembles. "Trying to replace me, I see."

Never. No one can replace you.

"This is complicated. I don't know what the hell to do."

"I know." She breaks down again, and I drag her closer.

I run my hand down her hair, kissing her forehead, and whisper, "We'll figure everything out."

"Will we?"

She peeks up at me, and my gut clenches at the sadness in the eyes I've fallen in love with, and when our gazes meet, it sets us on fire.

Eye contact has always been a dangerous game with us.

Always leads to trouble.

And feelings.

And touching.

To us hoping we can be more than what we're allowed to be.

"I wish this weren't so complicated," she whispers.

"Me too, baby. Me too."

She relaxes against my body, and even though they're not supposed to, our lips meet. I hesitate, waiting for her reaction, and she doesn't think twice before deepening our kiss.

It feels like home.

Like where we've always belonged.

We kiss hard.

As if we don't know when it'll happen again.

Or if it *will* ever happen again.

I cup her jaw as we kiss, using it as my way to tell her how much I care about her. I kiss her, using my mouth to show her how much I'm fucking falling in love with her.

She falls to her knees and starts unbuckling my jeans, my cock standing at full attention, waiting for her warm mouth.

I fail him when I pull her back to her feet. "I need to be inside you."

She nods, biting into her lip.

I retreat a few steps. "Take off your shirt."

My cock twitches when she does.

"Lose the bra."

She does.

"Your pants."

She starts tearing her pants down her legs.

"And your panties. I want to see every inch of you, every inch of you that belongs to me, whether you like it or not. That's why you came here, right?" I cup my aching cock against my jeans. "You came here because you belong to me."

"Yes," she whispers. "I belong to you and only you, Cohen."

"Damn fucking straight."

When she's fully naked, I charge toward her, wrap my hand around the back of her neck, and kiss her hard. She moans into my mouth, saying my name, and I walk her back to the couch and bend her over the arm of it. She glances back at me as I pull my shirt over my head, smack her ass, and drop my pants.

Our eye contact makes another appearance when I slam inside her.

She whimpers underneath me, arching her back, and I slide one hand down her spine while using the other to grip her waist.

"Fuck, baby," I groan, slapping her ass again as our bodies rub against each other's.

"Yes, Cohen," she moans. "I love you inside me."

"Yeah, you do." I change course, grind my hips, and move in circles, hitting every spot inside her that I can.

She bucks against me, her face pushed against the cushion, and when I know she's about to come, I pull out of her.

"What the—"

I twist her around, pull her legs around my waist, and hustle to the bedroom. Dropping her onto the bed, I waste no time before pushing back inside her.

"You feel so good," I say between breaths, grabbing her legs and tossing them over my shoulders.

"I'm coming," she moans.

"Yes, come on my dick, baby."

She does, and I curse with each rough thrust I give her until I find my own release.

I'm staring down at my cock still inside her pussy when another, "Fuck," hisses through my lips.

She glances up at me as I slowly pull out of her while dropping her legs at the same time.

"We didn't use a condom." I stare at her pussy, taking in the evidence that I was there. I love it, but I also know it was irresponsible as fuck. "Shit, this is on me. I'm sorry."

It got too heated.

We wanted each other too much.

"It's okay." She offers an easy smile.

"Are you on the pill?"

"No," she answers before glancing away. "But there's not much we can do about it now. I'll get a Plan B tomorrow."

Her response eases me, and I reach forward to run two fingers over her slit, pushing more of my juices inside her.

It's a bad move on my part, but her underneath me, with my come inside her, is a big fucking turn-on. She doesn't turn away, doesn't stop me, and I lean down to kiss her before falling on my back.

"Why does your cock feel so good?" she asks, her body still shaking, and she sounds almost annoyed.

"Why does your pussy feel so good?" I counter before shifting so I'm halfway on top of her, my semi rubbing against her thigh.

"We have to stop this," she says, widening her legs so my cock falls between them.

I run my hand up her stomach, cupping her breast, and thrust my hips forward, groaning while sliding my cock over her clit. "I like this."

Her nipple tightens as I play with it between my fingers, and she squirms beneath me. "I hate how much I love this."

"I love how much you love it."

"Heather wants to make things right with you."

I halt at the mention of her name.

There goes that mood.

I collapse onto my back and scrub a hand over my face—my cock not nearly as excited as it was. "Heather can fuck herself."

She turns onto her stomach and slides in closer to me. "My parents want her to make things right with you."

"No disrespect, but your parents can fuck themselves too."

Not trying to sound like an ass, but Heather isn't making shit right with us.

There's no making it right.

She'd better stay away from Noah and me.

Jamie thrums her fingers over my chest. "They're going to make me end things with you."

My chest caves in at the thought of losing her—*again.*

If she's still planning on leaving us, why is she here?

Her leaving isn't what's driving the anger through me.

It's *why* she's leaving.

She's walking away because someone else is telling her to—stomping on my heart, on her own, and on my son's heart because of *their* opinions.

Fuck their opinions.

Fuck them.

"With her situation—" she starts.

I cut her off, "Her situation doesn't have jack shit to do with us. Her being here won't change the fact that I'm falling in love with you or that I want to be with you. I don't care about her."

Her body goes still, her legs straightening, and her eyes widen in shock. "What?"

I blink. "What?"

"You said it ... those three words." A smile tilts at her lips.

Here goes.

I grab her knuckles and brush them against my lips before kissing the front of them. "I was an idiot not to say it then, but the timing felt forced, too expected, even though the moment I slid inside you, there was no uncertainty in my mind that I was falling in love with you. I wouldn't risk my heart, your heart, my son's heart for a quick fuck if mine didn't bleed for you. I love you, and I will fight for you. She can't tear us apart."

"Cohen," she breathes out, "I—"

She stops when my phone rings. I'd ignore it, given this is a critical moment in our relationship, but it's Georgia's ringtone. Since she has Noah, I give Jamie's knuckles a squeeze before sliding out of bed, my cock in full view, and step into my sweats.

"Hello?" I answer when I grab my phone from the living room.

"I'm in the driveway," Georgia says in a whisper, most likely not wanting Noah to hear her.

"All right?" I pay a glance at the front door before heading back to the bedroom.

"Jamie's car is here, so before we come in, I wanted to make sure everything is good."

Apparently, my sister can read me like a book because she knew something had happened between us at the realization that Jamie wasn't coming around anymore. I attempted to explain she was out of town, but with Noah complaining about his lack of FaceTiming with Jamie, my sister knew. We grew up and are too close for her not to know that Jamie and I slept together.

She claimed it was written all over my face—the love I had for Jamie and the loss over when she left us.

Understanding dawns on me. "Give us five."

"Gotcha."

I hang up the phone, toss it onto the dresser, and start collecting our clothes. "Georgia is outside with Noah."

"Shit," she hisses, getting up, and we start pulling our clothes on.

When we make it into the kitchen, Jamie's hair is a tangled mess, and my shirt is on backward. There's no question we look awkward as fuck. Jamie's face is puffy, her eyes red from her crying and our halfway there heart-to-heart. We're sipping on water when Georgia and Noah barge into the house.

"Hey, kids," Georgia chirps, her eyes pinging between Jamie and me.

"Jamie!" Noah shouts, bouncing from one foot to the other before exploding toward her. He hugs her legs. "I've missed you so much!"

My head spins when I notice the tears in Jamie's eyes.

She kneels to hug Noah. "And I've missed you so much."

He peeks up at her, excitement on every inch of his face. "Are you hanging out with us tonight?"

Georgia walks over to me, leans in, and whispers, "I can take him back out if you want to talk—or maybe light a candle to drown out the smell of sex in the air. I stashed a cinnamon candle in the guest room for when I stay the night. It smells like Fireball. I actually might have one in my car." She pauses. "A candle, not Fireball, unfortunately, because it appears you two could really use a shot of some strong shit right now."

Noah is blabbing about how he's been playing with the toys he got for his birthday.

I massage my throat before answering, "I think that's a good idea."

Jamie is on the verge of losing it the longer she hears Noah talk about everything she's been missing.

"Noah, my man," Georgia calls out, and Noah turns to look at her. "Let's go get some cupcakes!"

Jamie kisses the top of his head, tears hitting her cheeks, and scurries to the bathroom.

"Can I wait for Jamie to get back?" Noah asks. "She can come too!"

"No, I don't think Jamie is feeling well," Georgia says.

He frowns. "We'll bring her one back then. I know her favorite-favorite-ist."

Georgia squeezes his shoulders. "She'll love that. Let's get going before they're all gone." She glances at me. "I'll call before we come back."

"*Thanks,*" I mouth to her.

Noah hugs me good-bye, and they're out the door a minute later.

"They're gone," I shout, an edge to my voice, and I meet Jamie in the living room.

"I need to go," she rushes out before holding up her phone. "Everyone in my family is blowing me up."

"And?" I hiss. "It's your life."

"My family is also my life! You and I both know what we have is sex—"

The fuck?

"Is that how *you* feel? Can you clarify what you're thinking? Unless you forgot, fifteen minutes ago, I said I was *falling in love with you.* And correct me if I'm wrong, but you lit up like a fucking lamp when you heard me say it. That sure as hell doesn't scream it's only sex."

She throws her arms up. "Yes! I'm in love with you! Yes! Hearing those words was everything I've ever wanted to hear, but do you honestly think we can make this work? You've had sex with both me and *my sister!*"

"This is different," I grind out. "And you know it."

"My family won't see it that way." She repeatedly shakes her head. "Other people won't see it that way."

A knot forms in my stomach, twisting in defeat, and I sit down on the edge of the couch. "Heather fucking ruins shit again."

"I'm sorry," she whispers, her face just as broken as my heart.

"What was that then? A good-bye fuck?" Anger knots in my stomach next, overtaking the defeat. "Do you do that to all the guys you fuck over?"

She cringes at my harsh words. "Screw you! I didn't come over here with the intention of us having sex."

"What was your intention then?"

"I don't know." Her chin quivers. "I was sad. I needed someone."

"Needed someone or needed *me*?"

"You!" she screams. "Goddammit, you!"

Her answer ignites a fire inside me.

I stand when she starts pacing, wrap my arms around her waist to stop her, and spin her to face me. "Why are you walking away from us? Why are you breaking your own heart?"

She peers up at me, her face puffier, her body quaking. "I can't love you because I can't keep you."

I take a step back. "All right, I get it."

She winces. "What?"

"Run away like your sister. I already know how to handle it." I stalk across the room, open the door, and gesture for her to leave.

"Cohen," she whispers, her eyes wide.

Anger pivots through me.

Fuck this.

Just as I never tracked down my father, just as I haven't reached out to Heather, I'll never beg for someone to love me.

For someone to stay with me.

If you don't want me, you don't fucking want me.

I'll take it.

Sure, it'll kill me to move on, but I'll handle it.

I'm a strong man.

I can lock that cage back around my heart.

"You're right," I say, my throat tight. "We can't keep each other. I already let one woman fuck with my head, one woman who made me doubt our love, and I refuse to do it again."

"Cohen," she repeats.

"Get out!" I scream. "I'm not playing these bullshit heart games—not with my feelings and damn sure not with my son's on the line. We'll act like you and I never happened and go back to how it was. I won't take Noah away from you—*for him, not you*—but I won't be giving you one more goddamn piece of me."

She bows her head, the sobs back. "Okay."

We don't look at each other when she passes me.

When she lets us go.

I slam the door behind her.

Finn charges into my office.

I glance up from my paperwork and raise a brow.

He scratches his head. "You have a, uh ... visitor."

"Okay?"

"Heather is here."

I flex my fingers around the pen in my hand. "Are you shitting me?"

He shakes his head. "You want me to tell her to kick rocks?"

Finn is my only friend who knows what Heather looks like. He went to school with us.

"Nah, I'll handle it," I answer, blood rushing to my ears. "Can you bring her back here?"

I can't make a scene in my bar, and knowing Heather, there will be a scene.

Minutes later, Finn returns with Heather on crutches behind him. He doesn't say a word before turning and walking out, shutting the door behind us.

Heather stands in front of me and doesn't utter a word.

She's waiting for me to take the lead, like the coward she is.

She's different, she's aged, yet she is still attractive. Honey-blonde hair similar to Jamie's but thinner, no dimples like the woman I love, but she's dressed sexy enough that men will be hitting on her here.

Not me, though.

There isn't one cell in my body that wants her.

That will ever want her again.

She's not my type. She's not the one my heart beats for, who my body craves.

It's her sister who does that.

Her sister, who has gripped my heart and owns it.

Her sister, who is a goddamn pain in my ass.

Her sister, who I haven't spoken to in over a week.

I stand. "How dare you show up here? At my motherfucking *business.*"

She winces, shocked at my anger. "Jamie won't tell me where you live, so I asked around, and this is where I was told to find you. When can we sit down and talk?"

The name of the woman I love sends a knife through my chest.

"I'd prefer fucking never."

She releases a huff. "It's going to happen. I won't leave you alone until we talk this out."

"What do you want?" I hiss. "We have nothing to talk out."

"Hear me out."

"Nope. Leave."

"Please!"

Her begging sends a rush of memories through me.

Her begging reminds me of how I sounded when I was down on my knees, asking her not to leave us, pleading for her to at least stay for Noah.

"Fuck you," I snarl. "Did you hear me out when I begged you? You don't deserve one second of my time."

Her eyes lower, and she gestures toward the crutches. "I was shot."

"I'm sorry that happened to you, but it doesn't change our relationship. I wish you the best, but stay away from us."

"Why are you punishing our son from having a mother?"

"*My son,*" I seethe, hating that she referred to him as hers. "Not yours."

"You can think that all you want, but I'm still his mother. I gave birth to him."

"News flash, Heather: you signed over your rights. According to the state, you are nothing to him." The pressure from how hard my jaw is clamped down will give me a migraine by the end of this conversation.

"What about Jamie?" she snaps, jutting her chin out. "What is she to him? If I signed over my rights, she's *nothing* too."

I grip the edge of my desk, my nails biting into the wood. "This has nothing to do with Jamie."

Her voice rises. "Yes, it does. Out of all the people to sleep with, *my sister?*"

"Leave before I have you escorted out." The wood from my desk is chipping.

"Are you going to lie and say you aren't fucking her?"

"Nope."

We're not fucking at this moment, so I'm not lying.

"Bullshit," she spits. "I'm sure she didn't wait long before jumping on your dick."

Disgust sweeps up my throat that she's talking about Jamie like that. "You need to leave."

She scoffs. "God, what a whore. Sleeping with her sister's ex."

I slam my hand onto my desk, causing her to jump, and scream, "Don't you dare talk about her like that. Jamie has nothing to do with what you did or why I don't want you anywhere near *my son.*"

My voice is loud.

Booming.

Harsh enough that the entire bar can hear us.

At this point, when it comes to defending Jamie, I don't care who hears.

She curls her upper lip. "Do you want to be selfish and make Noah grow up without a mother?"

"You're the reason for that. Not me."

Her shoulders slump, her voice turning whiny as she takes this conversation another route. "Cohen. *Please.* I made a mistake."

Fuck, why does it seem like we're talking in circles?

"You did, and I won't make the mistake of letting you hurt my child again. Now, leave before I call someone to make you leave."

The tears start, the vulnerability she tries to hide creeping through.

Heather isn't heartless. There's something inside her but not much.

Selfishness is her main trait.

"I'm sorry, okay! I want my life back!" she cries out.

"How convenient. You want it now that the Vegas life didn't work out for you."

"Do you want to know why he shot me?"

I stay quiet.

No.

Because I don't want to feel sorry for her.

I want to keep hating her.

She doesn't care that I don't want to know. "He shot me because I didn't get my period, and he was scared I was pregnant."

I feel like an ass for rolling my eyes. "Considering he told you to leave your child, that isn't a shocker to me."

"I had a good man—*you*—and I messed it up." Her eyes are vacant, her words low, and it's almost as if she's reading this from a script. "I'll admit my wrongdoings. We weren't perfect, but we were good. We loved each other."

"That was the past."

"Is this because of my sister? You think you two will create this happy-go-lucky family? How in the world do you think that won't screw up Noah's head more than allowing me in his life?"

Circles.

That's all that's happening.

How do I kick her out of here?

The office door flies open.

"Sorry we're late," Georgia says, glancing back at Noah while they walk into the office. "This little guy talked me into stopping for ice cream."

She comes to a halt and shoves Noah behind her when she looks up and sees Heather. Disbelief and disgust cover her face, and I hold my breath, praying Heather doesn't utter a word to him.

The look on Georgia's face is terrifying to me.

I hope Heather feels the same way and doesn't want the wrath of my sister.

Georgia turns around, being sure she blocks Noah from seeing Heather, and kneels in front of him. "Why don't you go into Archer's office? He's in there." She playfully pokes him in the shoulder, but I notice her hand is shaking as she does it. "Let him know I told you where his candy stash is and to share with you."

Noah's eyes light up, and I'm happy Heather can't see them.

Can't see how great of a kid he is.

How his heart is so much different than hers.

"Really?" Noah says excitedly.

"Really," Georgia answers, whipping around and shutting the door as soon as he runs out of the room. A sneer is pointed in my direction. "What the fuck is she doing here?"

"I—" Heather starts.

Georgia raises her hand, cutting her off, and finally pays Heather a glance. "I didn't ask you. I asked my brother."

Heather glares at Georgia.

"If you're here to right your mistake, it's too late." Georgia's eyes, filled with fury, return to me. "I hope you agree with me."

I nod. "I've explained that a good hundred times."

Does it seem like we're ganging up on Heather?

Probably, but she can leave whenever she wants.

"If you need me to make her leave, I will," Georgia spits.

Heather rolls her eyes but doesn't move.

I tilt my head toward the door and rest my eyes on my sister. "Give us a minute. I don't want you getting in any trouble."

Curses fly from her mouth, and she gives Heather one last glare before leaving my office.

"He's so big." Heather releases a heavy sigh. "He looks like you, but he has my hair. He has my face."

He does, and I fucking hate it.

"Leave, Heather." I stalk to the door and jerk it open. "This is the last time I'll tell you. Leave. No one wants you here."

Her face falls, a single tear slipping down her cheek, and she slowly leaves the room, shooting me glances over her shoulder as if she's waiting for me to stop her.

I don't.

Call me a heartless bastard. I don't give a shit.

My heart beats for my son, and I'll stop anyone from hurting his.

CHAPTER
TWENTY-NINE

JAMIE

I'm walking out of the hospital, tired from a long shift, when my phone rings.

I pull it out of my bag to see Cohen's calling.

We haven't spoken since I left his house with tears in my eyes and regret in my heart.

I unlock my car with the remote in one hand and answer his call with the other, "Hello?"

"Tell your sister to stay the fuck away from us," he says, raw anger in his voice.

I stop before sliding into my car. "What?"

"She came to the bar, asking to see Noah, begging for her family back."

"What?" Apparently, that's the only word I can manage at the moment. I open the car door, toss my bag into the passenger seat, and get in.

"Make it clear that if she does it again, I'll have her arrested for trespassing."

"I told her it was a bad idea. I'm sorry." *I've told her multiple times, yet here I am, apologizing for Heather's bad behavior.*

"Tell her again. It should be easy since you're roommates."

"Not by choice and hopefully not much longer since I've told her to move out a few dozen times."

He stays quiet.

"I'll talk to my parents, ask them to make it clear she stay away from you. I'm sorry."

"I'm sorry too," he grumbles. "For being a dick." He releases a harsh breath. "I'm pissed, exhausted, and fed up with the bullshit."

I shut my eyes while taking in his miserable-sounding tone. "I understand."

"Noah wants to see you."

My eyes flash open, but before I can say anything, he continues, "Georgia is cool with you coming over and hanging out. She's watching him tonight if you want to stop by."

It's my turn to sound miserable. "We're back to that now? Back to having restrictions to hanging out with him? I thought you said you wouldn't do this, that you'd never take Noah away from me."

"This isn't me giving you *restrictions*. This is me making sure shit doesn't turn complicated."

My head aches. "What time?"

"Six."

"I'll be there."

"Cool. I'll give Georgia a heads-up."

We share a quick good-bye, nothing like the soft good-night tones he once gave me, and I hang up to call my mom.

Our relationship has taken a turn, and we've become distant since she questioned me about Cohen. When we do speak, he isn't brought up. Our conversations need to be centered around me asking when the hell Heather will be out of my house. If it wasn't for my mother's pleas not to kick her to the curb, it'd already be done. I tell her Cohen's threat about having Heather arrested for trespassing, and she swears to have a word with her.

"I said I wanted you out," I say when I walk into my house to find Heather on the couch, munching on my Cheetos.

It's become almost a daily game between us.

Like with my mother, our conversations are limited to me asking her to leave and her asking if it's because I'm sleeping with Cohen.

Heather tosses her head back. "Look, Jamie, I'm sorry for how everything went down and how shitty I've treated you since moving in. You're right. I should be grateful you're letting me into your home. I've been anything but that. I don't understand why you're so angry with me, though."

I drop my bag onto a chair but snatch it back up, not wanting to risk Heather rifling through it. I've already caught her in my bedroom a few times and lied about setting up a camera, so she'd stay out of it. Not that I have Cohen shoved into my closet or anything, but that's my private space.

"I'm angry because you called Mom and told her I was sleeping with Cohen," I reply with a straight face. "You damaged my relationship with Mom by spouting out shit you know nothing about."

"I was angry, which I have every right to be," she spews out, placing the Cheetos to the side. She delivers a forced smile. "We all make mistakes. I'm sure you regret sleeping with my son's father, and I forgive you."

I roll my eyes at her half-assed *forgiveness* and don't bother correcting the *my son* part.

She pats the space next to her with a smile as half-assed as her forgive-me speech. "Come on. Let's watch a movie. We've never had the chance to really hang out and have sister time. Maybe it's time we got to know each other."

We've never had sister time because you always kicked me out of the room and told me to go read a book.

"Sorry, but I have plans," I say.

"Can I come?" She raises a brow.

"Nope. There's no plus-one."

"You're going to see him, aren't you?"

"Nope." *Technically, I'm going to see Noah.*

She crosses her arms and scowls. "Why can't I come then?"

"I'm hanging out with Georgia, and word is, you're not her favorite person."

She curls up her lips before pinching them together. "Wow, you seem to really be cozying up to them, huh?"

I ignore her comment, go to my bedroom to change out of my scrubs, and leave.

I almost said no to going to La Mesa.

It'd only give me memories of coming here with Cohen.

Noah loves it, though, so I agreed.

I order something different than my usual.

Something different than what Cohen said he always ordered.

It's back to old times where I'm hanging out with Georgia and avoiding Cohen.

I hate it.

We devour our food, and then Noah goes to play in the arcade. I laugh as I watch him play some basketball game.

"You and Cohen need to talk about things," Georgia says from across the booth.

I glance at her as she sips on her margarita. "I take it, Cohen told you about us?"

I've been waiting for her to bring this up all night, and I'm surprised it took her this long. She knows something happened when she came over the day after my fight … and random sex with her brother. With how nosy Georgia can be, she probably had a list of questions for him.

"Told me?" she replies. "Cohen doesn't tell me anything, but I can read my brother." Concern etches on her tan face. "He's heartbroken, and I've only seen him this broken a few times. He cares about you, Jamie. He was ready to take that step with you. He's falling in love with you."

"He's falling in love with you."

I'm half-tempted to snatch that margarita and suck it down. "It's too messy," I croak out. "Ending it is for the best." I dip a chip in salsa and shove it in my mouth to stop from crying.

"How so? The only *messy* part of your relationship is Heather." Her nose turns into a snarl when she says my sister's name.

"She's my sister. It's too weird."

"Life's weird. Embrace that strange bitch and roll with it."

My shoulders slump as the truth pours out of me. "I want a boyfriend I can take home for the holidays. That'll never happen with Cohen. Sure, there was sexual tension. We hooked up, eased that tension, and now, it's over."

"Is that *tension* over because there was nothing there after you banged, or are you ending it because of Heather?"

Why does it seem like all I do is talk about Heather anymore?

"Either way," I say, "it can't happen. Better to end it now before we hate each other."

"I'll take, *Jamie, answer my question and stop bullshitting me* for two hundred dollars, please."

"I don't know." I throw my head back, wishing I'd ordered a shot of tequila. "Why do we always want the people we can't have?"

"Tell me about it," she grumbles. "Love can never be easy. What's that saying? *Love is patient, love is kind.* Bullshit. It's not that way with me. More along the lines of, *Love is painful, love is hell.*"

"And you're over here, telling me to throw myself *into* love?"

"The man you love loves you back. He wants to be with you. There's a difference."

"Is there a man you love, but he doesn't love you back?"

She shrugs. "Yep."

"Who is this man?" I'm almost positive I already know the answer.

"No one." She tightens one of her pigtails and looks away from me. "No one who matters anymore."

I drum my fingers along the table. "We've done enough talking about my love life tonight. Let's take a break for a moment and move to yours."

"That's not nearly as much fun." She frowns.

"Oh, come on. I have to live with Heather. Feel sorry for me and give me the scoop."

"Fine," she groans, her face going slack. "There's a guy, and things didn't work out between us. I kept holding on, hoping things would change, but I've come to the realization that I'm wasting my time. I told him I was done, and I'm at the point where I'm working through getting over it."

I hesitate before asking, "Does that guy happen to be Archer?"

Her eyes widen, and I've never seen her lost for words. "What?"

"Babe, I was secretly in love with your brother for years." My smile is compassionate. "I know what it looks like—the pain and longing for someone you can't have."

"Yet you can have that guy now." She leans closer to me, her voice lowering. "Archer and I have history, but when he found out Cohen was my brother, he pretty much told me to fuck myself. Now, I hate him."

"What do you mean, *have history*? Did you—"

"Aunt Georgia! Jamie," Noah yelps, appearing at the table with a stuffed frog in his hand. "Look what I won, you guys!"

Georgia stands up from the couch and looks down at me with a smile. "Cohen will be home soon, and I have a thing I need to get to."

"A thing?" I question, scrunching up my nose while in the kitchen with Georgia. "You can't have *a thing*. You're my babysitter, remember?"

And the person who helps me avoid Cohen.

I don't mind her leaving me with Noah.

"You're coming back after this thing *before* Cohen returns, right?" I ask.

"I trust you won't kidnap Noah," she answers.

Her words remind me of that night at the hospital when I asked Cohen if he thought I'd kidnap Noah.

"My brother was hurt and pissed about Heather's little visit when he enforced the whole *babysitter* rule," she says. "Everything will be peachy. I promise."

"Why do I feel like I'm being set up?"

Her hand moves to her chest. "I'm innocent, and I would never do anything like that." She laughs while I follow her into the living room where Noah is playing with Legos. "All right, big guy. Time for me to go. Jamie is going to stay with you until your dad gets home."

"Cool!" Noah jumps to his feet to deliver a kiss on her cheek, and she leaves me with the anxiety of having to face Cohen.

I help Noah with his homework, we build a pillow fort, and an hour later, he's asleep in it. Being with them tonight has helped ease my anxiousness from talking to Heather, but when Cohen gets home, it'll rebound in full force.

I bite at my nails when I hear the door open and footsteps approaching. This isn't a fear that it's a serial killer coming; it's fear of the impending conversation.

Be chill.

Act normal.

"Hey."

I turn back to see him from over the back of the couch. "Hi. I told Georgia you wouldn't be happy if she left me alone, but she ditched us."

"I told her it was fine," he answers. "She made it clear I was being a dick with the whole supervised-visit rule anyway, which I was. I'm sorry, Jamie."

There's nothing hotter than a man who apologizes.

Who owns his bullshit.

"I'm sorry too," I reply. "For everything."

My eyes follow him as he circles around the couch. He's wearing a shirt with the bar's logo on it, and he smirks at me as he takes in the pillow fort.

"Impressive."

I flip my hair over my shoulder. "They call me the Fort-Building Master."

He bends down to pick up Noah in his arms, and his son snuggles into his shoulder. I watch his back while he carries Noah down the hallway, and they disappear into his bedroom.

I chew at my nails again, then play with my hair, and then count my fingers while waiting for Cohen to return.

How will this go?

I'm not sure how much time has passed when he treks into the living room and collapses onto the chair next to the couch.

"You look exhausted," I can't stop myself from saying.

Good job, Jamie.

Start the convo with an insult.

Jamie Gentry, MD, Idiot of Relationships.

There's a distant look in his eyes before he rubs them. "I've had a lot going on these past weeks."

Guilt sweeps through me as I stare at him, speechless.

He sprawls out in the chair. "How have you been?"

I bite into my lip as I answer, "Do you want the truth or the fluffy answer?"

"The truth. I always want the truth from you."

I sag against the cushions. "I've been sucky."

His eyes, no longer as distant, meet mine in understanding. "We miss you, Jamie. *I* miss you."

Same.

So damn much.

I'm afraid to say those words, though. It'll only make things complicated, but I miss them so much that it physically hurts my heart. I cry in the shower, in my car while on my way home from work, and when I think about how much I miss being in Cohen's arms.

"I wish our situation were different," I whisper.

He scoots to the edge of the chair, spreads his legs, and rests his elbows on his knees, leaning in closer. "Our situation is what makes us, what brought us together. It's not fair to you, your heart, or me to break things off because of Heather's mistakes."

"You said you were falling in love with me," I blurt, moving toward a conversation I need to stay far, far away from. "Did you mean it?"

His words run through my mind day and night.

The look in his eyes, the emotion that was on his face, showed me the truth.

He meant it, but I want to hear him say them again.

I'm selfish.

"Do you think I throw those words around foolishly?"

"No." I shut my eyes.

He waits until I open my eyes before saying another word. "We can figure this out. Quit giving a shit what Heather thinks."

"It's not only Heather; it's also my parents. My entire damn family, Cohen. They're hardly speaking to me now."

I want to go back to the I love you *conversation.*

Those words from his mouth.

That's what I want to talk about.

Not Heather. Not my parents. Not the reasons we can't be together.

Tonight will be the last time I hear him say them to me.

"Explain the situation to them. Your parents are rational," he argues.

"It's hard not to look like an asshole when your sister was shot, and now, you're screwing her ex-boyfriend and the father of her child."

"Noah isn't her child."

"You know what I mean." Tears fill my eyes. "I'm sorry, Cohen. I really am. If things were different, had it been before Heather came home, it would've been easier for us to be together. But with her here, with what happened, it's changed everything." I wipe tears off my cheek, and my hands start shaking. "I hate losing you; trust me, it's the last thing I want. My heart is bleeding because of it, but I want to do the right thing, be a good person, and I don't want to let anyone down."

"You're letting me down."

My chin trembles. "I am."

"You're letting yourself down."

"I am."

"For other people."

"For other people," I repeat, covering my mouth in an attempt to stop the impending sobs.

It's the moment when I see it flash in his eyes.

Not anger.

Hurt, yes, but also understanding.

As if, in the pit of his heart, he knew this would backfire as much as I did.

That, no matter how badly we want it, it won't happen.

He grips the arms of the chair and pulls himself to his feet. "Guess it wasn't meant to be then."

I'm inhaling deep breaths when he stands in front of me and holds out his hand. I grab it, and he cups it tight as I stand, my body brushing against his.

He catches my chin between his thumb and forefinger with sadness in his eyes.

"Can we still be friends?" I whisper.

"Sure, fine, whatever."

I'm not sure who makes the first move, but our lips meet, and just like that, we fall into the same pattern we've had.

He groans my name into my mouth, grabbing my ass, pulling my front into his growing erection.

I pull away, my breathing ragged. "We can't."

His forehead rests against mine. "Gotcha."

It's after one when I get home.

"Where have you been?"

If there is any moment for Heather not to fuck with me, it's now.

I ignore her and start walking toward my bedroom.

"Were you with Cohen all night?" she shouts to my back. "Did you have sex with him?"

I whip around, and her eyes widen when I charge toward her. "You want the truth? Yes, I was with him."

Her mouth flies open. "You lied about hanging out with Georgia."

"I was with Georgia and Noah, and when Cohen got home, I was with him." I raise my voice. "And you want to know what we did, Heather? Do you really want to know?"

"I do."

"We didn't have sex."

We broke each other's hearts.

Which is worse than sex.

At least in just-sex situations, you don't feel broken after walking away.

She stutters for words.

"We broke things off." I inhale a deep breath to hold back tears. Unlike Cohen, she doesn't deserve them. "We broke things off *because of you.* Because, like the good sister I am, I don't want to hurt *you.* Like the good fucking person I am, I'm sacrificing my happiness for my family's—to do what everyone else thinks is right."

She wraps her arms around her, hugging her body. "I never asked you to do that."

I scoff, "Not directly, no, you didn't."

"You and he are wrong," she grinds out. "I've said it. Mom's said it. Anyone I've talked to has said it."

I can only imagine how many people she's told.

How many times she's played the victim.

I raise my arms before dropping them to my sides. "It doesn't matter who was right or who was wrong. It's done. To thank me, you can get the hell out of my house."

I turn around, ignoring her calling my name, and slam my bedroom door shut.

CHAPTER
THIRTY

COHEN

The Gentry girls.

They've been nothing but trouble in my life.

I'm on alert at all times now.

Nervous that Heather will pop up somewhere or that we'll run into her.

I've had nightmares where she tells Noah who she really is.

It's been two weeks since I've talked to Jamie.

She has been regularly hanging out with Georgia and Noah.

I won't take that away from my son.

No matter how hard she stomped on my heart.

I'm a big boy. I'll deal with it.

I pull my phone from my pocket when it rings, and I see the number of Noah's school flash onto the screen.

"Mr. Fox, Noah fell off the monkey bars at recess."

There's no freak-out this time.

No animosity.

Awkwardness, some.

Sadness, a little.

Jamie isn't shocked when she walks into the exam room to find Noah and me. The nurse, the same one who was with us before, must've given her a heads-up we were here. We share a quick smile before she moves to Noah, her forehead scrunched in concern.

Even in pain, Noah perks up when he sees her. "Hey, Jamie!"

"Hi, sweetie," she says. "I heard you had a little fall on the playground."

"It hurts," he whines, limply holding up his arm to show her the damage.

While on the monkey bars, he tried to jump from one bar to another. He fell, and while using his hand to break the fall, he ended up hurting his arm.

She carefully inspects his arm, telling him how good he's doing, before glancing back at me. "It seems like a broken arm, so let's get an X-ray and see what we're working with."

I nod. "He was bound to break something by the time he hit his teens."

"Young kids and broken bones are definitely not a rarity here." She lightly pats Noah's leg. "Someone will come in shortly, take you upstairs, and give you an X-ray of your arm."

"Will it hurt?" he asks with a trembling lip.

"It won't hurt. And when you get back, I'll get you a sucker. How's that sound?"

"That sounds awesome."

"I'll check on him when I can," Jamie says.

I nod again.

Ten minutes later, the X-ray tech comes in and wheels Noah out of the room in his bed. I sit back in my chair and text everyone an update on Noah's condition. I place the phone on my lap at the sound of a knock, expecting it to be Noah returning, but Jamie steps in the room with a handful of suckers.

She holds them up. "For when he gets back."

"Mind if I get one?" I say.

She tosses me a sucker before setting the rest down in the empty chair next to me.

"How have you been, babe?"

We both wince when I say *babe*.

It fell out naturally. I hadn't meant for it to.

She shoves her hands into the pockets of her jacket. "Busy. Working."

"Heather still crashing with you?"

"Unfortunately," she grumbles. "Which is probably why I'm working like crazy. Avoidance seems like my life at the moment."

"Avoiding your sister and me." I pull out my best teasing tone. "I don't blame you for dodging Heather."

As much as I've tried not to, I fucking miss Jamie.

"If you ever need time away from her, my places are open," I stupidly offer. "You can hang out with Noah at my place or grab a drink at the bar."

She sends me a wavering smile. "Thank you. I'll remember that."

This conversation seems so forced.

The friendliness such a fraud.

"I don't want shit to be weird with us, Jamie," I say, blowing out a long breath. "What we had happened. I don't regret it, and even though it's made shit complicated, I would hate myself if I wasn't up-front with you about my feelings. I respect you, and if you think a relationship with me will hurt your relationship with your family, which, in turn, will hurt you, I understand."

"Cohen"—her face falls—"it's not that I don't want a relationship with you. If there's anyone I want, it's you. It was you years ago, and it's you now."

"But it's not me."

"I'm sorry," she whispers, her voice choked with emotion. "Please don't hate me."

I stand, not wanting her to be upset at work, and wrap her into a tight hug. "I get it," I say into her hair. "I don't hate you."

This is me being a responsible adult.

Being respectful.

Putting my feelings aside for my son.

CHAPTER
THIRTY-ONE

JAMIE

"You two totally banged," Lauren says, stopping at the vending machine next to me and swiping her credit card.

"What are you talking about?" I ask, avoiding eye contact and pretending to focus on my cheese crackers.

"Your sister's abandoned baby daddy. Something happened between you two." She bends down to grab her candy bar and then bumps her hip against mine. "I'd say sex—or at least oral."

"Please never call him her abandoned baby daddy again."

"Look, I'm not one to throw out lectures because I hate hearing them myself."

"Cool. Then, don't."

"But I'll make an exception this time."

"No, you don't have to do that."

I turn around, strolling toward the doctors' lounge, and she scurries behind me like a lost duckling.

"I've told you about Gage and me, right?"

I nod. "Broke up, didn't speak for years, and he hated you?"

She snaps her fingers. "Correcto. When he came back into town, he didn't want anything to do with me, but then we realized we were being idiots and wasting valuable time." She perks up. "Now, we're happier than ever, married, and we have the cutest kids in the damn world. All because we got our heads out of our asses and took a chance, not knowing what'd happen after."

"Sorry, babe, but there's a big difference between you reconciling with your high school sweetheart and me banging my sister's ex."

Her face lights up. "Ah, so you did bang?"

I narrow my eyes at her.

"Have I ever told you about my brother Dallas?"

"Nope, but if it's another *take a chance on love* story, hard pass. Give me a murder mystery."

"Dallas was married with a daughter—perfect, award-winning life. Then his wife died. He was broken, but one night, he drunkenly hooked up with *and knocked up* a woman who he'd once worked with. Willow, the knocked-up character in this story, had known his wife. She was afraid of being hurt, of being second in line, of what people would think about her. They played a similar game as you and Hot Dad are." She taps my nose between her last words. "Quit playing games and at least try to make it work. What will it hurt?"

"My heart. His heart. His son's heart."

"Don't break them then." She shrugs. "It's as simple as that."

I sit down, and she collapses next to me.

"Oh! Tomorrow is my birthday, and I'm sure you haven't gotten me a present yet, *but* what you can get me is for you to give it a try." She pokes my shoulder. "Ask him to dinner."

I give her a death glare.

"Whatever. Just wait until he finds another woman to give him a chance. You'll regret it then, Dr. Chickenshit." She pats my thigh. "Noah wants you to sign his cast too, by the way. Make your move."

I stand, wiping my hands down my scrubs.

"And his father wants you to sign up for a date with him. Possibly another round in the sack."

I shake my head, leave my snack on the table, and head toward Noah's room.

Cohen is standing next to Noah, signing his bright green cast. He holds the pen out to me with a friendly smile. "Your turn."

Our hands graze each other's when I take the pen from him, and his hips brush against my mine when he steps back to give me room. Noah sucks on his sucker while I sign my name along with a giant heart and a smiley face.

When Cohen glances at me, I jerk my head toward the corner of the room, and he takes the hint, following me. I blow out a series of breaths.

Here goes.

My hand rests on his shoulder. "Do you want to have coffee or go to dinner or something this week?"

Shock fills his eyes as he scratches his cheek, confused by my sudden change of heart. "Are you asking me out on a date?"

My chest lightens at his humor. "I'm not sure what I'm asking, so work with me here."

He tips his head down, and he nuzzles my neck as he whispers his answer, "I'll work with you however you want, Doctor."

I hold my hand to his chest and push him away before I drag him out of this room and straddle his cock. "All right, Mr. Suggestive, we're in a hospital."

He grins, his lips on the edge of mine this time. "I'll pick you up tomorrow."

"Cool!" Noah says. "Are we going to get cupcakes?"

Oh, shit.

How do we explain he's not invited to this hangout?

"You need to let your arm heal, buddy," Cohen says. "How about I get you cupcakes, and you can eat them while Aunt Georgia babysits you?"

Noah perks up at Cohen's suggestion. "Okay! That'd be so cool! Sylvia can sign my cast too!"

"Saved by cupcakes," Cohen whispers to me.

"Always saved by cupcakes," I reply with a laugh.

I insisted on taking an Uber to the restaurant.

The last thing I need is Heather from Hell making a big deal if she sees Cohen picking me up. I shudder at the thought and the situation I'd have had to deal with.

"Where are you going?" Heather asks. She's sitting on my couch, which seems to be her favorite place, while watching some stupid TV show.

"Out," I answer.

She pauses her show. "You look pretty dressed up. Can I come?"

"Nope."

She crosses her arms, her nose wrinkling. "Is it a date?"

I whip around, snatch my clutch, and leave without answering. She texts me a few times on my ride to dinner, asking why I'm such a heartless sister, to which I send her a line full of middle-finger emojis.

What great sister bonding we have.

Cohen beat me to the restaurant and is waiting outside when my Uber pulls up. As soon as he sees me, he rushes to my side.

"Jesus, you look fucking gorgeous," he says, circling his arm around my hips and kissing my neck.

My cheeks warm. "Thank you."

I lick my lips.

He looks gorgeous himself. Since we've always been in more casual situations, I've never seen Cohen dressed up before. Tonight, he has on black pants and a fitted blue blazer with a long-sleeve button-down shirt underneath it—the top three buttons undone.

He grabs my hand, walks us to the entrance, and opens the door for me. The hostess smiles when we walk in and leads us to a table in the corner. Cohen scoots my chair out for me before taking his, and I smooth out my dress while the waitress pours our waters.

Cohen orders a draft beer, and I stay with my water.

He raises his brow. "No wine?"

"Water is fine for now," I answer, playing with the napkin in my hand while changing the subject. "Did you know this is my favorite restaurant?"

He stares at me with pride. "I'd love to say yes, but I'm not a liar. I don't exactly date, but Georgia said this was the place to go if you're trying to impress a woman and get her to date you."

"I have to give it to the girl. Georgia knows her shit."

"She wants us to ride off in the sunset together, so she made sure to steer me well."

"She did seem adamant on us talking about our relationship."

"She likes to see me happy."

I wiggle in my seat. "Is that what you are?"

"Happy?"

I nod.

"Can't say I've been having a blast since you dumped my ass." He stops and cocks his head to the side. "Or not dumped my ass but told me *fuck you* since I don't think we made it to the dating part yet."

I offer an apologetic smile. "We kind of went backward on that one, huh?"

"Just a little bit," he says with a hint of a smile. "We can start over and do it the right way? I'll wine and dine you." He gestures toward the room. "We can share flirty texts, maybe even sext a few times, and then we can progress back to sex from there. All I want from you is to get closer, to try this out, to see how we'd be together."

His words put me at ease, confirming I made the right decision in asking him out and that I'd been stupid to turn my back on him without us trying.

Who knows? Maybe, in the end, we'll hate each other.

Not likely, though.

Even in the short time we've spent together, my heart belongs to him.

I stare at him, affection in my eyes. "I want that too."

"What made you change your mind?"

I bite into my lip. "Lauren, the nurse, had a heart-to-heart with me."

Maybe it was Lauren's not very helpful and very random family history stories that hit me with the reality of what I'd be losing if I stepped away from Cohen for good. A relationship that seems wrong to other people is the one that makes me the happiest. It might be one stirred-up mess, but deep down, I'd regret turning my back on Cohen if I did.

If other people don't like it, who cares?

Opinions aren't worth breaking my heart.

Eventually, my parents will have to forgive me. They forgave Heather.

Seeing Noah and Cohen in the hospital room and realizing I could lose them made me view things with a different perspective.

Cohen reaches across the table and takes my hand. "We got this. Neither one of us would be taking this chance if we didn't think it'd work out in the end. I don't want anyone but you, and quite frankly, I sure as hell don't want there to be any other douchebag for you."

"No way in hell are you taking an Uber home," Cohen says, dragging me into his side as we walk out of the restaurant.

I laugh into his chest. "No way in hell are you taking me home, where Sisterzilla will see you."

He comes to a halt. "You don't have to go home. Want to come over and hang out?"

"I'm definitely game for that."

Cohen holds my hand on the car ride back to his house, and Georgia is on the couch watching TV when we walk in.

"Hey, you cute kids, you," she says in a squeaky voice while poking the air toward us. "The monster is in bed, knocked out, and I'm going home. Have fun. Practice safe sex, or don't practice safe sex. I'm down for being an aunt again."

Cohen gives her a stern look. "Good night. Be careful going home."

She gives each of us a hug good night—I love that she's more like a sister to me more than my own—and Cohen turns to look at me when she leaves.

"Food? TV? Bedroom?" he asks.

"TV in the bedroom?"

He jerks his head toward the bedroom and leads us there, his hand on the small of my back. "Let me give you some clothes to sleep in."

"Clothes to sleep in, huh?" I give him a flirty smile. "Being a bit optimistic that I'm staying the night, are we?"

"I'd be optimistic if I told you I wasn't giving you clothes to sleep in." He opens a drawer and pulls out a pair of sweatpants.

"What if I like the no-clothes idea better?"

His hand opens, dropping the pants onto the floor, and he takes three long strides in my direction before cupping my head and crushing his lips to mine. His tongue slides in my mouth without hesitation, his mouth tasting like beer and cinnamon, and I moan into it. I suck on the tip of his tongue, remembering how skilled it is and anticipating when it'll be pleasuring me again.

Soon, hopefully.

I drop my hand between our bodies, and he hisses when I squeeze his already-hard cock.

I love how hard he gets for me.

How much he wants me.

I unbuckle his pants and slide them to his feet at the same time I fall to my knees. His cock is in front of my face as I kneel before him, and I toss my hair over my shoulder. Another hiss leaves him when I fist his cock, pumping it a few times before taking it into my mouth. His head falls back, my name slipping from his lips like a curse, and I lightly tickle his balls. A hint of satisfaction runs through me when I take his entire cock in my mouth without gagging, deep-throating him the best that I can, and his knees buckle.

I suck him fast, and he's holding back, gripping my hair like he did last time.

"Yeah," he bites out. "Suck me just like that, Jamie." He groans, his words falling in rhythm with my sucking. "Just like that."

It's the reaction I craved.

He peeks down at me when I pull my mouth away and replace it with my hand, slowly stroking him.

"Pull my hair. Show me how fast and hard you want it."

His eyes shut, his hips jerking forward to match my hand. "You sure?"

I bite into my lip, nod, and then start sucking him again.

He, doing as I said, and plows his hand through my hair. I suck him harder, and he roughly pulls my mouth to his dick.

He warns me he's about to blow—a warning to pull away.

I don't.

I want to taste him.

Cohen's hand drops from my hair to my cheek, massaging it as I swallow his come. "My turn."

I yelp when I'm picked up from under my armpits and tossed onto the bed. I quickly cover my mouth.

"We have to be quiet," he says, leaning forward to pull my hand from my mouth and kiss me before drawing back.

He kicks off his pants as he walks to the door to lock it, and his shirt is next to go while he returns to the bed. I rub my thighs together to feed the arousal, anticipating what his turn will consist of, hoping it's something with his tongue.

Then his cock.

The determination and lust on his face as he comes back assure me that I won't be disappointed.

He kneels at the end of the bed, the same way I did at his feet, and slides my heels off.

"Where do you want my mouth first?" he asks, climbing up the bed and dragging his hand up my dress. He slips my panties to the side and pushes a finger inside me. "Here?"

I moan at the loss of his hand as he slips it higher, inching underneath my bra and cupping my breast.

"Or here?"

I gulp. "Between my legs. Most definitely between my legs."

He slides off my panties and rests my legs over his shoulders. "I've missed the taste of your pussy."

I shiver as he makes one long lick down my slit.

"Have you missed my mouth here?"

I nod, pushing my hips closer to him. "Every single day."

"Did you touch yourself, thinking about my mouth here?" He cups me before sliding three fingers inside me, causing me to yelp. "Shh …"

I throw my arm over my mouth, biting into it, hoping he doesn't attempt to get an answer out of me as he thrusts into me. If he does, it'll come out a lot louder than intended, and Noah might be a cockblock to us tonight.

He fingers me. He devours me with his tongue and his mouth. He doesn't stop until I'm writhing underneath him, biting my lip while saying his name and moaning.

One time.

Two times.

Three times.

He's torturing me, but it feels so good.

Cohen knows my body better than I do.

I push at his shoulder. "On your back."

The bed dips when he falls onto his back, and I straddle him, smashing our lips together.

Our kiss is hungry and passionate.

He smooths his hands over the backs of my thighs as we slowly make out, and I grind against him.

"Put it in, baby."

I suck on the tip of his tongue before pulling away, lifting, and falling down on his cock.

We both gasp as he fills me.

"So good," Cohen grumbles. Reaching up, he squeezes my breast, teasing my nipple. "So damn good." One of his hands falls, and he uses his thumb to play with my clit, moving it in circles with his hand.

I buck against him, biting into my lip so hard that I wouldn't be surprised if I drew blood. As I grow closer, I give him my weight, and my clit rubs against his groin as I rock into him.

It's coming. I'm coming. As soon as I hit my peak, I shove my face into his shoulder, sinking my teeth into his sweaty skin, and moan. He lets out a deep groan from the back of his throat, holding me in place, and thrusts underneath me until it's his turn to shove his face into my neck as he comes.

CHAPTER
THIRTY-TWO

JAMIE

H oly shit.
    Oh my God.
Is this really happening?

I stare at the stick in my shaking hand and set it alongside the others lined on my bathroom vanity.

"Jamie!"

I jump at Heather shouting my name on the other side of the door and banging on it.

"Are you alive in there?"

"Yes!" I shriek, fighting to control my breathing.

"What are you doing? You've been in there for over an hour!"

"I'm taking a shower." I dig my nails into the vanity. *Go the fuck away!*

"I haven't heard the shower running."

"I mean, I'm taking a bath."

"All right," she says, making it known that she doesn't believe me. "Have fun, taking your fake bath."

I flip off the door in frustration.

How will I explain this?

CHAPTER
THIRTY-THREE

COHEN

"You've got to be shitting me," I mutter when Heather takes a seat at the end of the bar, and I stalk to her. "I told you not to come here again."

"I'm a paying customer," Heather fires back with a smirk.

I dip my head down and lower my voice. "Go be a paying customer somewhere else."

She snarls, "What if I'm here to deliver good news?"

"I don't care."

The only good news she can deliver to me is that she's leaving town again and never coming back.

She settles her elbow on the bar. "Did Jamie tell you she's having a baby?"

My heart nearly stops. "Excuse me?"

A hint of a smile plays at her lips. She knows she's caught me off guard, and she's loving it. "Did my sister tell you she's knocked up?"

I grind my teeth, refusing to answer.

She snorts. "She didn't."

"Leave."

Heather flips her finger back and forth. "The question is, is she having *your* baby or another guy's baby?"

"Don't come in here, trying to start shit," I hiss. "It won't work."

She settles her duffel-sized purse onto the bar, pulls out a baggie, and pushes it toward me. "Don't believe me?"

"What the fuck?" I say around a gag before sliding it back to her. "What is wrong with you? Who walks around with a bag of pregnancy tests?"

"I found these tests in Jamie's bathroom."

"And?"

I won't grant her the satisfaction of reacting to her games. She knew she'd have me on the *bag of pregnancy tests* surprise.

"They're not my tests, and we don't have another roommate, so they have to be hers."

I stay quiet, clenching my jaw, and wait for her to get the hell out.

"Since you two were … or are banging each other, I thought it might be something you'd like to know."

She needs to get out before my heart jumps out of my chest and lands in front of her.

"Appreciate the concern, but you can leave."

"Do you think the baby is yours?"

"Leave, Heather."

She stares at me, unblinking and unmoving.

Fuck it.

Jamie.

I need to talk to Jamie.

I turn, walk away from the bar, and charge toward my office. I slam the door shut behind me, tug my phone from the charger on my desk, and find a text from Jamie.

Perfect fucking timing.

> Jamie: Is the offer to get some space at one of your places still open?

Do I ask her?

No way Jamie is sleeping around, and we've had sex a few times without protection.

That can mean only one thing: the baby is mine.

If those tests are even hers.

My hands shaking, I nearly drop my phone when I reply.

> **Me: Sure is.**

Are you pregnant with my baby?
Is that why you're coming here?

> **Jamie: Are you at the bar?**

> **Me: Yes. You want to have drinks?**

If she's pregnant, she can't drink. She'll decline. I flinch, remembering her not ordering wine at dinner. Jamie has made it clear that, in stressful situations, a glass of wine and Cheetos settle her nerves.

> **Jamie: No. Maybe just some company, someone to talk to, vent to.**

> **Me: I'll be here.**

Here waiting for you to break the news.
To ease the crazy-ass thoughts spiraling through my head.

I slump down in my chair and cover my face with my hands.

A baby?

So many mixed emotions pour through me, and the memory of when I found out Heather was pregnant with Noah surges through me. I was shocked but ecstatic, and damn it, my stomach flutters at the thought of having a baby with Jamie.

Fuck. It'd be awesome.

She'd be the best fucking mom in the world.

I fidget with my phone, then a pen on my desk, and then a

fucking paper clip while waiting for her. No way can I wait out in the bar. People will think I'm on speed, considering how pumped I am. I freeze, the paper clip falling through my fingers when there's a knock on the door.

I stand straight, expecting Jamie, but Archer walks in with the bag of pregnancy tests in his hand.

"Uh ... whoever that chick was, she left a present for you." He cringes, flicks the bag onto my desk, and grabs the hand sanitizer next to my computer. "I didn't want to throw them out, and it'd look pretty damn gross if I left them on the bar. I'm pissed I had to pick up those things that most likely have piss on them."

I silently stare at the bag of tests.

"Did you get someone pregnant? That chick? What about Jamie?"

"That chick is Jamie's sister."

His jaw drops. "What the fuck? You're banging her sister now too? Dude, from what you've told me about her, that's dumb as hell."

I recoil at the thought of being with Heather again. "No, Heather has been trying to get back with me, but I told her to piss off. She's living with Jamie, and she claims she found the tests in Jamie's bathroom."

"Have you asked Jamie about it?"

I shake my head. "When I got back to the office to call her, with perfect timing, she texted, asking if she could stop by the bar."

"That sounds like a pregnancy announcement to me."

I groan and rub my eyes. "Heather is known to be a liar, so I can't take her word on shit."

"If Heather wanted you back, why would she tell you Jamie was pregnant with your baby? Wouldn't you want Jamie?"

"She insinuated that Jamie is pregnant with someone else's baby. Heather knows something happened between Jamie and me, but I'm not sure how much she knows."

"Gotcha." He taps a loose fist to his chest. "Thank fuck I don't do relationships. Sounds like a major pain in the ass."

"If Jamie doesn't give me a heads-up she's here and comes into the bar, will you send her back here?"

"I got you."

When he leaves, I shove the bag of tests into a drawer. I pace in front of my desk, gripping my phone, and wait for her.

What if she doesn't tell me?

Do I bring it up?

Confront her?

I tense when there's another knock on the door, and Jamie walks in, a shy smile on her face.

"Hey, babe," I say, dropping my phone onto my desk.

"Hi." She glances around the room, running her hands up and down her arms. "Are you busy? I didn't mean to bombard you. I just needed to clear my head. Heather has been driving me nuts, and there are only so many hours I can work before they tell me I have to go home."

I sit on the edge of my desk to keep from falling flat on my face. "I'm never too busy for you." I stand, rush across the room to grab a chair, and pull it toward her. "Sit down."

Don't shake.

Stay cool.

Calm.

Collected.

She raises a brow and straightens out her dress before sitting. "Are you okay, Cohen? I can go—"

"No," I interrupt. "Stay."

She nods, hugging herself.

I lean against the desk and cross my ankles. "You look well."

Are you pregnant?

"I'm glad you think I look … *well.*" She laughs. "Even though you only saw me two days ago, and not much has changed."

"Do you *feel well?*"

"Do I *feel well?* Yes …"

"Anything big happen in those two days?"

"I mean, stuff has happened, yes. I've been working and—"

"Are you pregnant?" I blurt out.

Her eyes widen. "What?"

"Are you pregnant?"

"How did—" Her gaze moves from one side of the room to the other. "What the ...?"

"Is it true?"

She nods. "I was planning on telling you, just working up the nerve, but apparently, you're the baby whisperer."

I scrub my hand over my face.

"Are you mad?" she whispers.

"Is the baby mine?"

She winces. "Are you kidding me?"

I hold up my arms. "I'm a dick for asking, and never would I doubt you, but Heather was spitting out some bullshit about it being someone else's."

"Heather?" Her brows scrunch together. "When did you talk to Heather?"

"She came to the bar about an hour ago."

"She came to the bar," she slowly repeats.

I circle my desk, pull out the bag of tests, and hold it up. "She dropped these off and said she found them in your bathroom."

Her face turns bright red. "I don't know what's more mortifying. My sister going through my trash and packing up something so personal to me or that she brought them here or that you're holding them in front of me." She blows out a forceful breath. "Now, I'm really done with her."

I toss the bag on my desk, lock the door, and fall to my knees in front of her. "Come stay with me then. If you don't want to be near her and she won't leave, come to me."

She peers down at me, biting into her lip. "You'd be okay with me staying with you?"

"Absolutely."

I groan when she pinches my shoulder.

"And by the way, of course the baby is yours. Before you, I hadn't had sex in a year. You're lucky you only got a pinch and not a smack to the face."

I'm sporting a shit-eating smirk while running my hands up and down her thighs underneath the loose yellow dress she's wearing. "Are you really having my baby?"

She nods, flashing me a flirtatious grin. "I'm really having your baby."

"Wow." I kiss her knee. "This makes my fucking day."

"You're not worried that this happened too fast?"

I shake my head. "Sure, our relationship is new, but my feelings for you are strong enough that I'm ready for this—ready to jump headfirst and be with you, for us to be a family."

I groan deep in my throat as her eyes water, and I move my hand between her legs.

She laughs. "You're in a mood."

"Hell yes, I'm in a mood." I flip her dress up. "In the mood to show the woman who's having my baby how damn excited I am, how appreciative I am for her, and you deserve a reward for it."

She squeals when I move an arm to slip it around her waist, dragging her to the edge of the chair, and I part her thighs. Ducking my head, I drag her panties down her legs and yank her closer to my face. I savor the sound of her moan as I softly suck on her clit before thrusting two fingers inside her.

"Look at that. My baby mama is soaked for me."

Her eyes are shut, and she's licking her lips. "You're really going to play out this baby mama thing, aren't you?"

"Damn straight." My tongue joins my fingers, and I start devouring her—sucking and praising her pussy.

I love how sensitive she is to my touch—how goose bumps cover her soft skin and how she shivers with my every thrust.

She comes on my tongue, tasting delicious, and I suck on my finger before smearing her juices on my bottom lip.

CHAPTER
THIRTY-FOUR

JAMIE

Heat sweeps up my neck when Cohen walks me out of his office and through the bar. Archer raises a brow, taking in my wrinkled dress and the orgasmed-out expression on my face. When we reach my car, Cohen kisses me and asks me to come over later.

"That sounds nice."

I have some business to attend to real quick.

"See you later, baby mama."

"I'm so kicking your ass."

He winks and gives me one final kiss on my forehead.

When I arrive at my house, all the sweetness I had with Cohen evaporates, and my nails are drawn. I stomp up the porch steps, my hands itching to snatch Heather's shit and throw them out the window.

"Have you lost your fucking mind?" I screech before coming to a stop.

My parents, along with Heather, are sitting on the couch in my living room.

Heather's face is red with fake tears, my dad seems confused, and my mom looks hurt.

I zip my finger toward Heather. "I want her out of my house

now. I've been nice long enough. Put her in your house, get her an apartment—I don't care what you do, but if you don't make her leave, I'll do it myself."

"She wants me out, so she can hang out here, pregnant with Cohen's baby," Heather screeches.

"I want you out because you went all Oscar the Grouch and plucked pregnancy tests out of my trash can, bagged them up like you worked at a grocery store, and thought, *Gee, I think it'll be a good idea to take these to Cohen at his job.* You even insinuated that another man might be the father, like I sleep around!"

"Heather," my mother gasps, shooting her a concerned look, "did you do that?"

Heather stumbles for words. "She's having sex with Cohen, Mom! I think that gives me every right to be furious."

"Enough," my father yells.

Thank God.

"Heather, pack your shit," he demands.

Her eyes widen. "Wh-what?"

"Listen to your father," my mother says with an anger in her voice I've never heard before.

"Now," my father pushes, and she scrambles to her feet.

My mother jumps up to help her with her crutches, but Heather swats her away.

She points at me. "I can't believe you're taking *her* side. The woman who's having sex with the father of her sister's child. Your daughter is having his baby, and I'm the bad person?"

No one says a word, and when she realizes she's not getting the reaction she wants, she storms down the hallway to my guest bedroom, not even bothering with the crutches.

Heather is bitching as she throws her belongings into her suitcase.

I play with my hands in front of me to calm myself and dodge eye contact with my parents.

"Jamie," my mom says, causing me to look at her. "Is that true?" Her eyes drop to my stomach. "Are you pregnant?"

I nod. "Yes."

Not only did I take a million of the at-home pregnancy tests, but I also took a blood test at work to confirm.

Positive.

"That's your sister's ..." She stops as if she can't finish the sentence.

I nod. "He is."

My father scrubs a hand over his face. "Jamie, this puts all of us in a stressful situation."

I fall on the chair across from them. "You guys know my heart." I place my hand to my chest. "You know I don't make stupid decisions. I love him."

My father rises from the couch. "It's not fair for us to have this conversation while your sister is in the other room, throwing a tantrum. We'll take her home and discuss this later."

I nod. "Thank you."

He kisses the top of my head, and tears are in my mother's eyes as she hugs me.

I go to my bedroom to avoid any Heather drama and wait until she leaves before coming out.

My parents return an hour later, Heather-free, and we sit down in the living room.

"How did this happen?" my mother asks.

"I've been spending a lot of time with Cohen and Noah, and I don't know ... as we did, I developed feelings for Cohen. *Strong* feelings." A tear runs down my cheek. "This is complicated and puts you in a weird situation, and I get that. All I'm asking is for you to trust me, to believe in me, and to know that I've gone back and forth with Cohen. I've broken his heart, broken my own heart, by saying no to a relationship with him, but it's not fair to us."

"You're in love with him?" my father asks.

"I am."

He slaps his hands on his legs. "That's all that matters to me."

My mouth falls open. "What?"

"You were right about making responsible decisions. If this relationship wasn't that serious, if it wasn't *love*, then you wouldn't risk it."

I glance at my mother, tears also on her face.

"You're having a baby, honey," she says with excitement. "It's a shock, yes, and it'll create some issues, but nothing will ever cause us to turn our backs on you. We love you."

I'm full-on crying.

My fears dissolve.

They don't hate me.

They aren't disappointed in me.

They still love me.

"A big brother?" Noah shouts. "I'm going to be a big brother?"

Cohen nods, sitting next to me on the couch, and grabs my hand in his. "You're going to be a big brother, buddy."

Nothing will ever erase the memory of the beaming smile on his face.

He grabs my arm and jumps up and down. "I have a mom, and now, I'm going to be a big brother! This is so cool!"

Cohen and I shared countless talks on how to explain our relationship to Noah. Coming to a decision wasn't easy, and we hoped we were making the right one. We didn't ask for anyone's opinion, and in the end, we decided we wouldn't tell Noah I was his real mother's sister. Maybe, in the future, that will change, but he's too young to understand it now.

The risk of running into Heather is low. She started another online relationship, this one with Pat's cousin, and moved back to Vegas. My parents said when she left, she didn't utter a word of apology, a word about mending things with Noah and Cohen, and definitely nothing about me—not surprising. What she did ask for was money.

Cohen mentioned that she told him Joey shot her because she thought she was pregnant, but she took a test in the hospital, and it was negative.

A month ago, Cohen and I sat Noah down and told him that we were dating.

He didn't say, *Yucky yuck*, like he had when Seth told him he used to be my boyfriend.

It was the opposite reaction. He was as excited as he is now, bouncing on his tiptoes and then hugging me. The next day, he asked if I could become his new mom. I said I'd be there for him as much as any mom would.

We waited until now to break the big brother news. Other than Archer—given he had seen the pregnancy tests, which is mortifying—and my parents, we haven't broken the news to anyone else. As a doctor, I know things can happen early on in pregnancy, and I don't want to get anyone's hopes up. I also don't want to deal with questions if anything does happen.

"Do I get to pick the name?" he asks. "I bet I can come up with the best name ever."

Cohen laughs. "We'll have to see about that."

My hand breaks away from Cohen's hold when Noah plops down in the small space separating us and relaxes his head against my shoulder.

"This is the best day ever," he chirps.

I smooth my hand over his hair before kissing the top of his head.

Cohen asks Noah not to tell anyone yet and adds a bribe of three cupcakes if he doesn't.

Well, four cupcakes after negotiation.

COHEN

"Gender reveal party time," Georgia sings, strolling through my backyard with a giant-ass baby bottle—shaped piñata in her arms. "Someone find out how and where I can hang this thing up, please and thank you." She turns in a circle and points at Finn before shoving it into his arms. "You have been nominated as the official piñata boy!"

"What the—?" Finn stops before dropping the F-bomb.

Grace has been growing on him.

I'd never heard of a gender reveal party until Georgia announced she was throwing us one. I still don't get the concept of it, but Jamie was excited, so that's all that matters. Georgia and Ashley planned the party, and my backyard is packed with our friends and family. My mother is here, sitting in the corner, and I've barely spoken a word to her. Georgia insisted I invite her and wants us to work on our relationship. According to my sister, my mom is clean and has been trying to right her wrongs.

Jamie's parents are here, both of them excited as fuck, which is awesome. Jamie loves them so much, and it would've crushed her if they hadn't accepted our relationship,. At the moment, Noah is sitting on Regina's lap as he shows off his iPad.

Yes, iPad.

Somehow, he talked Jamie into upgrading the iPod.

"Lincoln, Lincoln, Lincoln," Georgia says, walking over to the tall, dark-haired guy, plopping down on his lap and wrapping her arms around his neck. "When are you going to take me out on a date?"

Lincoln is Archer's brother who recently started working at the bar. His employment caused a few arguments between Archer and me. Lincoln is fresh out of prison, and the thought of a felon working in the bar put a bad taste in my mouth. What bothers me more is how often Georgia flirts with him.

How he ended up at our gender reveal party is beyond me, but I'm sure it was Georgia's doing.

Lincoln wraps his arms around Georgia's waist, glancing down at her. "Whenever you're available, babe."

"Why did I agree to this shit?" Archer grumbles, his eyes cold. "I don't do baby shower shit."

"First, it's a gender reveal party," Jamie corrects. "And second, you're here because you love us." She pats his chest while walking past us.

I keep my eyes on Jamie, watching her practically waddle to her parents and talk to them. She looks breathtaking. Her hair is curled into loose waves, and my cock stirs as I eye her dress, her belly sticking out in the front. As soon as I saw her in it this morning, I tossed her onto the bed, peeled it off her body, and then made love to her.

She put it back on to torture me.

"What crawled up your ass?" I ask, turning back to Archer. "You were fine fifteen minutes ago."

He shrugs and scrubs a hand over his face. "Not trying to be a dick. I'm just stressed."

"Stressed about what? The bar?"

"Nah, some personal shit."

"You know you can talk to me about whatever, right?"

He nods.

"You ready, guys?" Ashley yells, skipping into the yard with a black balloon in her hand. "Cohen! Jamie! It's time!"

I was as frustrated as Archer is now when Jamie informed me that the sex of our baby would be kept secret until this party.

Until we popped a damn balloon.

I wanted to know right then and there at our ultrasound appointment, and the anticipation has been killing me. Every day, I changed my mind on whether I thought we were having a boy or a girl. I backed off on my frustrations and agreed to wait because my pregnant girlfriend has me wrapped around her fingers.

Jamie snags my hand in hers and leads us to where our guests are crowded around tables, all eyes on us. She's nearly bursting at the seams when Ashley hands us both a pin and the balloon.

This is it.

Our hands wrap around the thin string of the balloon, and the crowd counts down. My hand tightens around hers, excitement pouring through me, and we stab our pins into the balloon as soon as they yell, "One!"

Pink confetti rains down on us.

"A girl!" Jamie yelps.

"A girl," I repeat, holding pieces of confetti and staring at them in my hand, still comprehending what it means. And then it dawns on me. "We're having a baby girl!"

The crowd erupts in cheers, some crying, others ready to run to us with congratulations.

I can't let that happen.

Not yet.

I turn around, skimming the yard for Georgia, and relief hits me when I see she's running our way with another black balloon. She hands it to me and retreats back, and Jamie tilts her head to the side.

Her hand covers her mouth, her eyes meeting Georgia's. "Oh

my God!" Her hand leaves her mouth to grab mine. "Are we ... having twins?"

Oh hell, this isn't how I thought she'd react to this.

I grip the balloon in one hand and give her a pin with the other. "Pop it."

There's a hesitation before she does, and a frown covers her face at the lack of confetti.

"Wait, what?" The sound of her whimpering tells me when she's spotted it—the ring box falling to the ground at the same time I drop to one knee. "Holy shit," she hisses.

"Cuss word!" Noah yells at her.

She laughs. Her face is splotchy from the tears of finding out we're having a baby girl, and they're streaming down her face now.

"That ... that isn't confetti," she whispers, staring down at me.

I peer up at her, playing with the box in my hand before popping it open. "It's definitely not confetti."

"Is it a *thank you for having my baby* ring?" she asks with an unsteady breath.

I snatch the ring. "It's more along the lines of a *will you be my wife* ring?"

"Holy shit," she gasps, her voice so low only I hear her. "Holy shit."

"Does *holy shit* mean yes or no?" Fear settles through me that she's not ready for this yet.

That I jumped the gun.

She waves her hand next to her mouth as if she's struggling to produce words, and they come out between breaths. "Holy shit definitely means yes."

I grab the ring from the box, and both our hands shake as I slide it onto her finger.

"See how good I was at keeping a secret, Dad?" Noah says, running to us. "I didn't tell anyone!"

"You sure didn't," I say, rising to my feet. "I'm proud of you."

Noah, like the nosy kid he is, went through my drawers—looking for a pair of my underwear to wear over his jeans with the outfit Georgia demanded she wasn't going anywhere with him in—and found the ring.

Thank fuck Jamie wasn't there.

That meant that not only did Noah learn my secret, but with the way he came into the living room, waving it, Georgia found out too. I learned my son is great at hiding secrets—not once did he let the cat out of the bag when we told him about the pregnancy, and Jamie seemed to have no idea about my proposing.

The Georgia thing worked out because she helped me plan the perfect proposal.

Jamie's eyes meet mine, and she reaches out, running her hand along my cheek. "Are you going to cry, Cohen Fox?"

I repeatedly shake my head, fighting back my emotions. "Nope. I got this."

"Let me go grab the cake," Georgia says.

She's been hiding it from us. She wouldn't let us open the fridge all day, in fear we'd peek.

I'm pulling Jamie in for a kiss as Georgia disappears inside of the house. A crowd gathers around us, people inspecting the ring and offering their congratulations.

"Is Georgia in there, eating all the cake by herself?" Ashley asks.

I glance around the yard, now realizing she's been gone for a hot minute. "Let me see if she needs help."

She's not in the kitchen when I walk through the back door. I open the fridge, thinking she's probably in the bathroom, and snatch the cake box from it.

I set down the cake onto the counter and peel back the corner of the box at the same time I hear the sound of people arguing in Noah's bedroom. I follow the noise and stand on the other side of the shut door.

"Don't bullshit me," Archer says. "You're flirting with him to fuck with my head."

"Screw you, Archer. Maybe I like your brother. Maybe I'll go on a date with him, and I'll kiss him. And you know what? I might even fuck him too!"

I stiffen at my sister's voice.

"Don't say that shit," Archer grinds out.

"Why? Do you think that because you fucked me, you can tell me what to do now? You lost that right a long damn time ago."

I swing the door open and take in the scene in front of me. "What the fuck?"

CHAPTER
THIRTY-SIX

JAMIE

I hear, "What the fuck?" as soon as I hit the back door.

Oh no.

I was too slow.

Blame it on the pregnancy waddle.

Lola rushed over to me when she saw Cohen going inside to check on Georgia. She'd spotted Archer following her into the house with a pissed-off and determined look on his face, and she was positive they were about to argue.

Arguing that, knowing them, would lead to screaming.

I didn't say anything to Cohen because fistfights at your gender reveal party were so 2019, but Archer's anger had been pinned to Georgia, his nostrils flaring as she flirted with Lincoln earlier.

Georgia's secretive self still won't tell me what happened between them.

I turn down the hall to find Cohen standing in the doorway of Noah's bedroom with clenched fists. I peek around him into the room. Archer looks as if he's geared to block a punch to the face, and Georgia's eyes are as big as her mouth.

"She's my fucking sister," Cohen screams.

I grab his arm. "Nuh-uh. This isn't happening right now."

Make him think it'll hurt my feelings.

My pregnant, emotional feelings.

"Oh, it's happening," Cohen snaps.

Archer holds up his hands. "I'm out of here. You can rip me a new asshole tomorrow."

I take this opportunity to pull Cohen away. "Your *very* pregnant *fiancée* does not need the added stress of her *fiancé* fighting his best friend at their party."

Cohen's jaw works, and Archer's eyes stay on him as he leaves Noah's bedroom.

When I glance at Georgia, tears are in her eyes.

"Nope." She sniffles. "Today is about you two. Any dramatic conversations about my life will wait until later."

I snort.

Georgia isn't going to tell us shit.

"You know what the hardest part of having a baby is?" I ask Cohen while sitting at the kitchen table, exhausted from the party.

He scratches his head. "Uh ... having it?"

"Choosing a name."

He levels his eyes on me. "That's harder than pushing a tiny human out of your vagina?"

"You know what I mean. My list is fifty-seven names long. Be prepared for our child to have one long-ass name." I gesture to my list in frustration but smile when my diamond ring glistens underneath the light.

I love it.

The halo diamond has a vintage look to it, and the pavé diamonds along the band add more sparkle to it. I can't stop staring at it.

"If all else fails, we'll use Noah's idea," he suggests.

"We are not naming her Pizza Roll Spider-Man Diva."

"I think it's catchy." He massages my shoulders. "Put the list down. We have plenty of time before we need to choose a name. It'll come when we least expect it."

I frown. "Fine, but you're on *keep Jamie's mind occupied* duty then."

"Oh, I know how to keep you very occupied." He takes the seat next to me, and his tone turns serious. "Thank you for this."

"For the list of names?"

"No, for changing my life and sticking through the troubles with me even when I was an asshole. I never expected someone to come into our lives, and even though you were shoved into a messy-as-fuck situation, you stayed. You accept my son as much as you accept me. You love him as much as you love me. You stirred out emotions inside my heart that I never thought I was capable of having. Hell, you've stirred yourself perfectly into this family and made us whole." He clears his throat. "My engagement speech was something along those lines, but I didn't exactly get the chance to spit my game."

I rub my hand over his jaw before yawning. "I loved how it went down." I crack a cocky smile. "Admit it, you knew our lives were going to change after Noah's hospital visit."

He nods. "I was scared as hell and kept telling myself to stay away from you."

"Then you realized how amazing I am."

"I did."

"How sexy I am." I scrape my finger along the slice of half-eaten cake in front of me, collecting frosting, and lick it off, swirling my tongue along the tip. "How good I am in bed."

"Jesus," Cohen groans and grabs his dick before shutting my notebook and putting it to the side. "You need to get some rest."

I eye the erection forming underneath his jeans. "I actually need to get some dick."

"Dear God, pregnancy has made you extremely addicted to sex with me."

"Are you complaining?"

"Can't say that I am." He rubs my stomach. "We'll have this one, and then we can keep practicing for another."

"Wow, how many kids do you want running around here?"

"As many as *my wife* will have."

"Can we wait on the wife thing until after I have the baby? Homegirl doesn't want to miss out on champagne at her wedding."

"We can wait for whenever you're ready."

He helps me up and guides me to our bedroom.

Yes, our bedroom.

Georgia and Grace are renting my townhouse, and I moved in with Cohen and Noah.

I grin when he shuts the door behind us and wrap my arms around his neck, my eyes meeting his. "I can't believe we're having a baby." I hold out my left hand in the air, admiring the ring again. "And we're engaged. How did we get here?"

He sits me down on the edge of the bed, and my arms rise. He pulls my dress over my head and tosses it to the side. This has become a regular thing for us—him helping me undress since it's become harder for me to do with my belly.

"Well," he says, brushing his lips against mine before helping me up the bed, "you became a pain in my ass while also making me a happier man." He separates my thighs and splays his hand over my stomach, massaging my sensitive skin while staring at it in awe. "You made me fall in love with you, and now, I'm about to make you—my baby mama, the woman I love—my wife."

I smirk, running my finger along the seam of his lips. "I am pretty talented, huh?"

"Gotta give credit where credit is due, though, babe. I made you fall in love with me too." He dips his hand into my panties. "I also helped make this baby."

I roll my eyes. "The guy always loves to take the credit for shooting his sperm inside the woman."

He chuckles, and I raise my ass to help him drag my panties off.

"You did not make that sound romantic whatsoever."

"I wasn't trying to."

He laughs, and instead of him slipping his finger inside me, I ask for his cock.

He gives it to me, and with each thrust, he lists the reasons he can't wait for me to be his wife.

I'm amazing.

Beautiful.

Will look beautiful in a wedding dress.

Take cock so well.

He loves me.

I come, him doing the same minutes later.

As we catch our breaths, I glance over at him. "You know what one of my favorite things you do is?"

He raises a brow.

"It's weird, but the first night I came here, when Noah was sick, you told me good night in this sexy, heart-swooning voice. I almost fell for you right then. As I came around more, you kept doing it—even when we were nothing, fighting sexual tension, or hell, even breaking each other's hearts. Very rarely did you not give me a, 'Good night, Jamie.'"

"Good night, Jamie," he says in that rough, deep, but soft voice I love, and his lips meet mine. "I love you."

"*Swoon,*" I sing out before snuggling into his side.

"I have no idea what that means, but I'll take it." He kisses the top of my head. "I love you."

Cohen has stirred his way into my heart.

No drink is stronger than our love.

I can't wait for us to mix marriage and children into the cocktail that is our life.

ALSO BY CHARITY FERRELL

If you enjoyed Cohen & Jamie's story, check out the other books in the Twisted Fox series!

Twisted Fox Series

(each book can be read as a standalone)

Stirred (Cohen & Jamie's story)

Shaken (Archer & Georgia's story)

Straight Up (Lincoln & Cassidy's story)

Chaser (Finn & Grace's story)

Last Round (Silas & Lola's story)

Blue Beech Series

(each book can be read as a standalone)

Just A Fling

Just One Night

Just Exes

Just Neighbors

Just Roommates

Just Friends

Only You Series: A Blue Beech Second Generation

(each book can be read as a standalone)

Only Rivals

Only Coworkers

ABOUT THE AUTHOR

Charity Ferrell is a Wall Street Journal and USA Today
bestselling author. She resides in Indianapolis, Indiana with her
boyfriend and fur baby. Her passion is writing about broken
people finding love while adding a dash of humor and
heartbreak. Angst is her happy place.

When she's not writing, she's on a Starbucks run, shopping
online, or spending time with her family.

www.charityferrell.com

Printed in Great Britain
by Amazon

18409305R00160